T.I.M.E

T.I.M.E

Temporal Inconsistencies, Mythological Entities

James Moclair

authorHOUSE®

AuthorHouse™ UK Ltd.
1663 Liberty Drive
Bloomington, IN 47403 USA
www.authorhouse.co.uk
Phone: 0800.197.4150

Published by AuthorHouse   5/21/2014

ISBN: 978-1-4969-8156-1 (sc)
ISBN: 978-1-4969-8157-8 (hc)
ISBN: 978-1-4969-8158-5 (e)

CONTENTS

T.I.M.E.

(Temporal Inconsistencies, Mythological Entities)

A science fiction, fantasy and adventure novel

By James Moclair.

James Moclair is also the author of

S.P.A.C.E

(Spacial Populations and Cosmic Enigmas)

If you enjoyed S.P.A.C.E then

T.I.M.E will delight you as T.I.M.E naturally follows on where S.P.A.C.E

finishes.

James Moclair is also the author of the best selling martial arts books;

A Breath of Fresh Air, Kempo Karate. Novice to Intermediate.

A Breath of Fresh Air, Kempo Karate. Intermediate to Advanced

Ju-Jutsu, A Comprehensive Guide.

This book is dedicated to my loving wife Lorraine, who sadly passed away on 02.12.2013

We were married for thirty eight years and up until she was being diagnosed with terminal cancer, we both truly thought we had all the time in the world. Lorraine was the love of my life and my best friend. She was also a loving mother to my two daughters and the world's best grandmother to our granddaughter, Gabrielle.

Lorraine achieved many things in her short but, full life. Nevertheless for me and I say this with extreme pride; she was the best martial arts student I ever had! She held a 2nd Dan black belt in Ju-Jutsu and a 1st Dan Black Belt in Karate. In the dojo, (training hall) she was always respectful and would always address me, 'her husband' as Sensei (teacher). Throughout all the years she trained with me, she never once complained about the rigorous training or how hard I would push her.

Every student in my club respected Lorraine; this wasn't because she was the sensei's wife. She was respected because she worked hard and would take everyone under her wing and diligently help them with their techniques. This respect was shown at her funeral when, students past and present filled the chapel until there was hardly any standing room!

Away from the Dojo, we both enjoyed every second of our time together. I have a passion for fishing and when Lorraine would have a day off work, sunshine or more than likely because of the British weather, hail, rain or snow, she would come with me! That's true love. Now, I spend my time alone and wonder how our time on this planet, went so quick.

Until completing this book, I had not realised that I had included in the main character all of the qualities Lorraine had. Sincerity, courage and determination for everything she ever did, and the joie de vivre she had for life.

Time can be measured in nano seconds, and there is not one nano second in any day that I do not miss her.

The loss of a loved one is heartbreaking but I have been fortunate to have my family, friends and students to help me through this difficult time. From the bottom of my heart, thank you all.

James Moclair.

CHAPTER ONE

Time

It had only been a few earth hours since Captain Elaine Laurence had left the entrance of the micro universe. She should have been euphoric that she, Notus and the triloraptors had defeated the evil overlord! And that they had saved not only all who lived in her universe but, also all those who lived in the overlord's universe!

However Elaine's thoughts were elsewhere. All she could think about was her mission to rescue her fellow abducted passengers. And to be quite honest, she was more than a little annoyed! Her mentor, the being Notus had informed her that the rescue mission had been marred by the fact that time on the first planet they were going to was running at a different pace of time to that of her home planet Earth!

It was hard for Elaine to conceive that it had been just a little over a month ago that about four hundred and fifty nine guests and crew including herself had been abducted from two recreational space stations orbiting the planet Earth. This act was carried out by the race who was now aiding her, the triloraptors. And now, because of this time difference, some of her fellow a-bductees had aged at least forty years!

Being a medical doctor, Elaine decided that the best way for her to understand the intricacies of time was to try to analyse what she perceived of time itself. To do this, she could just ask Notus or the ships super trilo-computer for all the relevant information on time but, she chose the old fashioned way. She would write down all she personally knew of time.

Her first problem on board Notus One was that she did not have a pen or anything that resembled paper! "Blast" she thought. So Elaine then decided she would have to dictate her thoughts to the ships on-board super computer. Sitting in her command chair, Elaine activated the super computer and began her dictation headed, 'time';

"For me and my fellow humans, time seemed to begin when we as conscious, sentient beings became aware of it, but did it?"

As Elaine gathered her thoughts, she tried to frown but her blue crystal skin prevented her from most facial expressions! "Blast, blast and double blast," she thought and then with a lot of frustrated anger in her voice she yelled out at the top of her voice;

"When am I going to be able to control my adaptive DNA?"

After calming down, she mentally decided to put her adaptive DNA aside and then focus her thoughts back to the subject of time. At that, she continued her dictation;

"If we look back to our past, then we are looking back at periods of historical time. The creation of the universe and other universes started at some point of time, and since that point of time, all universes have constantly changed. These changes can be seen and documented throughout not just earth's time but, for all of the sentient beings in this and other universes.

Astronomers on earth using highly sophisticated land based telescopes and without a doubt, orbiting and spacial telescopes, have tried their best to map the known universe. In reality, the invention of the telescope was also the invention of the first time machine as it allows us to look back through time. The telescopes exploration has been taken further by using a spectrometer that analyses both visible and invisible light across all the electromagnetic spectrographic levels. And through their finding, they have been able to identify space properties and date their origins. To some scholars time is the fourth dimension. To others, time is merely a concept, or a tool for measuring from one moment to another in time.

Elaine deduced;

"Whatever is thought of time, it as a whole is an extremely complex subject and in its entirety, time offers many amazing variables! So to understand time a little better, time can be divided into three categories, planetary time, conceptual time and spacial time.

All three time categories have distinctive qualities that make them individual but, any one of the three can also overlap another, and they can even run parallel with each other. And just when you think your brain is about to explode just from analysing time. They all appear to be one and the same!

Elaine paused for a moment and then said to the super trilo-computer;

"Make a sub heading called; planetary time". She then continued;

"For a solar system and planets to form, it takes several million years. Gravity plays a big part in this and once a planet is formed, gravity also affects what is classed as planetary time. Logically you would assume that a small planet would rotate faster than a larger planet but, other spacial factors have to be taken into consideration. The overall size of the planet and its actual mass will have an effect on its rotational speed. Planets with molten cores will be less dense than those with metal cores and depending on other spacial factors, they will also rotate at different speeds.

The next important issue is the planets position in its solar system. Massive gravitational forces being applied by its sun will have a dramatic effect on its daily rotational speed. This variance will also be amplified or reduced depending on the age of the sun and what classification of star the sun is.

Closer to home the planet's planetary brothers and sisters will also influence its daily rotational speed with their own gravitational fields. This would be amplified if the planet has a planetary twin. And if we look on its immediate doorstep, the planet could have one or more moons; this too will have a substantial impact on its daily time calendar.

Put simply, a rotational day and night on one planet will not be the same as a day and night on another planet. And when you look to a year, even the planetary brothers and sisters in the same solar system will vary greatly. If you take the planet earth for example, it has three hundred and sixty five days in its year, except in a leap year. But, its closest brother mars, takes six hundred and eighty seven earth days to rotate around the sun. As you travel further out of the solar system, earth has a big sister; Uranus. This planet takes just over 30,799.095 earth days to rotate around the sun, which equates to one year on Uranus. While on earth 84.323326 earth years have passed!"

Elaine asked the super trilo-computer to play back her dictation and listened to it several times. She was reasonably happy with what she heard. Elaine then asked the super trilo-computer to start a new sub heading called; Conceptual time.

Once again Elaine began her dictation;

"As life develops on habitable planets, the emergent beings will have different concepts of planetary time. These concepts of time could also change depending on what type of intelligent life is emerging. For example cellular, land creatures, air, atmospheric, aquatics and energy beings, could all view time differently?

In the beginning, the majority of all species will understand that day brings night and night brings day and that combining these together is a way of measuring daily time. The planets seasons will also be of importance to an advancing civilisation. And now that they have a daily measurement, that measurement can then be divided into the planets seasons and a planetary yearly calendar will emerge. For a short period, this time measurement and awareness will be sufficient. However as intelligence increases, societies will find a need to divide day and night into a recognisable scale. It is therefore feasible that they would begin developing time measuring devises for that purpose.

From a land creatures view point, that being a human or similar type of species. One of the first possibilities is a time piece fashioned out of stone, similar to a sun dial that casts a shadow as their planet rotates around their sun. As we are aware, sun dials are primitive and therefore have their limitations as they are only good when the sun shines. So another possible solution would be to look to the stars. By looking at fixed points in the sky, these early astrologers could make charts and estimate the planets movements. It would also be plausible to think that some kind of telescope would be developed and utilised. The problem with this method is that it only works at night and in clear skies.

Out of need, it will not be long before they start to develop mechanical time devices that can be read both day and night. Perhaps they would even develop a time piece similar to a clock that measures time in hours, minutes and seconds. By constantly observing these time pieces, their lives will to the observers have seemed to have actually speeded up. And for some species, perhaps similar to humans, time down to the last second will become of paramount importance.

At some point of time in a developing culture, transportation will become necessary. This would apply to all land, air and sea civilizations. The transport to start with will be quite basic, perhaps at first riding a creature, and then a form of cart could be added and pulled or flown by the same species of creature. But as needs arise, a much faster and efficient form of transport will be required. To build such vehicles, they will need all the necessary resources and with that, industries will have to be developed. Efficient cost effective manufacturing will then become a priority and time schedules for production will become of paramount importance. Each day now ticks away at a much faster pace and the sentient beings that live on these planets will all be governed by precise and accurate time.

As populations grow, the production of food will become a major priority. Foods that were grown and allowed to flourish in nature's own time will be fed with growth enhancing chemicals and forced to grow throughout the planets calendar year. This will still not satisfy the swelling populace and over time, genetically enhanced plants will be introduced that will grow bigger and faster.

Almost all individuals in an evolving society will at some stage need medicine and medical help. While basic remedies seem crude but effective, advancements in these fields will lead to civilisations living longer and longer. Longevity will become a priority and DNA manipulation to extend life and increase intelligence will be seen by some species as a natural evolutionary progression".

Elaine paused and thought of her own adaptive DNA. As a human being she would not have survived her time on the planet Notus, so Notus, the being changed her DNA so she could now adapt to all planetary and spacial environments. Chuckling to herself, she said out loudly;

"Now that has to be top of any extreme DNA list!"

But then she thought of the triloraptors, as they had evolved they had taken DNA enhancement to a trilo-level! As raptors, the females were traditionally much larger than the males. But, through DNA enhancements, both males and females were now the same size. Still thinking of triloraptors, Elaine's thoughts immediately went to aggressive species and wars, the latter being something the triloraptors revelled in! She then continued her dictation;

"In a utopian society, wars would never exist! In reality, the majority of advancing civilisations will at some point of time have some form of tribal, boundary and then global conflict. In the early years of smaller skirmishes, blows, strikes or even the creatures own natural defence system could be used. As time moves on and things escalate, basic weapons such as sharpened sticks and rocks could be the first weaponry used. But war encourages advanced technology, and in a very short passage of time, these basic weapons would be superseded by more advanced ones.

As conflicts go global, the warring factions would want to strike their enemies at longer distances and for this, long range missiles would be developed. From basic propelled missiles, they then would in evolutionary war terms soon be looking into space to launch attacks! With this in mind, the warring factions would build technologically advanced weapons and even weapons of mass destruction! Sadly when it comes to this time in their evolution, their time on the planet could be running out and they may have to look to the stars for a new home. This is when they would possibly look to relocating to another planet where they would encounter spacial time".

Once again Elaine asked the super trilo-computer to pause her dictation/ she then asked the super computer to play back the sub heading, conceptual time. She listened to this only once and decided it was ok but, she would have to revise some of its contents later. She was eager to move on to the next sub heading, space time. Her dictation began;

"Time and space, according to Einstein's theories of relativity, are woven together, forming a four-dimensional fabric called, space-time".

Elaine tried to remember back to her university days when she had read up on Einstein's theories of relativity and then recalled an analogy of what was meant by a four-dimensional fabric. She continued her dictation;

"The mass of the Earth dimples this fabric, much like a heavy person sitting in the middle of a trampoline. Gravity, says Einstein, is simply the motion of objects following the curvaceous lines of the dimple."

To further explore Einstein's theory, Elaine recalled an experiment back in the year two thousand and four where physicists put four spinning gyroscopes into orbit around the Earth. With the spin axis pointed toward some distant star as a fixed reference point. Free from external forces, the gyroscope's axis should continue pointing at the star forever. But if space is twisted, the direction of the gyroscope's axis should drift over time. According to calculations, the twisted space-time around Earth should cause the axes of the gyros to drift merely 0.041 arc seconds over a year. An arc second is 1/3600th of a degree.

The results of the experiment were conclusive, what they measured was a geodetic precession of 6.600 plus or minus 0.017 arc seconds and a frame dragging effect of 0.039 plus or minus 0.007 arc seconds! This gave physicists renewed confidence that the strange predictions of Einstein's theory were indeed correct, and that these predictions may be applied elsewhere. The type of space time vortex that exists around Earth is duplicated and magnified elsewhere in the cosmos around massive neutron stars, black holes, and active galactic nuclei.

Concentrating hard, Elaine tried to recall what geodetic precession was, and then all of a sudden thanks to her adaptive DNA that had greatly improved her memory, it popped into her head! Geodetic precession is the amount of wobble caused by the static mass of the Earth (the dimple in space time) and the frame dragging effect is the amount of wobble caused by the spin of the Earth (the twist in space time). Both values are in precise accord with Einstein's predictions.

Elaine dictated her thoughts on Einstein's theory and then continued saying;

"Part of Isaac Newton's theory of relativity is also of importance; it is called the law of energy and goes under the heading of Energy time (E.T). Energy has always been in the universe and has always had the same level. Both Einstein and Newton's theories come to the same conclusion in that every planet has its own vortex of warped time. Newton goes further by speculating that a vortex can also absorb past ET. The energy is weak but can be amplified and through this, time travel to the past is possible. Time correction will change time in that vortex only and has no affect on the rest of the universe".

Stopping to think about what she had just dictated, Elaine decided that she would have to explore these theories more. After she finished her dictation she would also ask Notus for clarification on this. Her thoughts now began to wonder to time dilation, Elaine knew from her basic astronaut training that velocity and gravity each slow down time as they increase. However at times each seems to oppose the other.

Continuing with her thoughts, Elaine knew that for her to understand time dilation, it was best if she treated each one separately. She continued her dictation under the sub, sub heading, relative velocity time dilation;

"For me," she dictated, "velocity time dilation leads to one popular earth concept of time travel. If I were to get into a spaceship and travel close to the speed of light away from the planet Earth. Time inside the spaceship would slow down for me in comparison to that on the planet Earth. I could fly to our nearest star, Proxima Centauri, which is about four point two lights years away from earth and return again at nearly the speed of light. For those on the planet Earth, a few years would have passed. While for me, only a few weeks or months would pass."

Elaine then reflected on the current speed she was travelling at in her spacecraft named Notus One. Their current speed was in excess of ten gravitons; each graviton is measured by light speed (299.792.458 metres per second) times ten is one graviton. So she was now travelling over one hundred times faster than the speed of light! Elaine pondered momentarily on how this worked out with velocity time dilation but, the mathematical computations were beyond anything she could personally calculate.

Elaine's mind then jumped to another thought. How much 'relative time' had passed on earth since she had been abducted? For a moment she felt anxious but, she knew she would have to put these thoughts aside until she could speak to Notus about them. Elaine focused her mind and then continued her dictation, this time with a sub, sub heading on gravity time dilation;

"Gravitational time dilation was first described by Albert Einstein in the year 1907. Since that point of time several experiments have taken place that prove that there is an actual difference of elapsed time between two events as measured by observers differently situated from gravitational masses. The classic experiment and the one most documented that I recall where two atomic clocks are set at differing altitudes and therefore they have different gravitational potential. Over a short period of time they eventually showed different times. However as I recalls, the effects detected in this experiment were extremely small, with differences being measured in nanoseconds! A nanosecond (ns) as I recall is, one billionth of a second."

Trying to sum up gravity time dilation, Elaine guessed that over vast portions of space with spacial influences such as a collapsing star that could result in a black hole, the gravitational time dilation would be amplified extensively!

Concluding her dictation on time, Elaine said;

"It appears to me that the universal laws of nature are such that time itself will bend and change due to differences in either gravity or velocity, each of which affects planetary, conceptual and space time in different ways."

Elaine then asked the super trilo-computer to play back all of her dictation and thoughtfully listened to what she had dictated several times. It was at this point of time that Notus communicated telepathically with Elaine and said;

"I see you have a few questions for me on time. Well let me say first, that most of what you have dictated is good and falls in line with the physics you understand of this universe. However, as you are now aware, there are many other universes, and some are so different to your universe, that they have completely different laws of physics.

Next, let's look at your question on velocity time dilation. We are currently travelling at ten point two gravitons, that is, one hundred and two times faster than the speed of light. Simply put, that means we arrive at our destination a lot quicker than if we were travelling at a sub light speed. Velocity time dilation still happens, but it is reduced by our ability to travel at vast speeds.

Now let's look at your own situation. Since you have been abducted from the recreational space station orbiting earth, I calculate that the time that has passed on the planet Earth is just over a year and a quarter, yet the relative time for you has been only a month.

Lastly, both Einstein and Newton's theories that every planet has its own vortex of warped time is correct. I also believe that Newton was on to something with his theory on Energy time. Although Elaine, it is something I have never explored, as I have never had any reason to travel back through time."

Notus paused for Elaine to comment. However before she could say anything, one of the four trilo-raptors travelling with them entered Notus Ones command centre. It was wearing its full trilo-combat uniform and hovering by its side was its bladed trilo-tron weapon.

Without waiting, the triloraptor spoke;

"Captain Elaine Laurence, we shall arrive on the outskirts of our first planetary destinations solar system in twenty four of your earth hours. What orders do you have for the triloraptors?"

Elaine thought for a moment and then replied;

"At this point of time I do not have any orders for you but, if you don't mind, I do have a few questions."

Without hesitation the triloraptor replied;

"Captain Elaine Laurence, we are here to help you. Ask your questions."

Elaine jumped straight in;

"OK, just how many of my people did you drop off on this planet?"

Replying, the triloraptor said;

"Exactly one hundred and fifty human beings."

That surprised Elaine but, she continued with her questions;

"Tell me all you know of this planet and its system."

Without any emotion the triloraptor said;

"Proportionately the planet is three times larger than the planet Terra or Earth as you know it. The total land mass is 446,817,189.3989999 km (172,517,081.301 miles), which is about twenty nine point two percent of its total surface. Water covers approximately seventy point eight percent of the planet's surface. It has five oceans, six seas and numerous inland lakes and large rivers. Its planetary cycle around its sun takes one thousand and ninety five of your earth days and a daily planetary rotation takes, seventy two of your earth's hours.

The planet has two moons and its solar system has a total of fifteen planets. Ten of these are gas giants that occupy the outer areas of the solar system and the other five are inner planets that are made of various gases, rocks and metals.

Also like terra, the systems star is classified as a type G2 yellow dwarf, however it's mass is one third greater than terra's and it is approximately one billion years older.

Shortly before the overlord came to this universe, we visited this planet. The planetary environment and life forms fitted in with the Universal Interplanetary Congresses 'law of the way' and therefore it catered to our needs."

Elaine could feel herself getting annoyed and sharply said;

"That means you raped the hell out of this planet and left it and my people to rot!"

Without biting back, the two metre tall triloraptors feathers were not ruffled by Elaine's comments and calmly continued;

"Your people were not injured and were left with basic survival provisions. After that, the humans would have to provide for themselves. Half were dropped off in an area known as Brobryne marsh lands and the others were dropped off, five thousand earth miles to the East, in the vast flat grassy plains."

Elaine took a moment to absorb what the triloraptor had said and then asked;

"What are the chances of their survival?"

Without hesitation the triloraptor replied;

"We the triloraptors would not be on this mission if we thought there were no survivors. Given that we have visited your planet and our experiences with the humans, I would say that it is feasible that some of the one hundred and fifty would survive."

Elaine had another question;

"What do you know of the gravitational anomaly that is affecting the space time around the planet?"

Replying the triloraptor said;

"The gravitational anomaly as you call it is not just affecting that one planet; it is affecting the whole of its solar system. Our analysis has determined that it is a gravitational field that affects all matter and that results in a curvature in actual space time.

Our visits to this solar system and planet have been brief and therefore this anomaly was not of any concern to us."

Elaine thought that the triloraptors last statement was typical of the triloraptors. However, she needed to know more and asked;

"I have two more questions for you. Firstly long has this gravitational field or anomaly been there and second, how big is it?"

The triloraptor stood motionless for a few moments and Elaine guessed it was gathering information through its trilo-visor that is linked to the trilo-commands super computer. It then replied;

"We have no way of determining the age or presence of the gravitational field in this area. Now, to understand the scale of this gravitational field, please turn on your holographic display unit and I will uplink the data we have to your super computer."

Elaine had a telepathic link to Notus One's super computer and did as the triloraptor requested. Instantly, the holographic display showed the whole of the solar system with its sun, fifteen planets, asteroid belts, hundreds of comets and large dust clouds.

The triloraptor gave Elaine a few earth minutes to look at this and then said;

"The distance from the centre of the sun to the outer edge of the last planet is eleven billion, one million miles. Beyond that point and into space is hard to define where the solar system ends. But, you could add on at least another one and a half light years! The gravitational field is like a large globe and encompasses the whole of this solar system!"

This stunned Elaine and even surprised Notus. While Notus was trying to define the objective of such a vast gravitational field, Elaine was finding it difficult to comprehend its actual size. What confused her more was she had no way of mentally visualising how far these distances were. Notus jumped in and telepathically said;

"Elaine, to help you understand these numbers look at it this way. If you tried to count to eleven billion and one million at a pace of one number each second, it would take you over three hundred and sixty earth years!

Back on your own planet Earth, the distance from the sun to the outer regions of your solar system called the Oort cloud is approximately two light years or twelve trillion miles. To count that high, I would estimate that it would take three hundred and eighty thousand earth years."

Elaine began to laugh out loud and said telepathically to Notus;

> "Notus, at times you have a strange way of trying to explain things! But, yes, in a strange way, your explanation really does help."

At that, Elaine realised that the triloraptor was glancing at her strangely and in a sombre tone the triloraptor asked her;

> "Captain Elaine Laurence, was something I just said funny?"

Elaine stopped laughing and answered;

> "Oh no, not at all. I am just a little shocked at the vastness of the gravitational field."

Coldly replying, the triloraptor said;

> "In that case, you might want to take a seat for the next part!"

Elaine knew that she could show no signs of weakness to a triloraptor, so regaining her composure, she told the triloraptor to continue.

> "Trilo-command has done an analysis of the size of the gravitational field from when we first visited this solar system, to now. We have determined that the gravitational field is getting smaller and with that, gravity is becoming denser!"

As the triloraptor had paused, Elaine inquired;

> "Please elaborate on the implications of this."

The triloraptor seemed to be prepared for this question. It walked over to the holographic display unit. On the holographic display, a transparent globe had now been added to the outer regions of the solar system. The triloraptor answered;

> "This was the gravitational field's position when we first entered into this solar system."

A second globe then appeared inside the first one. The triloraptor continued;

"This was its position a little over one earth month ago, when we dropped your people off."

At that a third globe appeared, again showing that the field had shrunk. The triloraptor then said;

"The last globe is the gravitational field's current position. Our calculations state that its overall mass has shrunk by three percent and has increased its gravitational density by the same."

The triloraptor looked at Elaine and could see she was looking intently at the holographic projection. Then the triloraptor continued;

"If the gravitational field keeps shrinking and increasing its density at its present ratio, we estimate that it will be only a few of your earths months before this process becomes critical.

At that point of time, each planet, moon, asteroid and comet will be pulled out of their normal orbit. Given the laws of basic physics, the gravitational pull of those with a greater mass will attract the smaller ones and solar collisions will occur! This will continue with the planets also colliding and the debris from all of this chaos will then naturally be been drawn into the solar systems sun.

As the gravitational field continues to increase, the gases and atoms in and around the sun will begin to devour each other. And finally, jumping forward a few of your earth years, all that will be left is an enormous black hole.

Due to its size and extreme gravitational pulls, the black hole will then cause massive instability in this part of the universe."

To emphasize all of this, the triloraptor then had the holographic display unit re-create the sequence of events it had just explained. Elaine looked on in absolute horror!

CHAPTER TWO

Temporal Inconsistencies

Part One.

Space-time, forty earth years ago.

As Justin began to wake up, he instantly began to recall being in a room with others and being blasted by icy cold water! Opening his eyes, he could see he was no longer in that room and realised his body was partly submerged in slimy muddied water! Slithering to his feet, Justin wiped the pungent smelling mud from his face and upper parts of his body and tried to comprehend where he was. It was night fall and to his surprise, he could see two moons! The moons were bright in the sky and were the only source of light that he could see. As he scanned around he could see he was in some kind of marshland area.

Trying to get his bearings, Justin scanned the night sky but again to his surprise, the stars systems above were not recognisable to him.

Suddenly a male voice called out. The voice seemed to be only a few metres away from where he was standing, it said out loudly;

"Is there anyone out there?"

Justin replied;

"Yes it's me, Justin Harper, Captain of the Space Recreation Station, Darwin."

The male voice replied;

"Justin, it's me, John McNally. Help me; I'm stuck up to my waist in stinking mud."

Justin cautiously waded through the mud, shallow water, rushes and reeds until he came upon the stricken man. Reaching over, Justin said;

"Raise your arms above your head and I will try to pull you out."

John McNally did as he was told, and after several attempts, Justin managed to pull him free from the mud.

As John lay on the muddy wet ground, he asked Justin;

"Where in hells damnations are we? And how did we get here and what happened to our clothes?"

Justin helped him to his feet and replied;

"My friend, they are all good questions but, I do not have any answers. Look into the sky and tell me what you see."

"Holy flying cows!" John blurted out; "there are two moons!"

Jason laughed and said;

"I'm glad you can see them too, I thought I must have had a bump on my head and my vision was blurred."

As Jason was talking, John scanned the skies and said;

"Those stars don't sit right either."

Replying Jason said;

"Yep, I noticed that also. Do you remember being in a dark room with other's and being blasted with cold water?

John angrily replied;

"I sure do, god only knows what was happening there!"

Both men nodded in agreement and without any more talk, they both silently stood and for several minutes surveyed their surroundings. It was John who then broke the silence;

"Before the madness of the dark room, my last recollection was, we were both on board the Space Recreation Station, Darwin, orbiting the planet Earth.

Justin, looking at the sky, with its two moons and unrecognisable stars, I suspect this is not our planet, solar system or indeed our part of the universe!"

Justin nodded in agreement and then added;

"This area looks like some kind of marsh land, and out there in the darkness, there may be others from the Darwin"

Justin continued;

"I think it's a bit dangerous at the moment with poor light and treacherous deep muddy pools! But John, as soon as the sun rises, we had better begin to scout the area for other crew members and passengers."

John saluted and said;

"That's an affirmative Captain."

Both men smiled at each other, they had known each other since childhood and had gone to the same schools, played in the same soccer teams, gone to the same college and both became pilots in Britain's Royal air force. After that, they both underwent astronaut training and began working together as pilots for Virgin Galactic's space shuttles. And then they both enlisted, as captain and first officer on-board Virgins first Space Recreation Station called Darwin.

As the sun began to raise over the Brobryne marsh lands, Justin and John began their search of the immediate area. Both men set out in different directions, and being cautious of the depth of mud and water below their feet, they both had armed themselves with long sticks to probe the muddy waters.

It was agreed that at every twenty paces, they would communicate with each other. But John had only got to fourteen paces when to his horror, he discovered a female body. Calling to Justin, he said;

"Justin, Justin, come here quickly, I have found a body, and it's a female. Justin, she's laying face down! She appears to have drowned in the shallow water!

Justin cautiously made his way towards where John was standing but, that is when the groof struck! Just below the surface of the slimy mud, the four metre long amphibian had been patiently waiting for its next meal to come along, and Justin had just come onto the menu! Using its six legs, the groof leaped forward and with its razor sharp teeth, it tore Justin clean in two!

Hardly a second had passed before the groof's two metre wide mouth opened and its four meter long tongue shot out and grabbed the first part of its meal, Justin's lower torso and legs! Within another two seconds, the groof repeated the process and began to munch and crunch through the rest of Justin's body!

John was mortified, he opened his mouth and tried to call out to his friend but, no words came out! John's natural survival instincts kicked in, holding his stick like a throwing spear, John let out a roar and ran towards the feasting groof but, he only got a few paces, when a second groof struck.

Groof's have been living in these marsh lands for several thousands of years and over this period of time, they have adapted perfectly to this environment. Once submerged, to the untrained eye, you could not spot one of these primeval creatures, as their skins are camouflaged perfectly to blend in with the slimy muddied and coloured waters!

Until recently, the groof's had fed on the abundance of wildlife that lived and visited the marsh lands. However, since the triloraptors had decimated their food source, the groof's were left to scavenge on anything that came along. John had unwittingly stepped on one and within a few seconds, he was dead. His death was almost identical to that of his lifelong friend, Justin.

Sunrise was the groof's favourite time to feed. And on the same day that Justin and John died, the groof's also feasted on fifty nine other appetizing humans! Cunningly, the groof's had used the same hunting tactics for several thousands of years; they would leave a dead carcass out as bait. This in turn attracts other creatures, which would come to investigate and possibly feed on the carcass. In the case of the humans who had been dropped their by the triloraptors, some had inadvertently died from drowning! However, this served the groof's well, as dead meat was not appealing to the groof's. So they just left the dead human carcasses where they were, slithered into the muddied water close by, and then using their bodies inbuilt sonar to detect motion, they waited patiently for any vibrations in the mud or water!

Five thousand miles to the East of the marsh lands, lay the vast flat grassy plains. For thousands of years, these plains had been home to numerous vast herds of grazing beasts and wild life. Now, with the triloraptors need to feed, and desire to kill and to ransack this area, they had all gone.

Quite recently, the extermination of wildlife had been compounded by a raging trilo-phoon hitting this area. Within a few days it had destroyed this once fertile and beautiful landscape. As it continued to rage, it tore away thousands of kilometres of the rich top soil and left a desolate wasteland in its trail.

As part of their eco-destruction strategy, on a previous visit, the triloraptors had created several trilo-phoons. These trilo-phoons were, in their basic fundamental nature cyclones but, now they had triloraptor enhancements.

For normal cyclones in this universe, data had been collated and a scale for measuring the cyclones overall power had been made. The scale starts at one; this would be mild and goes up to five, which is extremely severe! A category five has winds with gusts of more than two hundred and eighty earth kilometre an hour. At this speed, the cyclone would cause almost total destruction! The triloraptors creation, the trilo-phoon was off any known universal scale! A classified cyclones life could last several earth weeks at sea and just about one earth's week once it hit land. The trilo-phoons were in a league all of their own! They would last for several earth months at sea and marginally less then that over land.

Dan Woverly's life's ambition was to go into outer space. Two years earlier, Dan's wife passed away, she had several cancerous tumours on her brain and after putting up a courageous fight for a few years, she succumbed to the ravages of the disease. She knew of Dan's desire to go into space and told him that once she was gone to go all out and do it. For the next two years, Dan devoted much of his time to researching all he could on a space trip to the newly constructed Space Recreation Stations. Dan also put up most of his life savings for the two week trip.

For his age, Dan was extremely fit and that helped him pass the space fitness test required for all prospective passengers to go on-board a Space Recreation Station. Dan had only been on-board the S.R.S a few earth hours, in that time Dan attended every lecture and signed up for every activity offered. As Dan retired to his luxury cabin, he sat and marvelled at the view of the planet Earth from his floor to ceiling transparent portal. He thought of his wife, and wished she was with him to share this wonderful experience. That's when he and everyone else on board went unconscious and were abducted by the triloraptors.

Dan would have loved the idea of visiting another planet. However, Dan's only recollection of waking up in an alien environment was feeling immense pain! His sixty two year old body was blown so hard across the hard and jagged terrain, that chunks of his skin were torn from his body! In one mighty gust, Dan was then hurled into alien oblivion by the raging trilo-phoon. Others in his party watched helplessly as Dan's body was carried away along with all debris in the trilo-phoons path! Fortunately for them, they had woken a little earlier from their drug induced sleep and had managed to scramble and find shelter in a deep ravine.

Part Two.

Space-time; approximately two and a half earth years ago.

Twenty four light years away from this trilo-phoon infested planet, is a star known as Gladious. This star is comparable to earth's star and the one in the solar system where the triloraptors dropped off the crew and passengers of the R.S.S. Darwin; it is a main sequence star. Main sequence stars are fuelled by nuclear fusion, converting hydrogen into helium. The life expectancy of these types of stars in their most stable part of their existence is generally about 5 billion years.

Gladious has twelve major planets and three planetoids. The fourth planet in orbit from Gladious has an atmosphere of 78.09% nitrogen, 20.95% oxygen, 0.93% argon, 0.039% carbon dioxide, and small amounts of other gases. This combination of gases is commonly known throughout the universe as air and is suitable for sustaining terrestrial plants and terrestrial animals similar to those found on earth. For the triloraptors, this planet was an ideal candidate to drop off more of their abducted humans!

The 1.6093 kilometres long black metallic trilo-craft entered the planet's atmosphere at a speed of 1,200 kilometres per hour. The trilo-craft with its sharp pointed nose cone that made it resemble a giant black crystal then slowed down and came to a dead stop just three metres above the sand dunes of a long white sanded beach.

Two sides of its metallic outer skin began to dissolve into a liquid state and twenty; three metre tall hatches appeared on both sides of the crafts body. As the hatches opened, forty, two metre tall trilo-bots began unloading their cargo, two hundred unconscious human beings! They had been abducted from the Recreational Space Station, Stephen Hawking.

As the trilo-bots continued to unload their hostages, cautious eyes watched from far-off. A group of mammals similar to Opossum marsupial had gathered to witness this strange goings on. These one metre tall creatures were social and as yet, primitively intelligent. They had seen many types of birds but they had never seen a flying object this big just hovering above the ground before. To say they had an inquisitive nature was an understatement. As they trilo-bots went about their business; the small group of mammals carefully crept forward.

From inside the trilo-craft, the presence of these small creatures had been detected and a single triloraptor fully clad in its trilo-combat uniform emerged from one of the hatches. Hovering just below the triloraptor was its one metre in diameter, obsidian-black metallic hexagon trilo-tron. The trilo-tron is the triloraptors personal weapon, (T.R.O.N stands for; transitional robotic organic neutraliser).

To control this weapon, the triloraptor uses a discrete translucent visor that is fitted around its eyes. The visor is connected to the triloraptors synaptic brain connections and neurological receptors. And in addition to linking the triloraptor to the trilo-crafts on board computer and central commands computer; it is also the command centre for the lethal trilo-tron.

As the triloraptor looked through the visor, it could see various symbols; which were activated by trilo-thought waves. Each major symbol had several sub menus. The symbol shape that was activated was that of a single hexagon weapon, this brought the option of guidance control into its sub menu. With this activated, the triloraptor could control the hexagons weapon flight in any direction, its speed and the overall flight range. It also brought up a menu bar at the bottom of the visor that allowed its controller to change the shape of the disc instantly.

In this instance, the triloraptor left the trilo-tron at its hexagon shape and through the sub menu that activated the trilo-trons guidance system, it locked the weapon onto all of the approaching creatures! At just under the speed of sound, the trilo-tron shot silently forward and cleanly sliced its first victims head off! Within another one earth second all the other creatures lay dead, having also been decapitated.

These kills were far too easy for the triloraptor! So it flew to a height of eighty five metres and using its excellent trilo-vision, that allowed it to see far more detail than most other living creatures, it spotted its next kill.

Inland, at just over 1.6093 kilometres (one mile) away was a large, four metre high and ten metre long beast that looked like a hairy prehistoric mammoth. At its top flight speed, the triloraptor headed for its unsuspecting prey. Callously, the triloraptor had decided that this beast would die slowly, and sent the trilo-tron ahead to slice at the beast's skin! With a rotational speed of 5000rpm and its outer edge sharper than any surgical scalpel, the trilo-tron sliced the poor helpless beast over two hundred times! The triloraptor then swooped in and using its powerful talons, it tore both the beast's eyes out.

Confused and in excruciating pain, the injured beast ran aimlessly around in circles! The triloraptor flew around the beast constantly taunting it! Periodically the triloraptor would swoop in and tear flesh from the beasts open wounds.

Knowing that it would take several hours for the beast to die, the triloraptor was satisfied with its meaningless carnage and swiftly headed back to the trilo-craft! Within a few earth minutes, the trilo-craft left the planet's atmosphere and from a safe distance, the triloraptors then armed a large array of spacial, air and ground booby traps! With all their tasks completed, the trilo-craft headed to its next destination, the planet Notus.

Part three.

Doctor Elaine Laurence's; space-time.

Due to massive solar eruptions and strange planetary gravitational forces, the last leg of the triloraptors trip through Notus's solar system was arduous. However, one year and four earth months ago, the triloraptors trilo-craft had touched down on the planet Notus! It was their first visit to this, one of the most distant solar systems and planets in this universe. And in the not too distant future, the triloraptors also planned another visit to this planet! However when they returned, they would change this, the largest planet in the universe with an abundance of life, into a trilo-grave yard!

The trilo-bots began to unload the last one hundred and thirty five human hostages. As they were going about their duties, trilo-central command sent an urgent message to the trilo-crafts commander's that they had received reliable information that the planet Notus was going to be the arena for a major battle! At this point of time, the trilo-raptors and the U.I.C were in the early throws of a universal war! The information obtained by the triloraptors indicated that the U.I.C intended to set a trap for the triloraptors fleet! The plan was to herd the triloraptors fleet towards the Planet Notus where the U.I.C would be waiting with a massive space and planetary ground force!

Without delay, the trilo-bots were ordered to reload their human cargo. That's when, without warning, a freak electrical magnetic rainstorm began and momentarily disabled the trilo-bots! As the electrical magnetic rain storm raged, the triloraptors rushed outside to see what was happening and witnessed one of the humans being swept away by a small whirl wind! To the triloraptors, one human being was inconsequential. So the other one hundred and thirty four were hastily reloaded and the trilo-craft hurriedly left the planet Notus!

Orders were sent by trilo-command to drop the human hostages off at the nearest habitable planet. Or if they could not find a suitable planet quickly, kill them all and then return at top speed to the main fleet! In this bleak outer region of the universe, there are only a few planets that fit the habitable bill. And the closest at just over twenty one light years away was the planet Arpeggio. Although the word Arpeggio can mean harmony, it was far from that!

Arpeggio was once a vibrant planet that had an advancing civilisation but now, that had all gone. Its total downfall happened within five earth decades of its scientists finding out how to split the atom! Now all that was left was a desolate chunk of rock! With a highly radioactive atmosphere! Knowing this, the trilo-bots injected all one hundred and thirty four humans with an anti radioactive isotope to help boost the frail human's immune systems! But, this isotope would only help for a few earth weeks!

The one hundred and thirty four remaining human hostages were a mixture of crew and passengers from the Recreational Space Station, Stephen Hawking and the Space Recreation Station, Darwin. These had been deliberately kept together by the triloraptors because they were all family groups. Strangely, despite the triloraptors killing nature, they always nurtured their young. So to ensure the human children's wellbeing, they also kept with this group the only remaining human medical doctor and two nurses.

From a deep drug induced slumber, two of the young children woke up first and thought they encountered a large glowing fairy or angel! As the six and eight year olds opened their eyes, a winged shimmering apparition flew around them and other members of their group and then the apparition disappeared! Moments later, both of the children's parents began to wake up. Excitedly both children reported what they had seen but, this was dismissed instantly by the parents and other adult members of this group had more important thing to consider. Like trying to comprehend what had happened and how they had got to this barren dusty place!

For several minutes chatter and speculation quickly got underway. One adult male even suggested that this might be an advanced holographic simulation game set up by the entertainments manager on board the recreational space station. However, this was quickly rubbished by a woman who scornfully said;

"Do you really think the multibillion dollar corporations that own the Recreational Space Stations would invent a game that would strip us of our clothing, and then put us in a godforsaken environment like this?"

The man instantly shut up but, Doctor William Tulsar had something to say;

"Ladies and Gentlemen, boys and girls, can I have your attention."

The group instantly came to a hushed silence and Doctor William Tulsar continued;

"Just in case you do not know who I am, I am Doctor William Tulsar, the medical doctor on board the Recreational Space Station, Darwin. For some reason, unbeknown to me and everyone else here, we seem to be on an alien planet?

While everyone was talking, I have been trying to evaluate our surroundings and if you look to the far left you will see the ruins of what looks like an alien town or city."

Everyone immediately looked to their far left and after a moment's silence; gasps could be heard. From their vantage point, which was on the top of a tall hill, the group could see in the far distance decaying domes that could be some kind of architectural structures. Doctor William Tulsar continued;

"I have also noticed that everyone is labouring for breath, I suspect that the atmosphere is not quite the same as on earth but, just take a lungful of air slowly and we should all be able to adjust in a short time."

One of the men in the group called out;

"Doc the sky looks very orangey; do you think that this has anything to do with it?"

Calmly Doctor William Tulsar replied;

"Sir, I have no idea but, let's get our priorities in order first. We can work on the orange sky and where we are. First we need to investigate the contents of those black containers?"

Everyone was silent, so Doctor William Tulsar continued;

"You men over there, could you please go and check for us. Hopefully the containers might hold food or water."

The men tried to run to where the twenty containers where but, they only got a few paces and then dropped to their knees. For the next few metres they crawled gasping for breath on their hands and knees. Exhausted, the men called back that ten contained liquid that could be water and the other ten some kind of seeded food.

"Good, that's good news," Doctor William Tulsar replied.

"Now", he continued;

"I have just done a head count, and we have one hundred and thirty four adults and children here. If we are careful, that food and water should last about seven days, so in that time, we need to find a fresh water supply and food.

Next, we need shelter and some of those structured domes over their might just do. I would estimate that it is about four miles (6.4372 kilometres) to the boundary of the domes. So we will need to bring that food and water containers with us. I think it would be a good idea if the men could take it in turns and try to slowly roll them down this hill to our potential new homes."

The journey to the domes was far more difficult than Doctor William Tulsar anticipated, within about thirty metres, everyone was puffing and panting and finding just the effort of walking, extremely difficult. The men who tried to push the food and water supply containers collapsed onto the ground and were clutching their chests and gasping for breath! Doctor William Tulsar had to rethink his initial strategy. Struggling for his own breath, the doctor said;

"OK everyone, just sit down and breathe slowly, I think we rushed this exercise!"

Now fighting to get his words out, the doctor breathlessly continued;

"We need more time to acclimatise to this atmosphere."

At that, the doctor slumped over and one by one, the group of humans passed out!

When the doctor regained consciousness, he found himself along with all the other humans in what appeared to be an underground cave chamber that was full of large Stalactites and Stalagmites. As he looked around, he could see a small amount of day light that filtered through from the caves large opening that was about one hundred and eighty metres away.

Cautiously in almost total darkness, he rose to his feet, took a few breaths and decided the air was a little better here. Confused as to what had happened, he called out to the group and asked if anyone knew how they got here.

From out of the shadows, a young girl answered him saying;

"Doctor, the angels brought us here."

Once again the child's parent tried to hush the child, saying;

"Rebecca dear, be quiet and let's not have any more of this nonsense about angels."

Doctor William Tulsar called back;

"Rebecca, could you and your mommy carefully head towards the light at the opening of this cave. I would like to find out more about the angels."

Out of nervous curiosity, every member of the group slowly followed Rebecca and her mother to the caves opening, but as they approached the opening, everyone's breathing became arduous. Greeting Rebecca, Doctor William Tulsar took a few slow deep breaths and said;

"Hello Rebecca, I guess from your smile and the fact that you have your two front teeth missing, that you are six years old."

Rebecca shook her head slowly from side to side and with a big toothless smile on her face she said;

"No, Doctor William Tulsar, I am six and a half years old."

The doctor laughed, took a deep breath and said;

"OK, miss six and a half year old Rebecca; tell me more about the angels?"

Rebecca looked around and could see that everyone, including her mommy was now keen to hear her story. Composing her little body so she could say her words out loud, Rebecca took a deep breath and said;

"When we all went to sleep, the angels flew in, picked us up and brought us to this cave."

In the light, Doctor William Tulsar could see extensive red marks on Rebecca's arms, legs and parts of her back. He then checked his own body and he too had similar red marks! Quickly, the doctor did a visual inspection of the people closest to him and they also had similar markings! He then ordered everyone to stand in line and as quick as he could, he examined all one hundred and thirty three humans. The examination revealed all had the same red marks. On a few, it looked like a bad heat rash but, on the majority, the marks resembled first or almost second degree burns, with nasty blisters forming on the surface skin!

Doctor William Tulsar did not want to alarm the group but, he suspected that whatever specie these angel like creatures were, their touch was toxic to human skin! He told everyone to go deeper into the cave where they could breathe easier. While this was happening, the doctor gave himself a few minutes to compose his thoughts and then announced;

"In addition to a difference in this planet's atmosphere, it would seem that we are not alone on this planet! The life forms we have encountered, now officially named 'Rebecca's Angels', must have seen that we were in distress and brought us into this cave to help us. It is my opinion that they are intelligent, sociable and do not mean us any harm. I also have to add a word of caution! If you see one, try to avoid any physical contact, as I think their touch maybe toxic to our human skin."

"Hey Doctor." A man called;

"I don't know if anyone noticed but, it would also seem that 'Rebecca's Angels' have moved the water and food containers. They are just outside the caves opening!"

CHAPTER THREE

Universal Interplanetary Congress 'Press'

The Universal Interplanetary Congress (U.I.C) had agreed in principal not to get involved in the rescue missions that Dr Elaine Laurence or as she was better known, Captain Elaine Laurence of the Newman Empire and the triloraptors were undertaking. However, after the recent universal war with the triloraptors and the overlord, they now felt it was their duty to be transparent and keep all Universal Interplanetary Congress members apprised of all new, newsworthy developments. So they contacted the Universal Interplanetary Congress media press office, and commissioned a special envoy to act on the Universal Interplanetary Congresses behalf in this matter.

Dalscar was an eight legged, three meter long four chameleon lizard with four separately mobile, stereoscopic eyes from the planet Crodus. He was head of the Universal Interplanetary Congresses media press office and the newly chosen press envoy. At this level, the technological resources available to Dalscar were first class, and for this highly newsworthy event, Dalscar intended to use them all.

First on the lizards agenda was to utilise one of the new press offices space craft and follow Captain Elaine Laurence of the Newman Empire on her noble quest. This way, the U.I.C and all of its planetary communities could have instant updates on Captain Elaine Laurence's progress.

Next, Dalscar had to appoint the journalists for a news team. This was easy, as the U.I.C press office had reporters on every U.I.C planet. Most of them would jump at this opportunity but, Dalscar had a few top notch reporters close at hand, and they were loyal to him. So Dalscar sent uni-net messages to the chosen few and within a few Crodus hours, Dalscar's news team had assembled and then headed for the 'new, news space craft'.

Because of its high level of advanced technology, the news space craft had itself been newsworthy a few Crudus weeks ago and this was its first deep space news mission. As the news team assembled, they were immediately impressed with their news room. Each species had its very own individualised work station, holographic display unit and uplink to the uni-net. Using their own uni-net link via their brains synaptic pathways and neurological receptors, the news reporters linked into uni-net online virtual news desk, where news could be analysed, cross referenced for other leads and then if need be, 'sensationalised' before going to universal public viewing.

As in all U.I.C news rooms, a large holographic display unit was situated in the centre of the news room and it had a direct link to the uni-net. Currently, it was running all up to date news feeds. The news feeds displayed the planet were the news was coming from, pictures of its geographical location and a live feed of the news event.

Wars can often spur on technology and in the years prior to the war, the Universal Interplanetary Congress had been lethargic in pushing for technological advancements but, since the war, all of that had now changed. Inter specie language communications had always been a problem but for the most, the uni-net language translator had solved that. For the minority however, it was still a problem. That problem was now being resolved as the on board uni-net communications language translator now had the latest hardware and software upgrades.

The space craft also had newly designed sensors strategically fitted that were linked into the uni-net translator and could decipher into understandable language, a species that communicates with just body language. Another innovation was it was now able to translate the meaning of those specie who communicate with changeable colours on their bodies. And finally, through the sensitivity of the sensors, it also had odour detection analyses for species who communicate with pheromones.

Arblaa Diplad was the news space craft's captain and was a large round, multi limbed, multi coloured landlocked puffer-gill hermaphrodite from a planetoid that has a large amount of methane in its atmosphere. One of the new technologies on-board was computer controlled gravity and atmospheric mobile containment force fields. With the exception of aquatics, these force fields accommodated most of the Universal Interplanetary Congress specie. Now the captain and every other specie could wonder freely around the space craft and not have to be confined to their own gravity and atmospheric chambers.

With everyone on board, the captain ordered that the graviton engines be brought online and after the standard safety checks had been cleared, the news craft left its space dock in pursuit of Captain Elaine Laurence and the triloraptors on board the space craft Notus One.

In a discussion with Captain Diplad; Dalscar was not happy to find that at their present speed of ten gravitons, it would take several rotations of his planet to catch up to Notus One. This discussion became quite heated as Dalscar tried to insist that Captain Diplad ignore safety protocols of running the graviton engines in and increase the crafts speed to at least twelve and a half gravitons. Angry at being told what to do, the captain's puffer-gill body began to swell and as a chameleon lizard, Dalscar body changed from green to an angry red! This was not a good start to their voyage and both went off in a huff!

Both forgot their little tiff when the long range scanner's picked up what appeared to be an unidentified space craft almost mirroring their route? Under the Universal Interplanetary Congresses rules on space protocol, all space craft are required to identify each other. So, Captain Diplad sent a message on all known communications media to the unidentified space craft, informing the craft that they were an Interplanetary Universal Congress news craft and asking the unidentified space craft for identification. That's when they felt a slight shudder and the propulsion from the graviton new engines died!

Puzzled at what just happened? Captain Diplad immediately asked the engine room for an update. The reply he got back was not what he was expecting!

"Captain," the chief engineer replied. "The graviton engine has disappeared and if you check the long range sensors, so had that unidentified space craft!"

If Dalscar hadn't been on-board, he would have found this story hard to believe but, it was true and after reporting what had happened to the Universal Interplanetary Congress, he next put out on the uni-net his exclusive headline story; UFO Steals Graviton Engine from New I.U.C News Space Craft!

An immediate U.I.C rescue mission and investigation into this extraordinary incident was launched. Also, while the Universal Interplanetary Congresses investigation team got to the bottom of this unexplained phenomena, all Universal Interplanetary Congresses space craft's with graviton engines were advised not to travel!

As a large proportion of the U.I.C members had more conventional engines in their space crafts, the new graviton engine restrictions would not affect them. This however was not true of one species, the triloraptors; almost every space craft in their fleet had now been fitted with this new drive graviton system. Another problem the triloraptors had with this new directive is; they are nomadic and live in space. Being triloraptors, they chose the only path open to them, ignore the directive and hunt the graviton engine thieves!

On record, the U.I.C was not happy with the triloraptors for ignoring their directive. Off the record however, they could not argue with them as they could see that being a nomadic space species, they had no choice in this matter. So they agreed to share any information their investigators found. For the triloraptors, this gesture meant nothing and they planned to proceed as always, doing things their own way!

Both the U.I.C investigation team and a fleet of ten trilo-craft turned up within the vicinity of the incapacitated news space craft together. The first problem was trying to board the space craft that was still travelling out of control, at a speed of almost ten gravitons! If the news craft had still got its graviton engine it could use it to help it de-accelerate but without it, it would take several Crudus years just to slow down to light speed! Another major problem was, at this immense speed, to the rear of the news space craft, the spacial turbulence was enormous!

It was the triloraptors that took the initiative. They used their trilo-super computer to re-create this scenario and within a few trilo-seconds it came up with a feasible solution. Five trilo-craft accelerated to twelve gravitons and shot passed the news space craft, they then strategically positioned themselves so they were now 160 934.4 kilometres (one hundred thousand miles) directly in front of the news craft and with nano second timing, all five fired the reverse thrusters of their own graviton engines. The blasts from all five sent a spacial wake backwards that acted like a buffer and the news craft slowly began to de-accelerate.

As the five trilo-craft continued to fire their rear graviton thrusters, another four trilo-craft strategically positioned themselves at a safe 80 467.2 kilometres (fifty thousand miles) distance to the left, right, top and bottom of the news space craft. When their on board trilo-computers detected that the news craft speed was at exactly eight gravitons, all four trilo-craft angled themselves at forty five degrees in relation the news craft space ship and then fired their graviton rear thrusters at five trilo-second bursts, this helped slow the news craft down to just over five gravitons.

The tenth trilo-craft had kept its distance and was doing long range surveillance, when it faintly detected several other unidentified space craft. Before it and all the other nine trilo-craft could react, each trilo-craft felt a small shudder and within half a nano second, their graviton engines disappeared!

Before heading for this rescue mission, the triloraptors had anticipated this possibility and had installed small but efficient old fashioned plasma matter-antimatter back up engines. Immediately sensing the problem, their on-board trilo-computers automatically fired up these old but reliable back up engines and each trilo-craft began to slowly accelerate away.

Back on board the Universal Interplanetary Congresses news ship, Dalscar and his team were in reporter's heaven! They normally reported the news, now they and all that was happening around them were the news! The news room was a frantic hive of actively with news feeds going live every few Crudus minutes.

More excitingly, with its ultra smooth ceramic glazed exterior. The news ships body acted as one big external camera lens and had captured in superb three dimensional, high quality, holographic definition and amazingly, from every conceivable angle, the news ships rescue mission and all the drama's to date! What it recorded next would go down in Universal Interplanetary Congresses news history! In unison, all ten triloraptor ships and the Universal Interplanetary Congresses craft just disappeared!

Captain Diplad immediately tried opening the uni-net and all other communications frequencies to attempt to contact the eleven missing space craft, when he was joined by Dalscar. Dalscar indicated that Captain Diplad should carry on but, frustratingly Captain Diplad's body began to swell, and the multi limbed puffer-gill hermaphrodite raised all its limbs to indicate to Dalscar that all communications were dead! Perplexed by the rescue crafts disappearance, the next course of action was for both of them to use their emergency uni-net links and meet instantly with all U.I.C delegates at their virtual congressional meeting hall.

As this was an undoubted crisis, all three thousand five hundred elected delegates' uni-links instantly activated and within a few nano seconds, every delegate was present in the virtual congressional meeting hall. In order to avoid any inter specie bigotries, the normal specie protocols had also been activated and every delegate appeared as a different coloured orb.

Rather than go through lengthy explanations, Captain Diplad in agreement with Dalscar used the uni-net holographic recording of the incident and let the congressional U.I.C members view the eleven space craft just disappear. All members instantly began to speculate over what had happened until the chair elect, an highly intelligent aquatic from the oceanic planet Ramlindos, called out and said;

> "Members of this esteemed congress, let's stop this speculation and deal with the hard facts. At present, we know that eleven graviton engines have gone missing from eleven space craft. We also know is that . . . ."

The chair elects words dried up as the triloraptor delegate, dressed in its full obsidian black trilo-combat uniform, with its trilo-tron at its side, joined the meeting. Ignoring the normal protocols of U.I.C Congress meetings, the triloraptor jumped in and said;

> "What you know is nothing; we the triloraptors also have nothing, our ten trilo-craft have vanished without a trace!

Like all members of the Universal Interplanetary Congress, we thought the theft of the graviton engine was an act of space piracy but, this now goes beyond that! It now appears we have a new cowardly enemy, one who hides in the darkness of space but, has technology that we do not have. We are at war again!"

Pausing for a moment so that all three thousand five hundred elected delegates could digest his words, the triloraptor tried to continue but was heckled by a light green orb who shouted;

"This is a typical over reaction from the triloraptors; all they want is to fight and kill!

Calmly the triloraptor delegate replied;

"Delegates of the Universal Interplanetary Congress, we are what we are and as you are aware, adhere to the Universal Interplanetary Congresses law of the way. But when an unknown adversary abducts our crews and steals out technology along with ten of our trilo-craft, we do not cower behind our orbs. We do what we do best!"

At that, the triloraptor disengaged its uni-net link and left the emergency Universal Interplanetary Congresses Congressional meeting.

As soon as the triloraptor delegate left, numerous discussions took place concerning the risk of a new war and clearly, the bitter memories of the last one still lingered on! Discussions then took place on trying to resolve this issue with diplomacy. So until the mystery of what had happened to the missing space craft's along with crews and why this unknown faction had wanted their graviton engines was solved. All three thousand, five hundred delegates agreed that they had the uni-net virtual links for all business communications and leisure activities. In view of this, it was then unanimously agreed that space travel was not necessary and could be restricted to emergency and essential needs only for the foreseeable future!

Both Dalsca and Captain Diplad objected strongly to this lily-livered approach but, both were unanimously overruled! The chair elect told them in no uncertain words that they and the crew on board the news space craft were in no imminent danger. The chair elect then pointed out they had plenty of provisions, top class facilities and could survive comfortably drifting in space for quite some time! This decision was then endorsed by all three thousand, five hundred Universal Interplanetary Congress Congressional delegates!

Infuriated, Dalsca and Captain Diplad immediately turned off their uni-net links and headed for the news room. Their intentions were to broadcast this outrageous judgment to all Universal Interplanetary Congress Congressional members! But, before they could get there, the inside of the news craft went into total darkness and like the other eleven space craft, the news craft disappeared!

CHAPTER FOUR

Really angry!

Upon hearing the decision of the Universal Interplanetary Congress, the triloraptor central commands elders convened for an emergency meeting. The trilo-super computer had already sensed the annoyance in this group and had analysed all the data available. To save its masters any further anguish, it had already come up with several suggestions.

Each triloraptor elder stood in front of its own three dimensional holographic display unit. Triloraptors do not need any frills, niceties or welcomes, so the unit displayed a priority listing that each elder could consider. The list read as follows;

1. Contact Captain Elaine Laurence and the triloraptor rescue team immediately and inform them of what has happened. Also inform them that there is a ninety nine point nine percent chance that they too are also in danger.
2. Immediately upgrade all cloaking devices with variable multi energy force fields.
3. Expand the multi energy force fields to encompass the whole trilo-fleet.
4. Send trilo-drones investigation crafts to the sites that have had space craft stolen and collate further information.
5. Restrict triloraptor space flight until further information is gathered.
6. Once enough information has been gathered and processed, annihilate this unknown enemy!

Number five on the list did not please the triloraptor elders but, number six excited them and for number six to work they had to concede that number five would have to be implemented.

Within a few trilo-minutes the elders had contacted Captain Elaine Laurence and their advanced technology department was working on ways of upgrading their cloaking devices with variable multi energy force fields that could also expand around one, several or if need be their whole fleet.

Elaine took the news of what had happened calmly but, the four triloraptors travelling with her were extremely agitated. In a calm voice, Elaine told them;

> "We have a mission to complete and I am confident that trilo-central command will be able to handle this issue. For now, our mission is all I intend to concentrate on but, I think we should be more vigilant and for that I will need you to increase long range scans and our on-board security. I also want regular updates on any developments from trilo-central command."

It was difficult for Elaine to try to gauge if this had pacified the triloraptors as they took their instructions and without commenting they just walked away. But she needed to ask Notus for some advice on the missing space craft. Before she could telepathically say anything, Notus said;

> "Elaine, the space craft that have gone missing seem to have somehow been moved into a temporal field that exists four earth seconds outside this universes own space time continuum!"

Elaine had no idea what that meant and said to Notus;

> "What exactly does that mean?"

Replying Notus explained;

> "The explanation is extremely complex but to simplify it, they have been trapped in a time pocket that appears to be four earth seconds out of phase with this universe. How this has happened, I do not know and I also do not know what affect it will have on the crews of the space craft's!"

Elaine's calm demeanour began to crumble and she now felt apprehensive. She then asked Notus;

"Do you think this has anything to do with our rescue mission?"

Notus was aware of Elaine's anxiety and replied;

"Elaine, I wish I could say yes or no but, I really do not know. Although I am old, my own experience of temporal fields and time is limited. Temporal fields like this one are extremely rare and for me to gain more insight into this, I will have to contact some of my specie who might be able to supply more information. In the mean time, let's just carry on with our objective and rescue your fellow humans."

Still puzzled Elaine had another two questions;

"Notus, how do you know that they vanished into a temporal field or time pocket? And what or who owned the other alien spaceships sited?"

Notus laughed and replied;

"Your question about the temporal field or time pocket is the easy bit. Seventy percent of space in this universe is full of dark matter and dark energy. I and all my specie are sensitive to all matter in this and other universes. I can sense that the whole area where the space craft have gone missing is also completely empty of dark matter and dark energy. It is therefore logical to assume that they had no other place to go.

As to the four seconds, well I have estimated this based on how long it would take to open a temporal field that big, envelop the space craft and then close the field.

I know you are thinking that I have overlooked the missing graviton engines but, I have to concede, that is a mystery to me, and at this point of time I can offer no plausible explanation.

As too the alien spaceships positioned close to the ones that have gone missing. This is the hard bit and again my answer is just a guess. But, I think as the temporal fields were opening, they caused several manifestations. And what were seen were mirror images of the triloraptor and U.I.C spaceships!"

Elaine could not mention Notus's evaluation of what had happened to the triloraptors central command or U.I.C as both parties did not know of Notus's the beings existence. So she decided to put forward a hypothesis from herself and hoped that they would take a serious look into this mysterious temporal field.

Elaine mentally asked Notus One's super computer to open a uni-net link to the U.I.C and triloraptors central command and after a quick greeting from the chair elect and the triloraptor delegate, Elaine informed them of her theory and also asked them to send any data they had on temporal fields or any other related time anomalies.

In the past few earth months Elaine had, had a few uni-net virtual conversations but, she had never had one with an aquatic! The chair elect was swimming in a virtual tank of what looked like sparkling blue water and she was stunningly beautiful. Her forty metre long body was covered in mirrored gold scales that glistened in the clear liquid. What Elaine found even more surprising was her face, it looked as if she had almost the same amount of face muscles that a human being has, the chair elect could smile and frown. On earth, this beautiful creature could easily pass as a gigantic fabled mermaid.

As Elaine finished her presentation, both chair elect and triloraptor delegate thanked Captain Elaine Laurence for her conjecture and said that they would investigate this further. Elaine was also promised that they would keep her up to date on their findings and send her any relevant data they had. As Elaine asked the super computer to close her uni-net link, she realised a triloraptor was standing close by. Elaine mentally smiled but her crystal blue adapted D.N.A face would not let her do this. Politely she asked the triloraptor;

"Can I help you?"

Replying the triloraptor said;

"We are now at the edge of the solar system and we need to prepare to disarm the outer systems spacial trilo-nuclear mines before we can proceed."

Elaine thought it a little strange that the triloraptor was informing her of this and said;

"Please proceed with this, or is there a problem?

Looking straight into Elaine's eyes, the triloraptor said with its normal detachment of emotion;

"We would like to proceed but, we do not have the disarm codes. They were lost when you destroyed our mother ship and most of our main fleet!"

A little shocked by this, Elaine said;

"We returned your trilo-super computers black box. Didn't that have the disarm data?"

Again without any sentiment, the triloraptor answered;

"No, they were lost along with the trilo-craft that placed the trilo-nuclear mines here in the first place. Now we need to concentrate on disarming them, the ones on the outer region of the solar system are the easiest. They are just nano-bot controlled, random floating nuclear mines with laser, motion and heat detection!"

To Elaine that sounded horrendous but trying to act cool, Elaine inquired;

"How many were placed in the outer region of this solar system?"

Triloraptors do not have facial muscles but as it replied, Elaine could have sworn she had seen it grin as it said;

"I estimate the number to be in excess of two hundred and fifty thousand!"

Flabbergasted and now angry, Elaine said;

"Over a quarter of a million, how the hell are we going to disarm all of these? Surely this will take fore ever!"

Confidently, the triloraptor answered;

"Once we get past the first one, we will then programme our trilo-drones with the codes and then use them to then clear a path for us. While we continue on our journey, they can then continue working in the outer regions of this solar system and disarm all of the others!"

Elaine thought that this was going to be a walk in the park until the triloraptor mentioned;

"You will need to collect your trilo-combat uniform and accompany me to the trilo-shuttle craft. We can then go over the plan of how you can disarm the first one!

Without hesitation Elaine said;

"Hang on, didn't the trilo-drones disarm similar spacial mines outside the worm hole that led to the overlord's universe and they did it without me?"

"You are correct," the triloraptor replied. "But as I mention earlier, these are different. They have a disarm code and that has to be input manually."

Elaine had another question that she thought might please the triloraptors;

"Why can't we just blow them up?"

"We could," the triloraptor replied "but, as you are aware this solar system is collapsing under a massive gravitational field. Detonating over two hundred and fifty thousand nuclear bombs would only add to its destabilisation."

Elaine did not like what she had just heard and asked;

"Does this mean what I think it means, I have to go into space and then disarm a nuclear mine that you do not have the disarm codes for?"

The triloraptor began walking towards the shuttle bay corridor and using one of its wings it beckoned Elaine to follow it, and answered;

"That is correct, that is the plan."

CHAPTER FIVE

Nerves of steel

As Elaine sat in the trilo-shuttle craft, she put on her trilo-combat uniform and visor and then studied the trilo-symbols on the inside of her trilo-visors screen. Each symbol was a numerical number in the triloraptors language and ranged from zero to one thousand. Any one of these numbers in an eight number combination could be the deactivation code!

The trilo-shuttle headed out from Notus One's launch bay and its objective was to find the closest trilo-nuclear mine! Their first problem was trying to identify them as they were individually camouflaged to look like chunks of space debris. Using both long and short range scanners, the triloraptor piloting the trilo-shuttle said;

> "We have one just twenty five thousand metres ahead, it looks like a small piece of space ice about ten metres wide. Captain Elaine Laurence, are you ready for your space walk?"

Without saying a word, Elaine just nodded and walked over to the air lock and waited for the triloraptor to open the air lock door. She then walked in and the air lock door closed behind her. Depressurisation only took four earth seconds. As this was happening, Elaine counted three, two, one and then using her ability to manipulate gravity, she mentally activated a spherical shaped anti-gravity force field around herself!

As the exterior doors opened, Elaine's visor showed her the exact location of the camouflaged nuclear mine. Concentrating hard, with her anti-gravity force field around her, Elaine drifted out of the air hatch and into open space. The triloraptors had assured her that the trilo-spacial mines motion detection would only activate if it detected motion from something as large as a small shuttle or space craft. They also mentioned that as she was less than two metre tall and now a pure energy being, the trilo-mine should not detect her motion and she should be alright. That was not a comfort to Elaine, in the back of her mind she still did not trust the triloraptors; after all, they had already tried to kill her once before!

Putting those thoughts aside, Elaine paused and made sure her trilo-combat uniform was not radiating any heat. She also set her trilo combat uniform so that it appeared to allow a laser beams light to go straight through it. Satisfied that everything was functioning correctly, Elaine moved slowly forward another two hundred and fifty metres and then stopped again. Through her visor communications one of the triloraptors said;

> "When you get close to the trilo-spacial mine, activate the icon now showing in your visors display. This will open the mines control unit. Our trilo-super computer has narrowed the code down to fourteen thousand possibilities but, you only get one chance and if it is wrong the mine will activate the tamper device and in one nano second the mine will detonate!

Hearing that, Elaine's heart nearly jumped out of her trilo combat uniform! She took a few deep breaths to calm herself and then realising what she had just done, Elaine mentally laughed to herself and thought;

> "Old habits die hard, come on Elaine, you're immortal now, you don't need air."

But then a horrible thought jumped into her head;

> "You may be immortal but, remember what killed Notus's offspring Olotinium who was a lot more powerful that you are. A massive nuclear explosion!"

With that thought in her mind, Elaine went back to taking a few more deep breaths and edged herself closer to the trilo-spacial mine. When she was just one metre away, she stopped and activated the icon that opened the trilo-spacial mines control panel. The panel instantly opened and then it linked automatically with her trilo visor. In front of Elaine's eyes a trilo-numerical key pad appeared. All she had to do now was mentally input the correct code! Before she attempted to input any numbers, she telepathically asked Notus for help. Notus immediately said;

"Elaine, I have been working with Notus One's super computer but regrettably, I do not have the correct code for you. Just remember that you are unique in this universe, so close your eyes and try to visualise each trilo-number."

What Notus said really did not help, Elaine realised she was on her own and out of desperation she closed her eyes and tried to visualise the trilo-numbers but as hard as she tried, nothing happened! All that kept distracting her in the silence of space was the heavy thumping of her heart!

That's when a thought hit her; she knew it was stupid and illogical but, she had no other option. She began to count how many heart beats she had in a minute. In the first minute she had sixty eight beats. Elaine then spent the next seven minutes monitoring her heart rate that slowed down each minute. Now with eight different numbers, Elaine used her trilo-visor and called up the triloraptors numerical equivalents. Each number was then converted into a trilo symbol and with that, Elaine had a trilo-numbered code. Wasting no time, Elaine immediately cross referenced her code with the fourteen thousand that the trilo-super computers had come up and it came up blank except for one that had five trilo-symbols in the same order! The other three of the trilo-symbols were completely different!

Elaine felt she was on the right road but she had to make a decision. Use all of her codes or the triloraptors codes? Logically choosing the triloraptor ones would make sense as it was their trilo-spatial mine. But, Elaine still had that niggling doubt! She knew in that instant that she would go for her own combination and as quickly as she could, she mentally entered her own eight digit code and pressed enter. The inside of her visor flashed a message that the mine had been de-activated and Elaine began to cry with relief! Offering Elaine some comfort, Notus telepathically said;

"Well done warrior princess, you now have a new skill, deactivating trilo-nuclear bombs!"

Elaine could not respond for a few moments as she began to shake and tremble! And finally after a few earth minutes she tried to inject a little humour into this situation by saying;

"Notus, if I were still human, my hair would be snow white by now!"

Notus could feel how shaken Elaine was and replied;

"Elaine, it's time to head back to the shuttle and when you get back. Ask the triloraptor pilot to give you a big hug!"

This made Elaine laugh; she looked back at the shuttle and within an earth second she was at the airlock door. Instantly the air lock opened and Elaine entered the decompression chamber. As the chamber pressurised, Elaine mentally closed her anti-gravity force field. The inner door then opened and to her relief, she stepped into the trilo-shuttle. Inside, her triloraptor companion was waiting for her and he began stamping his feet.

"Thump, thump, thump, thump, thump, thump, thump, thump, thump, thump."

This was a sign of respect from the triloraptor but, as Elaine took of her trilo-visor, the triloraptor pilot stopped stamping and just stared at Elaine. This began to unnerve Elaine and she said sharply;

"OK, what's wrong, why are you staring at me?"

The triloraptor instantly spoke up and replied;

"Captain Elaine Laurence, I meant no disrespect to you, but, your skin has changed colour, and you are now metallic silver!"

The trilo-shuttle craft interior was quite bland; its walls were a dull black and had no shiny surfaces, so a mirror was definitely out of the question. Elaine sat down and began to slip off her trilo-combat uniform and sure enough her skin was metallic silver! She attempted to smile at the pilot triloraptor and as she could not, she said;

"This my feathered trilo-friend is my adaptive DNA in action!"

Nodding as if he understood, he then carried on with his duties, Elaine however telepathically said to Notus;

"Doctor Frankenstein, what's with the metal silver girl?"

Answering in a Swiss Doctor Frankenstein accent, Notus replied;

"I think we have a new you, cosmic woman! This must be your adaptive DNA protective skin colour when you spacewalk."

In a serious tone, Elaine asked;

"Do you think this metal skin would have protected me if that trilo-nuclear mine had exploded?"

Trying to keep Elaine calm, Notus replied;

"Let's hope we never have to put it to the test. Oh by the way, you may have been surprised that you could decipher the nuclear mines code just by listening to your heart. As I said earlier you are unique and you have some of my species abilities, one of those is to be at one with your surroundings. As for your metallic skin, I think silver is definitely your colour."

Mentally laughing, Elaine said;

"Flattery will get you everywhere. However, it is not very flattering to know I am at one with a trilo-spatial nuclear mine!"

At that, both Notus and Elaine burst out laughing. However, Elaine was still in the company of her triloraptor companion and her outburst of laughter got a few more strange glances? When Elaine stopped laughing, the triloraptor said;

"We are about to dock in Notus Ones shuttle bay. We need to head immediately for the command centre so we can go over our next objective, disarming the planetary defence network!"

This to Elaine had a sound of foreboding to it. And she then recalled what the triloraptor had said;

"The ones on the outer region of the solar system are the easiest"!

As Elaine and the four triloraptors walked into Notus Ones command centre. The three dimensional holographic display unit light up and display the planet and its two moons that Elaine's team were heading to. One of the triloraptors walked forward and said;

"Turn on the holographic planetary defence network."

A grid appeared around the planet, each grids gap was tiny and Elaine estimated that you could only fit something the size of a small bird through it. The triloraptor continued;

"As you can see the lattice on the grid is small. If an object hits the grid, the grid distorts with its impact, and in five nano seconds, the grids nerve centres evaluates if the object is a threat. If it is not a threat, like a small meteor, it allows it to pass through harmlessly. However, if any weapon or spacecraft known to the triloraptors is detected, the grid rejects the object instantly with a high powered pulse wave. At the same time, thousands of trilo-proton nano mines are released that attach themselves to the object! As the object is thrust back into space by the pulse wave, it is destroyed instantly!

I also need to add, if for any reason the grid is breached by a hostile weapon or craft, a microscopic tamper device is activated in each human on the planet's surface and they all die instantly!"

Out loud Elaine said;

"Wow, that's impressive, it's a shame Earth did not have one of these when you and the U.I.C came calling! So, how do we turn it off?"

Almost excitedly, the triloraptor asked the holographic display unit to show phase two and then answered;

"That's where things get more impressive. The planetary defence network has four nerve command centres. When they were originally activated, two were exactly aligned with the North and South poles of the planet. The other two were positioned along the equatorial line, one in the East the other at its exact opposite in the west.

Since that point of time, every ten trilo-minutes they automatically realign themselves by ten degrees North to South, South to North and East to West and West to East.

Disarming them will not be easy as they have holographic camouflage that allows them to blend in with natural colours displayed in the upper atmosphere. We also have to calculate their relative planetary position now. Additionally, we have to use two space craft for the disarm procedure! We will concentrate on the ones positioned along the North and South line first and then in less than ten trilo-minutes, disarm the two positioned along East to West line.

Should we fail to do this in the specified time, all of the tamper devices will be activated and we will be treated as hostiles! As soon as this happens, a second defence grid that is positioned around the outer regions of the planets second moon will also be activated, therefore making survivable escape impossible! Needless to say, the tamper device will also kill the humans on the planet's surface!"

In Elaine's mind, this reminded her of an old classic television series and movies, mission impossible. All that was missing was the music! Elaine then took a few more moments to take in this new mission and said;

"As I see it, the first thing we need to do is split Notus One from the trilo-mother ship. We then need to feed the co-ordinates of the four nerve command centres into our two crafts super computers so that we co-ordinate our disarm procedures down to one nano second."

All four triloraptors seemed to be in agreement with this and their spokesperson said;

"We shall start the crafts separation procedure immediately."

Notus One was created by Notus the being so that Elaine could travel in space. As space craft's come, Notus One was spectacular. Its shape was of a crystal blue Marquise-Cut boat shaped diamond that was 2953 metres long and 1476.5 metres wide. This magnificent space craft was made by mixing some of the deceased Olotinium's pure energy atoms with the four pure carbon atoms that normally make diamonds. The result is a super strong pure energy structured diamond which also has a unique pure energy drive system.

After Notus and Elaine defeated the triloraptors fleet and destroyed their mother ship. The triloraptors devised an elaborate plan to capture Elaine's space craft, Notus One! They made a space craft that looked exactly like Notus One and called it their 'new mother ship'.

This new mother ship had a few radical difference's; it colour was obsidian-black and at least twenty times bigger than Notus One! This clever but devious plan was to capture Notus One and use its advanced technology to further the triloraptors trilo-goals. They first blasted Notus One with a powerful electro-pulse wave that affected its con.rol and computer functions! Once Notus One was temporarily disabled, they manoeuvred their new trilo-space craft into position alongside Notus One and from its centre; it slowly began to divide into two.

The trilo crafts 'new mother ships' two sections then manoeuvred themselves so one was above and the other was below Notus One. Then with triloraptor precision, the two sections then manoeuvred themselves so Notus One was completely imprisoned. Being made of R.I.T.S (robomatic inter transdimensional substance), the same substance that their other trilo-craft and trilo combat suits are made of, the two sections then sealed themselves together and the space craft appeared to be one whole vessel again!

However, the triloraptors plan backfired and Notus the being ingeniously took control of the triloraptors Trojan horse, their alleged 'mother ship' and decided to utilise this spacecraft to aid in the rescue of Elaine's people. Now for the first time since they had merged, they were about to separate the two space craft's!

Because of past dealing, both Elaine and Notus were a little apprehensive of the triloraptors. But to Elaine's surprise, the triloraptors spokesperson stayed in Notus Ones command centre. The other three triloraptors went to their own command centre to organise the separation of the trilo-mother ship from Notus One. A few trilo-minutes later, Elaine's three dimensional holographic display unit lit up showing the diamond shaped obsidian-black Marquise-Cut boat shaped trilo craft. It looked magnificent. In triloraptor numerals a countdown began and as it reached the equivalent of zero, the centre of the trilo-mother ship began to dissolve and slowly from its centre the space craft split into two!

Both sections continued to rise until Elaine could see clearly her own beautiful crystal blue space craft. Within another few trilo-minutes the two trilo craft sections had manoeuvred themselves so that they were clear of Notus One. They then aligned themselves back up and the trilo-mother craft was whole again.

For a moment, Elaine began to remember back to her days on-board the recreational space station where she was the on-board doctor. The whole crew were always put on standby as docking and undocking procedures were complex and a little dangerous. Elaine had to admire the triloraptors skill on this as the whole procedure was over in less than fifteen earth minutes and was probably two hundred times more complex.

A holographic triloraptor then appeared on Elaine's display unit and said;

> "We have linked our on-board trilo-super computer to yours so that we can synchronize both our arrivals at the North and South poles of the planet precisely. Once there, we will begin the procedure for disarmament of the trilo-planetary defence network."

At that, the three dimensional holographic unit turned itself off.

Before joining the triloraptors towards the planet they had never given a name to. Elaine took another moment and looked around. The exterior of Notus One was transparent and although each facet on its outer surface fractionally distorted the view, the view into space was stunning! She then decided to give a name to the planet, she said out loud;

> "Computer the planet we are heading to will be called 'Hope', please proceed to the planet 'Hope'."

CHAPTER SIX

Planet Hope

Both space craft arrived at their designated co-ordinates at precisely the same time. Elaine was just outside the planet Hopes upper atmosphere at its North Pole and the triloraptors were at its South Pole. Each space ships super computer took less than a few nano seconds to plot the approximate locations of the first two trilo-planetary defence network command nerve centres. The super computers also ascertained that the four nerve command centres had realigned themselves exactly eight trilo-minutes ago. Elaine made a decision to wait until the next alignment before proceeding, that way they would have their full ten trilo-minutes.

While they waited, the triloraptor who stayed with Elaine went over the disarm procedure;

> "As soon as we are both in position, we will simultaneously fire a trilo-drone that is armed with a liquid oxygen instant neutraliser (L.O.I.N.) towards where we consider the command nerve centres are. The trilo-drone will fire a serious of short bursts from the neutraliser revealing the camouflaged command nerve centres and at the same time this will temporally freeze the anti tamper device. We then need our super computers to communicate with each command nerve centres and request their disarming trilo-codes.

> Each command nerve centre has a different trilo-code and that has to be inputted by our super computers within five nano seconds. Once this is inputted, we need to move as quickly as we can move to our next location and then repeat the same procedure."

Smiling and being a little sarcastic Elaine said;

"This sounds like a walk in the park."

But then looking at the blank expression on the triloraptors face, Elaine mentally summarised that triloraptors do not have parks or indeed the ability to deal with satirical humour.

The triloraptor did however ask Elaine to look at the holographic display unit. The display jumped to life with a large trilo-countdown clock. From what Elaine could establish they had less than one trilo-minute before the next alignment. Looking at Elaine the triloraptor said;

"For speed and accuracy, I suggest you let Notus Ones super computer handle flight control for the next few manoeuvres."

Elaine nodded and mentally ordered the Notus One super computer to take over the helm. The clock then hit the triloraptors equivalent of zero and Notus One shot off to its next destination. Again, the holographic display unit lit up and was now showing a real time simulation of both space craft's at their new planetary positions. From each craft a trilo-drone emerged and within a few trilo-seconds they fired their L.O.I.Ns and located their target. Almost instantly, the holographic display unit displayed a message that successful disarms had been completed, and both space craft's swiftly moved to their East West positions. With excellent trilo-efficiency, the procedure was then duplicated and the awesome trilo-planetary defence network was disarmed.

While the final disarm procedure only took a few trilo-minutes to complete, Elaine realised that without the triloraptors help this far, her rescue mission would have failed. She would probably have been killed trying to disarm the trilo-spacial nuclear mines. Even if she got passed the solar systems outer spacial trilo-nuclear mine traps, the trilo-planetary defence network would have definitely got her and almost certainly, Notus One would have also been destroyed!

More alarmingly, had the evil overlord tried this, her fellow humans on the planet Hope would have almost certainly been killed! Conversely, not by the overlord, but by the microscopic tamper device implanted into them by the triloraptors!

Elaine decided that she had to stop thinking 'what if' and had to focus on 'what now,' so she turned to the triloraptor spokesperson and said;

"Now that the trilo-planetary defence network is disarmed, lets head on down to the planet's surface and make contact with my fellow human beings."

Completely dampening Elaine's enthusiasm, the triloraptor replied;

"We have to get past the trilo-ground to air defence systems first!"

If the triloraptor could have pulled out one of its smallest feathers, it would have been able to knock Elaine over with it with what is had just said. Exasperated, Elaine replied;

"Bloody hell, why in the name of the entire god's in this universe did you have to install more Trilo-booby traps?"

Without any emotion in its voice the triloraptor answered;

"We have just fought a war with the overlord who is one of the most intelligent beings in this and his own universe. Had he have won, he would by now be in control of this universe and the only species left that would be able to fight him would be the triloraptors! Any good military force knows that in war, to wear the enemy down, you have to make every step they take as arduous as possible."

Elaine could not argue with this trilo-strategy, and calming down a little, she asked;

"How do we disarm the trilo-ground to air defence systems?"

With a strange enthusiasm in its voice, the triloraptor replied;

"We do not disarm this system, we have to destroy them!"

Elaine kept quiet and gestured with her hands for the triloraptor to continue;

"Each one is camouflaged with a hologram that blends in perfectly with its background. They only work on planets that have an atmosphere and discharge acoustically propelled plasma light emissions (A.P.P.L.E) that instantly shatter the hostile crafts exterior and will destroy most known space craft.

Elaine began to laugh out loud and said;

"You throw apples at hostile space ships!"

Ignoring Elaine's humorous but irrelevant remark, the triloraptor continued;

"To be safe, we will need to stay outside the planet's atmosphere and deploy decoy trilo-siles to draw the A.P.P.L.E's fire. Once we have located them, we can destroy them with our on-board trilo-space to ground high velocity pulse cannons."

All Elaine could do was nod in agreement and then watch the action on the three dimensional holographic display unit.

The three dimensional holographic display unit lit up with a stunning display of the planet Hope and the trilo-mother ship in orbit above its Northern hemisphere. Elaine assumed that Notus One was not included in this as it did not have any decoy trilo-siles on board. Within a few trilo-seconds, several hundred decoy trilo-siles were fired into the atmosphere above the planets Northern hemisphere. Elaine could not calculate their speed but, from what she could see, she knew they were incredibly fast! As they entered the planet Hopes atmosphere, the A.P.P.L.E's defence system instantly destroyed them!

On-board the trilo-mother ship, the triloraptors had within a few nano seconds gathered the information they needed to establish the exact co-ordinates of the A.P.P.L.E's defence systems in this hemisphere and had programmed their weapons defence systems to automatically return fire. Silently, the trilo-space to ground high velocity pulse cannons burst into action. All that could be seen on the three dimensional holographic display unit as each high velocity pulse hit its target, was a tiny ripple on the surface of the planet Hope.

Satisfied that all A.P.P.L.E's had been destroyed in the Northern hemisphere, the trilo-mother ship swiftly headed to the planets Southern, Eastern and Western hemispheres and time after time repeated the process. To any other species, this trouble-free procedure would have been a mere military manoeuvre. But, for all four triloraptors who normally revel in killing, firing there high velocity pulse cannons was a much needed release!

At the end of this, one of the three triloraptors came onto the three dimensional holographic display unit and announced that all of the A.P.P.L.E's defence systems had been completely destroyed! When Elaine was ready, the trilo-mother ship was now ready to link back up with Notus One in readiness for their descent to the planet's surface.

Elaine's heart began to race; she knew that due to time dilation, over forty years had passed since seeing some of her fellow humans and colleagues. Nevertheless, she was really excited by the thought of the re-union. Her next thought was what to wear? The only clothing she had was her trilo-combat uniform. Deciding that this was better than nothing, while the two space craft's linked up she began to put it on. It was then she realised her skin was crystal blue! Once again this was thanks to her 'at times' annoying adaptive DNA! Elaine just hoped that when she meet up with her fellow humans colleagues that her skin would change to it normal 'human' mode. If not, she would have a bit of explaining to do!

Notus One and the trilo mother craft linked up effortlessly and with the co-ordinates already known by the triloraptors. Elaine and her trilo-chums made their way to the Brobryne marsh lands on the planet's surface.

It was just approaching dawn as the 59,060 metre long obsidian black craft smoothly touchdown almost at the centre of the Brobryne marsh lands. Elaine had asked Notus Ones super computer to scan for human life forms but, it had come up with nothing! Elaine thought that maybe the sight of this big black diamond space craft could have spooked her people or more realistically, over time they could have moved away.

So initially, she thought it would be easier to search the area with the triloraptors in flight. With trilo-precision, each triloraptor took to the air and searched an individual 160.9344 kilometres (one hundred miles) grid that came up on inside their trilo-visor. Elaine's plan was first to do it the old earth way by initially walking and calling out "Hello." And if this proved fruitless, she would create an anti-gravity sphere around herself and float just above the tall marsh grass and shrubs.

Since the previous incursions of this area by the triloraptors, the Brobryne marsh lands had suffered badly. In reality this meant that for the last forty years there had been a lack of food and the groof's populations had dwindled. The lucky ones to survive were the largest, most ferocious and they were desperate for some fresh meat! The vibrations caused through the landing of Notus One had sent a signal across the marshlands! The groof's did not need an invitation, within one earth second, every hungry groof scurried towards Notus One!

Elaine stepped out of Notus One's loading bay door and immediately, she was up to her knees in brown slimy, muddied water! This did not concern her but what did was, her adaptive DNA! She hoped that she would not turn into 'Swamp Thing' woman!

Plodding through the knee deep water, Elaine thought she seen something move but then, a four metre long amphibian leapt out of the water and using its mammoth two metre wide mouth it grabbed Elaine around her waist! The six legged beast shook Elaine ferociously from side to side like a rag doll and then in an attempt to drown her, it pulled her under the muddied water! As Elaine was pulled and tossed along the silted bottom, another amphibian joined in with the attack and grabbed Elaine's right leg! It too pulled ferociously; it was trying to tear her leg away from her body!

Although she was shocked by the attack, Elaine struggled to break free but the both beasts' huge teeth held her fast! Suddenly there was a whoosh, whoosh in the water and both amphibians were sliced clean in two! Something then grabbed Elaine by her shoulders and lifted her out of the now blooded waters, it was a triloraptor. With a flick, the triloraptor released Elaine from its powerful talons and threw her headlong into Notus One's open loading bay door! It then joined its fellow triloraptors who were using their trilo-trons to massacre the frenzied groof's, who out of desperation and hunger, were now feeding off their own species dead bodies!

Dazed, Elaine lay on the loading bay floor and then to her horror realised that most of the dead groof's upper body was still attached to her waistline! Using her hands, she prised its two metre wide jaws open; she then wriggled herself backwards away from the dead beast's razor sharp teeth. Elaine closed her eyes and lay motionless for a moment and as she re-opened them rage set in and Elaine began to scream and without thinking, she began kicking the dead carcass several times, driving it back out of the loading bay and into the muddied water's.

Within less than an earth second of the dead carcass hitting the water, an enormous groof leapt out of the water and began devouring this welcomed meal! What the groof had not realised is it had caught the attention of a triloraptor! Using its trilo-tron so it was now a spear shape, the triloraptor targeted its prey and mentally thrust the spear so it went straight through its mouth and out through its tail. The triloraptor then swooped down, grabbed the amphibian beast by one of its legs and tossed it high into the air.

Several other groof's reacted instinctively to this and leapt upward in an attempt to catch the airborne meal but, that was exactly what the triloraptor had wanted! Its trilo-tron instantly changed shape and it returned to its original octagon shape and with lightning speed. The lethal bladed weapon sliced effortlessly through five airborne groof's and before the body parts fell back into the muddied and blooded water; the trilo-tron struck again and neatly quartered each one!

Still stunned by her grim ordeal, Elaine tottered to her feet and looked at her unmarked trilo-combat uniform and thought with relief;

"Thank heavens I put this on!"

Just as she was about to turn and walk back up to Notus One command centre, she saw something flash out the corner of her eye. A massive groof had leapt out of the muddy water and was heading straight for her! Instinctively Elaine caught the wide mouthed monster in an anti gravitational field and hurled it thirty metres backwards. As the large groof smashed into the marshy water it was simultaneously killed by four trilo-trons that sliced it to pieces! Pleased with their work, the four triloraptors then feasted on their last kill of the day!

Elaine flopped into her crystal blue diamond command chair and telepathically said to Notus;

"I was just hoping that once we had disarmed all the triloraptors spacial and land booby traps that this rescue mission was going to be easy. But I was wrong, what are those ugly sons of a bitch creatures that tried to eat me?"

Calmly Notus replied;

"It is my understanding that the amphibians that tried to eat you are called groof's. They have lived in this marshland for thousands of years and today, our four triloraptors friends have killed the last few hundred in existence! Elaine thanks to the triloraptors killing every animal and bird in this area forty years ago, these amphibian beasts was starving and unfortunately, you were the only morsel on the menu!"

Notus then paused and said;

"Oh, sorry I did not ask earlier, Elaine, are you OK? Your trilo-combat uniform made from trilo-R.I.T.S, (R.I.T.S stands for; robomatic inter transdimensional substance) certainly came in handy!"

Sighing, Elaine replied;

"Notus to be honest, this has really shaken me up but, luckily I will live. It seems as if I owe my life to the triloraptors and at least a limb or two and a few other body parts to my trilo-combat uniform!"

As for Notus's explanation about the groof's, at this point of time, Elaine felt no sympathy towards them and if Notus was trying to make Elaine feel bad, it wasn't working. Starving or not, Elaine definitely didn't want to be on anyone's food menu! But one thing Elaine did realise is, if she was attacked by the groof's, it also stood a good chance that some of her fellow humans colleagues could have also been on the groof's menu!

Turning the food tables around, the groof's were definitely on the triloraptors menu. After they had finished feasting, they eagerly got their trilo-bots to gather up all the dead groof's carcases and take them to the on-board trilo-refrigeration chamber for storage and future consumption.

With the triloraptors back on-board, Elaine went to thank them for saving her. As she greeted them, her human emotions took over and with tears in her eyes; she gave each one a big hug. Triloraptors are not a sociable species and did not know how to react to this show of warmth and gratitude, so they just let Elaine hug them and without saying a word, they tried to continue with their business. However, Elaine decided that the search in the marshlands was fruitless and before letting them go asked for more information about the other drop off point on the planet Hope. They re-affirmed that there was only one more, the vast flat grass lands 8 046.72 kilometres (five thousand miles) to the East of the marsh lands.

Within a few earth minutes, Elaine was in her command chair and Notus One was heading for their next destination. Elaine kept Notus Ones speed down to just below the speed of sound and at a fraction under 338 kph (approximately 750 Mph) she took a leisurely flight to the vast flat grassy plains. The flight took over five earth hours and Elaine wanted to see some of the planets Hopes surface, so she asked the on-board super computer to show on the holographic display unit a live feed of their short journey. To Elaine's utter disgust the sights were not pleasant; the landscapes were now barren and a forty year old ice age had scarred what should have been a beautiful fertile countryside! As Notus One flew over what should have been the grassy plains, they had gone! And all that was left was a cold, desolate, snow-white wasteland!

Notus Ones on-board super computer had been continually doing scans of the area for life forms but, it had come up with a negative! This did not dash Elaine's hopes. She knew the super computer was good but, she suspected that it might not be able to detect life forms if they were shielded by large rock formations or if they were deep underground.

One feature that caught Elaine's eye was a large deep land ravine and she thought it might be a good place to seek shelter, so she landed Notus One close by and then went on foot to explore. At the same time, the four triloraptors took to the air and as before, each had a geographical search grid.

As soon as Elaine stepped outside Notus One, the high winds nearly knocked her off her feet and the icy cold snow showers restricted her vision. Looking up to the sky, Elaine wondered how the triloraptors were doing but she found that this was not a good idea as she slipped on the ice underfoot and tumbled to the ground! Picking herself back up, Elaine slowly made her way to the edge of the ridge. The going was treacherous and the only way she could see down into the rift without falling over its mirrored iced edges was to create an anti-gravity field around her and then float over the edge.

Looking down, all that Elaine could see on the ridge floor was thick ice and snow. Checking her trilo-visor, the air temperature was minus thirty degrees Celsius and even at the bottom of the ridge; the temperature was a frosty minus twenty eight degrees! If anyone had been here, they had long since moved on or had died in this extremely cold climate!

Disappointed, Elaine returned back to Notus One and found the triloraptors were already waiting for her. They seemed a little edgy and without delay reported to Elaine that even with their superior eye sight, the severe weather had hampered their vision and they could not see any life forms. All four then stood silently and after a few moments of awkward silence their spokesperson said;

"Captain Elaine Laurence, we have something for you."

At that, the triloraptors presented Elaine with her own personal trilo-tron. The weapon immediately flew to Elaine's side and inside her trilo-visor a new menu appeared for control of the weapon. Elaine new they must have been concerned about her safety and to be given a trilo-tron was a great honour. She thanked them for this but, before she could give them all another hug, they hurried swiftly away.

With her new trilo-tron at her side, Elaine made her way back to Notus Ones command centre and was pondering on what to do next. She then telepathically asked Notus for advice. Notus instantly replied;

"Elaine, I believe you have a couple of options, first you could do a low level search of the whole planet, it will take time but, it would show conclusively that there are or are not human's survivors. If you go for this option, it might be a good idea for Notus One and the triloraptors mother ship to split and that way you could do the search faster. If this search proves fruitless, the next option is to abandon this planet and move onto the next planetary location."

Elaine had now reached Notus One's command centre and while she was mentally evaluating what Notus had said, she began to remove her trilo-combat uniform. To her surprise and amusement, her skin was covered in short but dense white hair! Apparently her adaptive DNA had kicked in while she was outside in the sub-zero temperatures and had turned her into Polar Woman! Replying to Notus she telepathically said;

"I thought I was quite warm when I was outside but, it seems Doctor Frankenstein that you have a new creation, Polar Woman!"

Notus laughed and said;

"It seems as if your adaptive DNA has malfunctioned, for extreme cold temperatures, I had been planning on Yeti Woman!"

Both Elaine and Notus laughed at this and then Elaine brought the conversation back to the problem at hand by saying;

"I think your first option is practical, I will get the triloraptors to divide our two ships immediately and we will then do a full planet search. The second option is not going to happen as I still want to explore an option you missed out, going back in time and saving my people."

By now Notus had to concede that once Elaine got something into her head she was immovable and replied;

"OK polar woman, do your planetary search first and then after that, I have a few ideas that we can discuss about time travel."

With trilo-efficiency the dividing of both space craft was done with ease within the planet Hopes atmosphere and then, without delay, each craft set off to carry out their searches. With Elaine and the triloraptor spokesperson on-board, Notus One began its search in the Northern hemisphere and covered all ice land's, tiny islands and small and large land masses. The trilo mother ship did the same in the Southern hemisphere. The plan was, if they found nothing they would eventually meet at the planets equator.

The joint search took thirty two frustrating earth hours and produced absolutely nothing! What did become apparent to Elaine was that the whole of the planets eco system had been destroyed by the triloraptors and the chances of any of her fellow humans and colleagues surviving for any length of time on this bleak almost barren planet were close to absolute zero! Elaine asked the triloraptors to link both space craft's again and while they were doing that, she needed to talk to Notus about the possibilities of time travel.

CHAPTER SEVEN

Energy

To say Elaine felt disappointed at not having been able to find any of her fellow humans and colleagues on the planet Hope was an understatement! However, being a pragmatist, she knew she had to move on. And moving on was exploring her next option, time travel. Elaine was sitting comfortably in her command chair and telepathically fired the question of travelling backwards in time to Notus. Within a few seconds Notus replied;

"Elaine, as I told you before, although I am extremely old, I have never had any need for time travel. So my personal knowledge on this subject is limited. I have however telepathically spoken with several of my species on this. They have informed me that throughout this universe, numerous temporal experiments have been carried out. They also informed me that to date, no species known to any of the planetary guardians has ever successfully travelled back or indeed forward in time!

What can be established is, every planet has its own vortex of warped time and numerous universal scholars have theorised that energy time can also be absorbed by this vortex. I have to point out that the energy would be extremely weak! But, if it does exist, I have an idea on how to amplify it!"

Notus could sense Elaine's excitement and continued;

"First, we need to take samples of energy waves within the planetary vortex and for this, Notus One must move outside of the planetary vortex. I also need the use of a trilo-drone for modification. Once modified it will be used to gather and transmit the energy samples. I have designed and installed a computer programme that recognises all forms of energy and will categorise them into their various forms. The programme will be specifically looking for unusual forms of energy that fall into the energy time category. If energy time exists, the programme will then analyse its energy wave content and attempt to date the time it was originally created."

If and this is a big if, we have an accurate calendar of energy time events. Notus One super computer can then calculate exactly the precise time the triloraptors dropped of your people and then we can start the next phase, the energy amplification programme!"

Elaine realised that Notus was taking energy time and time travel serious and excitedly asked;

"Why do you need to use a trilo-drone to gather the energy samples? Can't we just use Notus One?"

Eagerly replying Notus said;

"The warped time in a planetary vortex is delicate and a large space craft can upset the balance of energy time waves within it. A trilo-drone is small and will create less spacial disturbance and using it will give us a better chance of collecting uncontaminated energy time wave samples."

Mentally nodding in agreement, Elaine then asked;

"How do you propose to amplify the energy time within the planetary vortex?"

If Elaine had a trillion dollars to bet, she would bet it on the answer Notus was about to say. Laughing Notus answered;

"You already know the answer. You won your bet. We use Notus One as a transformer. You have to admit, it was almost made for this purpose. It is a pure energy space craft, so amplifying an energy field will not be a problem."

Elaine laughed and then asked a question she definitely did not have an answer for;

"If all of this works how do we actually travel back and forth through time?"

With a tremendous air of confidence Notus replied;

"Once we establish we have the correct energy time co-ordinates, the computer programme controlling the energy amplification running through Notus One will be able to put a small discrete break in the energy time flow. That will be your doorway or time portal. Through our on-board computer, the time portal will be tied into the holographic display unit right here on the command centre. At this side or the other side, the exterior of the time portal can use the holographic program and blend in with anything you like."

Inside Elaine's head, all of this sounded way too easy! Telepathically, Notus picked up on these thoughts and said;

"I know what you are thinking but, you have to remember that we already have the resources to try this. You must also remember that, this is all based on the assumption that we can find energy time within the planetary vortex."

Satisfied with what Notus had said, Elaine called the four triloraptors into a meeting and explained the overall time travel plan. Elaine could only assume that they liked the plan and could see no flaws in it, as they did not ask any questions about it. Continuing, she then showed then the computerised instructions needed for the modification of a trilo-drone. They browsed over them with interest and again, without asking any questions on how she designed or came about the modifications; they informed her that the work would be done in less than three earth hours. While Elaine waited for the trilo-drone to be ready, she took Notus One to the co-ordinates Notus had set, just outside the planet Hopes vortex of warped time.

True to their word, the trilo-drone was ready for action in two and a half hours. Its small on-board computer had had the new software installed and this had been synchronised with Notus One's super computer. Without any pomp or ceremony, the trilo-drone was launched and within a few earth minutes, it was gathering energy data from the planets vortex. Elaine had no idea how long this would take? So while she was waiting, she thought it prudent to check on the plan for accommodating her fellow humans in the triloraptors mother ship.

As she walked around its dark walled corridors, Elaine thought it was a shame that the triloraptors did not appreciate a splash of bright colour. Each room she looked in had the same black walls and minimal un-human furnishings. However, on the bright side, the lighting seemed reasonable. Chuckling to herself, Elaine thought;

> "This is definitely not a five star hotel! Our guests won't have any tables or chairs and even worse, they won't have beds, pillows or bedding!"

Then another thought hit Elaine and this time she said it out loud;

> "Oh my god, we do not have any food on board!"

She then began to laugh and again said out loud;

> "They will have to eat boiled groof! Mind you, the triloraptors might have something to say about that!"

One thing Elaine did notice was that there was practical but definitely not human, medical and sanitation facilities. They could however be adapted with a little trilo-ingenuity to accommodate her human colleagues. Elaine ended her tour and summarised that her guests would have to rough it for a while, and maybe shed a pound or two unless they came across a twenty four seven space store!

For some reason, Elaine thought that analysing the energy waves within a planets vortex would be a fast process but, even with Notus One's super computer that is probably more powerful then every computer on the planet Earth. It took five and a half mind-numbing Earth days! The results however were astounding! Energy time had been found and logged in years, days, hours, minutes, seconds and even nano seconds!

What was even more astounding was, the super computer had been able to isolate the exact energy time down to the last nano second of when Elaine's fellow humans and colleagues had been dropped off in the

Brobryne marsh lands. And it was now amplifying this energy time with pure energy through Notus One!

Brimming with excitement, Elaine telepathically said to Notus;

"Your ideas all seem to be working brilliantly! It's a shame I can't actually touch you because, I would give you a big hug right now!"

Feeling a little proud and adding a bit of humour, Notus replied;

"Pure energy offspring of mine, don't you know that brilliance runs in the family. Oh, and being telepathically linked, you could give me a mental hug."

Laughing, Elaine thought a big hug and Notus said;

"That was real nice, but now we have to get down to the business at hand. As soon as the time portal opens, you must be ready. I recommend you put on your trilo-combat uniform and once you are in the other time zone you will need to have your trilo-tron ready just in case there are any groof's around! I further recommend that you transport your people while they are still under the influence of the propofol gas to the triloraptors part of this space ship as quickly as you can. The best way of transporting them quickly is by using some of the trilo-bots. Once everyone is safely on-board and awake, you can then explain who you are, about yours and their abductions and the reasons for time travel."

Clearly, Notus was on the ball and Elaine thought this was a good rescue plan. Without delay, Elaine put on her trilo-combat uniform and called the triloraptors to another meeting. At the meeting, Elaine briefed the triloraptors on the rescue plan and asked if there was anything they could add to it.

The triloraptor spokesperson said;

"Your rescue plan sounds good. I do have a suggestion; the four of us should accompany you through the time portal. We can then give you air support in case any groof's are around and if need be we can also assist in transporting your people."

To Elaine, that sounded very positive. She also knew that the triloraptors would relish the thought of another encounter with the rather tasty but vicious groof's!

Continuing the triloraptor added;

> "Assuming that this works, we will have to do the same for the rest of the humans at the grassy flat lands?"

Elaine had not thought that far ahead but; the triloraptor was right and replied;

> "You're right, yes we will. Do you have any thoughts on this?"

Replying the triloraptor said;

> "By the time we start this phase of the rescue mission, the propofol gas would have worn off from the humans rescued from the marsh lands. I believe with them awake, they could get in the way and slow down the next part of the rescue mission."

The triloraptor had a point and Elaine had to agree, it was a good one, so she asked;

> "Do we have anything on board that can sedate them a little longer?"

Nodding the triloraptor answered;

> "When I was chosen for this mission, I ordered several canisters of propofol gas as I thought it might be useful. They are in one of the cargo bays along with some dried nutritional food that is fit for human consumption."

While the triloraptors original motives for having several canisters of propofol gas on-board may have been a bit shady, Elaine was pleased to have the gas now and the food was a real bonus. Elaine thanked the triloraptors for their input and with butterflies in her stomach, she along with the triloraptors and three dozen trilo-bots, waited patiently for Notus One's super computer to do its work and for the time portal to open.

While Elaine waited, she thought about time travelling and the possible consequences of travelling back in time. All of these negative thoughts were put aside when she thought that she would be the first human and possibly the first sentient being to ever travel back in time. If she wanted to be honest, this thought really excited her!

Then, without any fireworks, flashing lights or Hollywood's exaggerated drama, a three metre tall and three metre wide time portal suddenly opened in the command centre of Notus One. With her heart pounding, Elaine walked to its opening and then hesitated. She peered through the time portal opening and amazingly she could see it was a clear night over the Brobryne marsh lands! Feeling really excited, Elaine did not know if a small speech was appropriate at this historical point of time? She looked back at each of the four triloraptors for some support but, all she could see was blank emotionless expression on their faces. Instantly, Elaine decided that a speech would be a waste of time and nervously stepped into the time portal opening.

For Elaine this should have been a momentous occasion but, the first thing she noticed as she stepped into the muddied water was the stench of marsh gas! The next thing she saw was a very large obsidian black trilo-craft crossing the night sky. She assumed that it had dropped off its gassed and unconscious human cargo and then had just taken off, Notus One's super computers timing was perfect! Without wasting time, Elaine stepped aside and allowed the triloraptors to take to the air and then she ordered the three dozen trilo-bots to collect the humans from the marsh land.

While the trilo-bots busied themselves with the collection of humans, Elaine created an anti-gravity field around her body and explored the immediate area. The first human she came across was someone she recognised immediately; it was Justin Harper, Captain of the Space Recreation Station, Darwin! Elaine immediately created an anti-gravity field around Justin and mentally lifted him off the marshes. As she turned around, Elaine noticed another body a few metres away. It was John McNally, first officer of the Space Recreation Station, Darwin! Before she could intervene, two trilo-bots came rushing over. One picked up John McNally and the other waited for Elaine to hand over Justin Harper. Elaine gently handed him over and then continued her own search.

About fifteen metres away, Elaine came across an adult female who was face down in the muddied water! Elaine immediately collapsed her anti-gravity field and dropped to the side of the woman. Without thinking, Elaine's medical training kicked in, she rolled the woman over on to her back, turned her head to one side and then checked her pulse. It was faint but irregular. Immediately Elaine began the first aid procedure for water inhalation rescue followed by cardio pulmonary resuscitation. After a few moments, the woman coughed up some water and then after a little CPR, she began to breathe normally! Elaine then called over a trilo-bot and told it to take the woman to the infirmary part of the trilo-mother ship.

In less than ten earth minutes, sixty one humans had been rescued from the Brobryne marsh lands and were now safe and still sound asleep in their new trilo-quarters. As it was still about an hour and a half until dawn, the groof's had not stirred! This was a disappointment to the four triloraptors and a relief to Elaine. It was also a blessing and a potential life saver to the sixty one humans!

Through Elaine's trilo-visor communicator that linked Elaine's brain to Notus Ones' super computer via her synaptic pathways and neurological receptors. Elaine mentally informed the triloraptors that the rescue mission had been successful. All of the humans in the marshlands were safely on-board and they should return to the time portal. It only took a few trilo-minutes for the four triloraptors to re-enter the time portal, Elaine then asked Notus Ones super computer to close it behind them and begin work without delay on their next destination, the vast grassy flat planes.

As Elaine sat and patiently waited for Notus Ones super computer to amplify the next energy time wave through Notus One, she began to think about time. At this moment in time, every minute waiting seemed to drag and felt more like an hour! But, when she was at the Brobryne marsh lands, every minute seemed like a second! In fact for Elaine, the whole rescue seemed to be over in the blink of a human eye. Elaine decided that time from one moment to another still has the same value as when she was a mortal being. And all sentient beings in the universe must experience the same individual time variations.

At that, the time portal opened. Instantly an icy cold draft filled Notus One's command centre and all present could hear the trilo-winds howling!

Elaine thought;

"Here comes Polar Woman!" as she braced herself and stepped through the time portal and into a massive snow storm and raging winds! Short of being blown away, the only thing Elaine could do to stabilise her footing was create a sphere-shaped anti-gravity field around her and mentally hold it close to the ground! The plan was the same as before, however with a trilo-phoon raging, the four triloraptors wisely stayed on the ground!

Once again, Notus One's super computer's timing was impeccable. Elaine guessed that the triloraptors must have dropped their human cargo no more than two to three earth minutes ago as the tracks in the snow still looked fresh! Elaine could also see ten round black containers; she guessed that these were the trilo-survival food and water containers the triloraptors had mentioned earlier. They were a welcome sight and she would have these loaded into one of Notus One's cargo bays once her people were safely on-board.

Through the snowy blizzard, Elaine spotted an unconscious elderly man on the ground not far from where she was standing. Suddenly a powerful gust of wind picked him up as if he were a leaf and began hurling him through the icy air! Acting on Instinct, Elaine immediately created an anti-gravity field around him and gently drew him towards the time portal. A trilo-bot then took over and carried him into the safety of Notus One's trilo-quarters.

From Elaine's last visit to this area, she knew that the deep ravine was only a few hundred meters away, she hoped with these powerful winds that none of her fellow humans and colleagues had been blown in there and thought it prudent to check it out. Using her anti-gravity field, Elaine flew over to the ravines edge and then surveyed the area. Looking down, Elaine could see that the walls of the ravine were a sheer drop into what she could estimate at its deepest, was fifty metres to its ice covered floor! She thought if anyone had been blown into this icy pit, they would have surely died! Elaine however did not give up, she methodically flew up and down the ravine until she was satisfied there were no survivors or bodies!

The extreme weather made the going much slower than Elaine would have liked. But after almost twenty earth minutes, thanks to the hard work by the triloraptors and the trilo-bots, one by one all sixty four unconscious human beings were rescued and taken to the safety and warmth of their trilo-quarters.

With the food and water now on-board, Elaine and the four triloraptors stood briefly at the time portal and without saying a word, they were glad to re-enter Notus Ones command centre away from the snow storms and icy cold winds. As soon as they entered the command centre, the time portal closed and it was nearly time for Elaine to wake her human guests and inform them of all that had been happening!

CHAPTER EIGHT

A new beginning!

Before waking up her guests, Elaine was in a psychological quandary! Her adaptive DNA had kicked in and she was 'Polar Woman' and no matter how hard she tried her adaptive DNA would not change! On top of that, she had to assemble one hundred and fifty people in an alien environment and tell them that while they had been unconscious for months that the world that they once knew had radically changed!

Notus could sense Elaine's mental anxiety and telepathically said;

"Elaine, congratulations to you and the triloraptors for becoming the first time travelling team in this universe, however you really need to calm down! The last few earth hours has had your emotions running wild."

Snapping back at Notus, Elaine replied;

"That's easy for you to say! But how do you think my fellow humans and colleagues are going to react when the first thing they see when they wake up is me as Polar Woman? And then to compound this, four ferocious looking two metre tall eagle like aliens that they cannot communicate with? I know how I would react, with shock and horror!

Notus had to concede that this picture had its downfalls and after a few moments of serious thought, replied;

"Elaine, you have a good point, how about this for a proposal? While they are still unconscious you get the triloraptors to implant uni-net links into all the humans' synaptic pathways and neurological receptors. In the meantime, you contact the Universal Interplanetary Congresses uni-net engineers and ask them to set up a virtual meeting area that looks like the main reception area of an earth space recreational station. I think the plans for this are in Notus One's data base, if not; the uni-net engineers will have them in their own data bases from when they visited your planet.

You can also ask the Universal Interplanetary Congresses uni-net engineers to activate their uni-net links just as they are on the threshold of waking up. Once the uni-net links are activated, you could then hold a virtual meeting with them, with you looking like your old earth self.

And when you introduce the triloraptors and virtual members of the Universal Interplanetary Congress, the uni-nets language translator will be online and that would solve the communications problem?"

Elaine thought that this was a brilliant proposal and with a little embarrassment telepathically said;

"Notus I'm sorry I snapped at you, I know none of this is your fault . . . . well except the adaptive DNA.

Notus laughed and allowed Elaine to continue;

"Your plan as always is just what the doctor ordered. I will contact the triloraptors immediately and get them to install the uni-net links and then contact the Universal Interplanetary Congresses uni-net engineers. Do you think I should tell the U.I.C about the time portal rescue?"

Without any hesitation, Notus said;

"Tell them that the humans from the planet Hope have been rescued but do not mention time travel or the time portal! Elaine as you are aware, there are some unscrupulous beings in this and other universes that would love to exploit time travel! I also think you should ask the four triloraptors to withhold the time travel information from their central command!"

Taking on-board everything that Notus had just said, Elaine busied herself and within one earth hour, Elaine's fellow humans and colleagues on board Notus One were linked up to the uni-net and the uni-net engineers had set up the virtual earth space recreational station meeting area.

Time was now moving fast and within a few earth minutes of Elaine informing the universal inter-planetary congress of her initial success; Elaine had a virtual uni-net call from the chair elect who eagerly inquired about the rescue mission. Elaine responded and told her;

> "Madam Chair elect, the first phase has been a success; we have rescued one hundred and fifty humans. But, our rescue mission is far from over; we still have to go to the planet's Gladious and Arpeggio to rescue the remaining crew and passengers."

What Elaine said was the truth; she however avoided the actual rescue details, as she did not want to lie to the chair elect.

The chair elect seemed genuinely excited and said;

> "Captain Elaine Laurence, it was a shame that the U.I.C news ship was not there to document this gallant rescue and share this event with the Universal Interplanetary Congresses members. However, I and the U.I.C understood the complex circumstances for them not being there and we would look forward to a full report when you have completed your rescue missions."

At that, the Universal Interplanetary Congresses chair elect signed off.

Elaine's next job was to meet with her four on-board triloraptors and discuss their previous time travel mission. This however did not go well, as they informed her that they had already informed trilo-central command of all that had transpired, including the time travel! This was not what Elaine or Notus had wanted but, Elaine realised that she could not do anything about this now and she had other important priorities. The only thing that she, and she bet Notus hoped for was, that this would not come back and bite them on their preverbal bums, now, in the past or in the future!

To semi-wake up and activate the uni-net links of one hundred and fifty humans at precisely the same time, was an easy task for the uni-net engineers. They sent a small programme to each uni-net link that simultaneously sent a small electrical charge through each recipient's synaptic pathways and neurological receptors. This in turn instantly activated the uni-net link and took the recipient's straight to the virtual reception area of an earth space recreational station.

Justin Harper, Captain of the Space Recreation Station Darwin, woke up with a start! He was sitting in the space stations reception area? He could not recall why he was there. As he looked around, there were a large number of guests and crew who seemed to be as confused as he was! Standing up, he called out to everyone;

> "Ladies and gentlemen, can I have your attention. Please except my apologies. We have all congregated here but, I for one seemed to have fallen asleep and have no idea why. Perhaps one of the other crew members can explain?"

To his and the other crew members utter surprise, Doctor Elaine Laurence from the Recreational Space Station, Stephen Hawking walked in and said;

> "Hello everyone, my name is Doctor Elaine Laurence. Please do not be alarmed, what I am about to tell you will take some time so please sit down, relax and listen. I will answer all your questions once you have heard all I have to say."

Everyone looked at Captain Justin Harper but he complied and just sat down. He put his hands in the air and said;

> "If Doctor Laurence has something important to say, then I think we had all better listen."

Elaine smiled at Captain Justin Harper and then paused to make sure she had everyone's attention. With all eyes on her, she then continued;

> "Each person sitting in this reception area has been unconscious for a little over five weeks! In that time, the Planet Earth has undergone some radical changes! It all started with a being from another universe whose species was dying and then coming to this universe with the intention of conquering and dominating it!

This highly intelligent being used some ingenious technology and within a short period of time he conquered the majority of intelligent life bearing planets in this universe! He then manipulated an assembly of intelligent life forms known as the Universal Interplanetary Congress to come to the planet Earth and conquer it! As far as I am aware, his goal was to use human beings as physical hosts for his own species!

To frustrate this evil beings efforts; a nomadic space specie called the triloraptors, kidnapped us from the recreational space stations, Darwin and Stephen Hawking and put us on different planets in this universe.

The good news is, the overlord has now been defeated and I and a small team have been on a mission to rescue you, and you are the first one hundred and fifty to be saved. The rescue mission has been extremely difficult due to several factors but, the biggest has been a thing called time dilation. To cut a long story shorter, over forty earth years have passed since you were first abducted! But, thanks to us developing time travel, we have been able to travel back through time and rescue you!"

As Elaine stopped speaking, she immediately realised how ludicrous all of this sounded! And her human audience was one step ahead of her, they all began to laugh and clap! Embarrassed, Elaine tried to re-take control but by now, her audience was convinced that this was an elaborate space station hoax. What made it worse was even Captain Harper was clapping and laughing! However, the laughter died down as four triloraptors dressed in full trilo-combat uniforms suddenly appeared at either side of Elaine.

Standing to his feet, it was Captain Harper who spoke first;

"Elaine, this is absolutely brilliant, I don't know how you pulled this off but, well done. Come on ladies and gentlemen; please give Doctor Elaine Laurence and her backing group a big round of applause!"

To Elaine's total embarrassment, the virtual space station reception area filled with the sound of applause and cheering.

Looking at Elaine the triloraptor spokesperson quietly said;

"This is not going well; a change of tactics is needed."

Elaine nodded in agreement and instantaneously the virtual reality programme ended! All one hundred and fifty humans were now awake, naked and in a cargo hold in the triloraptors part of Notus One! Once again Elaine walked in but, instead of wearing her red virgin galactic uniform, she was wearing her full trilo-combat uniforms and the skin visible on her hairless head was crystal blue!

It was hard to work out what had shocked the people most. Their nakedness or the crystal blue Elaine! But, whatever it was, Captain Justin Harper was having none of it! Angrily he roared;

"Elaine you have taken this too far! I don't know how you are doing this but, you must stop it now!"

Everyone hushed to hear Elaine's reply,

"Captain Harper, all I have told you is true! I knew this would come as a shock to everyone so I tried to ease you into what has happened by creating a virtual environment that you were familiar with. This sadly did not work and now we are in reality. This is one of the cargo holds on my spaceship named Notus One."

Justin Harper's mind was racing at what seemed like a million miles per hour. Was she still playing an elaborate hoax or was this for real? Captain Justin Harper decided to call Elaine's bluff and said;

"OK Elaine, if this is a spaceship; I want you to take me and my first officer, John McNally on a tour."

Elaine immediately agreed and asked everyone else to stay calm and where they were until they came back.

Captain Justin Harper and John McNally followed Elaine out of the cargo bay doors and then through numerous passageways, on the way Elaine opened several doors so her two guests could peer in. After several minutes they came to Notus Ones stunning command centre. Its interior was made from a crystal blue diamond! And what really caught both Justin's and John's eyes were the three meter tall, three dimensional virtual display unit towards the rear of the command centre. It was displaying the planet Hope, its sun and solar system. They both walked around in awe and then John McNally commented;

"This is all very impressive but Elaine; do you really need to have your skin colour co-ordinated to the command centre?"

Elaine sat in her crystal blue command chair and said;

"Gentlemen, I got dropped off on a different planet to you, my skin had to adapt or I would have died. Now when I go into different environments, my skin automatically changes. It's called adaptive DNA."

John McNally smiled and replied;

"That's real cool. Can I touch it?"

Elaine nodded and John apprehensively prodded Elaine's head. From Johns approach, Elaine thought he might think she had some kind of contagious disease. She even saw him glance at the end of his finger to possibly see if it went blue! Satisfied with his probing, John then said;

"Now if you don't mind, I have another question. Where did a little blue earth girl like you get this fantastic spaceship from?"

Elaine tried to smile but, as usual her crystal blue skin would not bend. So she laughed out loud and said;

"It's a long story; I will fill you in on that later, now I want you to meet my rescue team, the triloraptors."

On cue, the four triloraptors walked into the command centre. It was Captain Justin Harper who spoke first;

"So it was you feathery fellows that kidnapped us in the first place?"

The triloraptor spokesperson replied;

"That is correct and it was the triloraptors who helped defeat the overlord and again it is the triloraptors who have assisted Captain Elaine Laurence in this rescue mission."

John McNally's curiosity got the better of him and asked;

"This is really weird, how are we communicating with you?"

The triloraptor responded by saying;

"You have had a device installed in your synaptic pathways and neurological receptors, called a uni-net link. The uni-link allows you to have virtual meetings like the one we had before. It also has a built in universal language translator and that's how we can communicate with each other."

It was now Captain Justin Harper's turn to ask another question;

"Can I also assume that it was the triloraptors who took our clothes and sprayed us with icy cold water while we were unconscious?"

Looking straight at him the triloraptor replied;

"Your assumption is correct. While we were transporting you and your people to other worlds, we had to sanitise you!"

Elaine could feel a little hostility building up and said;

"OK Justin and John the spaceship tour is over. Now do you believe what I have told you?"

Both men looked at each other and John asked Justin;

"What do you think captain?"

Justin looked around him and said;

"Well my friend, seeing is believing. This is indeed a strange tale but, it would seem as if we are all going to have great stories to tell our grandchildren!"

Elaine and John both laughed but, the triloraptors just stood still and exchanged glances at each other.

Elaine briefed both men on the food and water situation and then escorted them back to the cargo bay. Upon arriving, Elaine thought it wise to let Captain Justin Harper and the first officer John McNally explain the whole situation to the passengers and crew. After a lengthy debate, a few questions popped up and as Justin and John could not answer them, they passed them over to Elaine. The first was;

"Can we communicate with the people back on earth and let them know we are alive?

It was a good question and one Elaine did not have a ready answer too but, she said she would look into it. The next general question was;

"When could they expect to be back on earth?"

Elaine explained;

"As Captain Harper has already said, we still have others to rescue. It's difficult to put a time scale on this but, I will stick my neck out and say that this should only take a few earth weeks. Once we have all our people, I think we could have you back home in about another eight to ten earth weeks."

Pausing for a moment, Elaine let everyone take this in and then she continued;

"Another thing everyone has to bear in mind is due to time dilation. Earths time will have passed quicker than our space time. So according to our super computers calculations, the people on the planet Earth would have aged about one year and ten month!"

No sooner than Elaine had finished speaking, a man called out and said;

"You said you can time travel, why don't we travel back in time and arrive on earth earlier?"

Justin looked at Elaine; he raised his eyebrows and in an agreeing tone said;

"Elaine that's a good question, the man has a point!"

To be candid, this stopped Elaine in her tracks; she was no expert on time travel, so why couldn't they travel back in earth's time? Notus immediately jumped in and telepathically said;

"Elaine, time should be as time was meant to be. If you mess with time you could create temporal inconsistencies that may affect the whole of earth's time line."

Notus's words were wise and Elaine looked at her one hundred and fifty guests and said;

"When you were rescued from the planet Hope, we did not have to worry about interfering with any intelligent life's time lines. If we did travel back in earth's time, we would unravel events that may have dire consequences! I also think the earth and its inhabitants have gone through enough in the past few years without us messing up temporal events!"

As far as Elaine could tell, everyone seemed happy with this explanation and one final question was asked that was concerning everyone but was voiced by one rather over weight, middle aged lady who called out;

"As you can see, I'm a bit fat and being naked is embarrassing! Do you have any clothes on-board?"

Elaine restrained herself from laughing and in a true doctor's sympathetic tone, she said;

"Sorry ladies and gentlemen, I do not have any clothes on-board. And unless we come across something that you can use on the planets we are about to visit, you will have to wait until we reach the planet Earth."

It was now time for Elaine to delegate some of her inherited duties. So she asked Captain Justin Harper and the first officer John McNally to take responsibility for the passengers, show them to their sleeping quarters and ration out the food. Captain Harper replied;

"Elaine you might be the Captain of this fine star ship but, until we plant our feet firmly on the planet Earth, I and John as Captain and first officers of the Space Recreation Station Darwin still have a duty of care. And that duty of care is to look after the crew and passengers. We will do our utmost to make sure that everyone is well looked after on-board Notus One and we will also provide any assistance you need in rescuing the passengers and crew from the Darwin and Stephen Hawking."

Elaine thanked them and left for Notus Ones command centre. She wanted to set a course immediately for the planet Gladious and get the next rescue underway.

CHAPTER NINE

Planet Gladious

Looking at the virtual three dimensional unit; Elaine could see that Gladious solar system was small compared with the planet Earths own system. It has only three major planets and in its outer solar regions, it has two small ice covered planetoids. Gladious sun is a G-type main-sequence star with a diameter of 696 342 kilometres. That is approximately half the size of the planet Earth's sun.

It appeared that Gladious was a typical goldilocks planet that falls within a star's habitable zone and that meant it was able to develop life! Hopefully for Elaine that meant it would possibly also support human life! From what she could see as she walked around the virtual three dimensional unit, the planet's surface was about sixty percent water with vast land masses that formed huge continents.

Counting the moons around Gladious proved a little difficult as it had three huge external planetary rings around it. These three rings held numerous large formations within them that could or could not be counted as moons? However, Elaine did count five small moons outside the rings so for now; she would stick with the five until she was told different.

While Elaine waited for the triloraptors to join her in the command centre, she tried to envisage the spacial and planetary trilo mines and traps the triloraptors would have installed before leaving her fellow humans and colleagues on the planet Gladious. Elaine hopes were on a similar set up as it was on the planet Hope. But, she had to throw that aside when the triloraptors joined her and their spokesperson said;

"As you can see, this is a small solar system. So we were able to install and activate a defensive volatile plasma field that extends out a far as the third planet! Any spacecraft known to the triloraptors passing through this would detonate the volatile plasma! As a result of the spacial plasma explosion, a massive spacial shock wave would swell out into the solar system and destroy anything in its path. That would include all other spacecrafts and the two outer planetoids!"

The first thought that came into Elaine's head was; this was true triloraptor tactics, destroy everything! However, Elaine knew that they had done this for two valid reasons. The first was to stop the overlord from getting the human hostages and the second was; when they installed this, the triloraptors were still at war with the Universal Interplanetary Congress. If the U.I.C were unfortunate enough to come to this solar system, they would have suffered massive losses! Putting this aside, what was relevant now was how they disarm the plasma field and Elaine asked;

"Where are the disarm control devises located for the plasma field?"

Replying immediately the triloraptors spokesperson answered;

"There is only one, and that is on the planet surface along with the other trilo-planetary booby traps and their deactivation devices!"

This puzzled Elaine and she asked;

"So how do we get to the planet surface without all being killed and destroying part of the solar system?"

Clearly, the triloraptors spokesperson had already thought this scenario through and replied;

"In this instance, only a trilo-craft made from R.I.T.S (robomatic inter transdimensional substance) can pass through the plasma defence field. Also, if the device detects any other life forms on-board, the plasma field will explode and activate our other planetary booby traps!

So we will need to put all the humans in Notus One and then separate it from our mother ship. The mother ship can then safely proceed to the planet's surface and disarm all the spacial and planetary booby traps."

Under normal circumstance this would be an easy plan but, it had created one big logistical problem! They had just taken on-board one hundred and fifty people! So for this to work, Elaine would have to squeeze one hundred and fifty people into the 'compact' Notus One.

With the uni-net devices installed, Elaine could now easily contact Captain Harper. She opened her own uni-net link and requested a virtual meeting with the Captain. In seconds they were both in a virtual booth. There, Elaine briefed Captain Harper on the disarmament plan and having to separate the two space ships and cram everyone into Notus One. Captain Harper said;

"Elaine, you are full of surprises, so Notus One is actually two space crafts and the triloraptors section actually surrounds your craft, the original Notus One?"

Nodding Elaine answered;

"That's correct, it's an awfully long story but a little while ago, the triloraptors tried to capture Notus One but things backfired for them! I ended up commandeering their mother ship and then using it help with this rescue mission."

It took a few moments for Captain Harper to take this in and then he said;

"Wow that's some conquest, while we have been asleep, you have been really busy! You know Elaine, this uni-net is fantastic; when we get back to earth; we really need to get this for everyone!

Elaine laughed and then explained;

"When the earth was conquered by the Universal Interplanetary Congress, the first thing they did was install a uni-net devise in every human being. Justin, as far as I know, all that is needed for it to be turned on is the installation of some spacial hubs and the uni net engineers flicking the on switch."

Enthusiastically Captain Harper replied;

"That's incredible, now as for cramming our people into the original Notus One, if we need to stand on each other shoulders then, that's what needs to be done!"

Captain Harper's last comment gave Elaine an idea; she would create anti-gravity fields and stack the people up! She just hoped that she could mentally keep this up until the triloraptors mother ship returned! While Elaine thought this was a good idea, she also had to deal with explaining her ability to control gravity to her rescued guests! While she pondered on this, Notus telepathically said;

"Elaine, this is not a problem, just tell them that it is one of many features that Notus One has, and then leave it at that."

For Elaine, that sounded like a reasonable explanation. So she thanked Notus and then began to put into operation plan 'squash them in, pile them high'.

Before the triloraptors could start with the separation procedure of their mother ship from Notus One, they had to wait for the humans to be moved into Notus One's command centre. This took a good couple of earth hours as on Captain Elaine Laurence's order's everyone had to be given food and then toileted before they could be squashed for several earth hours into in the small command centre of Notus One!

Once the niceties were over, the one hundred and fifty humans filed into Notus One's command centre. As the first sixty three entered the command centre, Elaine created an anti-gravity walk way that took them up above her head; she then held them there with a large anti-gravity field. To save any unnecessary embarrassment from upward glances, she aided a nice touch by also frosting the floor of anti-gravity field. The next sixty two filed in and had to stand in and around Elaine. With everyone packed in, Elaine closed the outer air lock hatch and the triloraptors began to separate the mother ship from Notus One.

In was only then that Elaine rescued guests began to appreciate how spectacular both space craft's were! As the two crafts separated and then the two sections of triloraptors mother ship seamlessly joined together. Several loud 'wows' could be heard as they watched in awe through Notus One's crystal blue translucent walls!

Excited vocal chatter filled the command centre as the people began to realise that both space craft's shapes were that of a Marquise-Cut boat diamond. Elaine asked for everyone attention and like a professional tour guide, she explained that Notus One's interior and exterior was actually a real diamond that was energised with pure energy! She then went on to explain about the construction of the triloraptors mother ship and the material it was made of. With questions and answers about the two space craft this filled about fifteen earth minutes or so and then true to form for humans, the people started to moan about the cramped conditions!

It was then time for Elaine to put plan B into effect. She again called for everyone's attention and said it would be a good idea while they were waiting for them to use their uni-net links to find out more about the triloraptors and the Universal Interplanetary Congress. Almost instantly, this exercise seemed to backfire on Elaine and it produced some really negative results!

Up until now, Elaine's rescued human guests had only been briefly informed about what had transpired on Earth. Now they had more information than they could handle through the uni-net in a virtual surrounding that seemed like a reality! Each watched in horror as their planet was invaded and then they witnessed the pandemonium it caused along with the horrendous unjustifiable killings!

From what they just experienced, the people were shocked and extremely angry! They voiced their thoughts and stated that the Universal Interplanetary Congress were a cowardly shameful bunch for their behaviour towards earth and its vulnerable people! Most thought the U.I.C should be held accountable for war crimes against humanity! When it came to comments about the triloraptors, it was generally felt that they are absolute psychopathic killers and should never be trusted!

While Elaine tried to calm everyone down, the triloraptors had been able to stealthily get too the planet's surface in the dark of night and successfully disarmed all the spacial and planetary booby traps. They also scanned the surface for bio signs and what they found really surprised them but, one thing was for sure, it was really going to upset Captain Elaine Laurence's rescue plans!

After five long earth hours of angry heated debate, Elaine was pleased to get a message from the triloraptors that they disarmed all the booby traps and were about to re-join Notus One. They also said that they needed to speak with her as soon as possible.

As soon as the triloraptor mother ship re-joined Notus One, Elaine got Captain Harper and first officer John McNally to escort her guests back to their trilo-quarters. While she felt really sorry for what had happened on earth and indeed for what had happened to all the kidnapped victims. Elaine knew earth and its people would not forgive the U.I.C or the triloraptors for their invasion of the planet Earth!

It was then that she decided that once all the rescue missions were complete, she would take this up with the U.I.C and see what could be done to help the citizens of earth. Now she had something else on her mind, what did the triloraptors need to tell her urgently?

All four triloraptors entered the command centre and it was their spokesperson who said;

"Captain Elaine Laurence, as you are aware the deactivation of our spacial and ground to air booby traps has gone well. While we were on the planet's surface we did a bio scan for the humans and found them all alive. Since these humans left earth, the variance in time dilation is about two and a half years. In that time, they have set up what seems like a colony that has expanded! There are now two hundred and fifteen of them!

Elaine began to laugh, clapped her hands together and said;

"That's good, in fact that's really good news! You know, I was expecting some kind of horrendous horror story."

Again the triloraptor spokesperson spoke;

"I do not think you have grasped the severity of what I just said. They are alive and well and now that they have children that have been born on this planet. They may not want to leave their new home!

What the triloraptor said was true, Elaine had only thought of rescuing them and returning them safely back to earth. What she had not anticipated is that they would have had children and could be happy in their new planetary environment.

After thinking for a moment Elaine said;

> "We still have to give them the option of returning to the planet Earth. We also have to show them that they were not abandoned by earth and that the people of earth care."

The triloraptors spokesperson nodded in agreement and then compassionately said something that surprised Elaine;

> "I have a suggestion; when you made first contact with the humans from the planet Hope, the meeting did not go very well. Perhaps this time, you could let some of the other humans we have on-board make first contact?"

It was a good proposition but, an amazing one coming from what everyone assumed was a cold hearted triloraptor! Elaine instantly agreed to this and said she would seek the help of Captain Justin Harper and his first officer, John McNally. Sensing that Elaine was about to give them another 'human hug' the four triloraptors then made a quick exit.

Without delay, Elaine contacted Captain Harper and John McNally and asked them to meet her in the command centre. When they arrived, Elaine greeted them and then informed them that the people on the planet were alive and from bio scans had given birth to some children. Before either man could respond, Elaine then told them of her concerns, the triloraptors suggestion and asked them if they would consider helping. John McNally responded instantly and said;

> "Elaine, we would be happy to help. Have you thought how we would initially approach these people?

Elaine shrugged and answered;

> "John, at this point of time, I am open to suggestions from both of you."

Captain Harper thought for a moment and said;

> "A few years ago, these people woke up on an alien planet; over that time they must have discussed how they got there? If that were me; I would also think that whoever put us on this planet, would one day

come back! I think landing the triloraptors big black mother ship or Notus One will only panic them. How about we scale things down and use the trilo-shuttle craft? We could fly at a reasonable altitude over there settlement a few times and then land on its outskirts. Both I and John can then get out and wait for a response?"

John McNally asked his Captain a question;

"What if they think we are hostile and attack us?"

Smiling, Captain Harper answered;

"That my friend is a risk we will have to take. I hope that when they see that we are also human, they will in the first instance be curious and in the second instance be peaceable."

Seeing that this was the only realistic plan on the table, Elaine agreed to it and said that they should implement the plan just as dawn breaks on the planet. That way, it would give the human colony a whole day to respond and if all goes well, they would have ample time to open up discussions on what the people of the planet Gladious wanted to do. She also thought that they would only need a small team for this; Captain Harper and John McNally would head the team, a triloraptor would pilot the trilo-shuttle craft and she would be on hand to administer medical attention if any hostilities took place.

With everyone in agreement, Elaine said that Captain Harper and John McNally should get some sleep as they would be in orbit around the planet within five earth hours and she wanted to launch the trilo-shuttle craft as soon as they could thereafter. Being immortal, Elaine did not need sleep anymore but, she still found it mentally comforting to have a long catnap. She slipped off her trilo-combat uniform, reclined her crystal command chair, switched on the anti-gravity cushion and dozed blissfully for a few hours.

As she woke up, Notus One's super computer informed her that they were now in a high orbit around the planet Gladious. Elaine felt quite excited; she really hoped this phase of the rescue mission would go well. Her only regret was, with her crystal blue skin she did not look human! So she put her trilo-combat uniform back on and then headed for the shuttle bay.

As she arrived, the triloraptor, Captain Harper and John McNally were already there and both Justin and John greeted her by saying together;

"Good morning Elaine."

It was only then that Elaine realised that this little earthly greeting and all the other earthly welcomes, goodbyes, good nights and other salutations was something she had really missed and responded by saying;

"Good morning to you all. Today is a new day and we have a new venture ahead of us, I have a little idea. When we fly over the human colony, we use the trilo-external speaker system and greet everyone with a 'Good morning everyone'?"

Captain Harper laughed and said;

"Its novel but, it would certainly break the ice. Let's do it!"

Within a few earth minutes the trilo-shuttle craft left its docking bay and headed for the earth colony. While they were entering the planet's atmosphere, Elaine asked Captain Harper if he would record their greetings message and they could play it on a continuous loop as they flew over the colony. Justin had already given this some thought and recorded;

"Good morning, this is Justin Harper, Captain of Earth's Space Recreation Station, Darwin. We will be landing shortly and need to talk to everyone in the colony."

Laughing, Elaine said Justin sounded just like a commercial aeroplane Captain back on earth giving out his announcements. They both laughed at this, but Elaine also said that the recording was perfect and as soon as they were in position, they began their broadcast.

CHAPTER TEN

Mixed feelings

Within a few earth seconds of hearing the spaceship broadcasts, the people of the Novus Inceptio (meaning, new beginning) district began to put their defence plans into action. They had excavated a deep fortified moat around the whole district and immediately raised the drawbridges. Trained volunteers then armed the giant wheeled catapults and waited to see where the space craft would land. Each dwelling had its own arsenal of deadly weapons and now every man, woman and child above the age of ten was armed.They watched with trepidation as the small space craft flew overhead a few times, and then slowly landed in their South territory. As soon as the space craft touched down, the local people and militia moved their giant wheeled catapults into striking range! To an outside force, these people had only crude weaponry but, that was exactly what the Novus Inceptio district people wanted them to think!.

In the two and a half years that they had been on this planet they had been very industrious. They had been able to mine for various metals and minerals and within a short period of time they had the ingredients for gun powder! Using a mixture of sulphur, charcoal, and potassium nitrate (saltpeter) they began to manufacture fireworks. From this, they turned their hands into making small firearms. From that, one weapon led to another and now they had several long range artillery cannons, numerous machine guns, sniper rifles and quite a few highly accurate hand guns! They even had a half tracked tank that ran on steam!

The people of the Novus Inceptio district had also been diligent in the construction of a network of underground tunnels that spread out in all directions from their colony. In just a few earth minutes of the space craft landing, the militia of Novus Inceptio district had covertly surrounded it!

Back on board the trilo-shuttle craft the triloraptor pilot had been closely monitoring the human's movement. Calling for everyone's attention, the triloraptor said;

"Before you go outside, you need to be aware that the human's have weapons. My scans tell me that they have what you call in your medieval times, giant wheeled catapults, crossbows and spears! This however is just a primitive but clever distraction! They also have heavy field artillery, a tank and various bulleted guns!

Captain Harper nodded and replied;

"That, my feathered friend, is what human's will do when you kidnap them, they fight back."

Ignoring the sarcasm, the triloraptor continued;

"You also need to know two more important things. There is a network of tunnels running throughout this area, and you already have a human armed reception party waiting for you! Plus I have also detected several thousand other life forms in this area!

The second part caught Elaine's attention and she inquired;

"Can you identify the other life forms?"

Nodding the triloraptor replied."

"They are mammals similar to Opossum Marsupial on the planet Earth. We have seen these before; they are a species whose intelligence is developing. I would speculate that the humans have been using them for work animals."

It was John McNally that asked the next question;

"Do you think these animals have been trained to attack strangers?"

Looking a John McNally, the triloraptor replied;

"It is possible but, if you are worried, I can deal with them!"

Jumping in straight away, Elaine said;

"No! We will not hurt anyone or anything! We have come to rescue these people and when Justin and John step out of this trilo-shuttle craft. I want them to emphasize that they are only here to take those interested back to earth!"

Captain Harper looked at John McNally and said;

"John, I think it's time to hit the road."

Both men walked towards the trilo-shuttle door and the triloraptor pilot opened it for them and slowly. Then both men stepped out of the trilo-shuttle into the planet Gladious fresh air.

From his elevated observation post. Captain Ron Walker of the Recreational Space Station, Stephen Hawking, looked through his hand made telescope at the two men who just got out of the obsidian black space craft. Both were naked and unshaven but, he knew both of them. It was Justin Harper, Captain of the Space Recreation Station, Darwin and his first officer John McNally?

Captain Ron Walker's mind was racing. His first thought was, is this some kind of a trap? Could this be a clever distraction and other space craft are flying in and trying to outflank them? Cautiously looking around himself, he picked up a cone he used as a loud hailer and called;

"This is Captain Ron Walker of the Recreational Space Station, Stephen Hawking, state clearly what you want."

The triloraptor had coupled Justin Harper and John McNally voices into the external sound system of the trilo-shuttle craft, so when Justin Harper replied. His voice boomed across the colony as he called;

"Hello Captain Ron Walker, this is Justin Harper, Captain of the Space Recreation Station Darwin. We are here on a rescue mission. If you want to, we have come to take you and your people home!"

Captain Ron Walker was a shrewd, no nonsense man! He knew that if something sounded too good, it had to be a trick! And as Ron Walker looked through his hand made telescope at the two unshaven, naked men. It certainly did not look like a rescue mission! He called back;

> "Why don't you two fellows get back into that space craft and leave us alone!"

Justin Harper guessed that Captain Ron Walker thought something was not right and called back saying;

> "Ron, we have come a long way to rescue you. The craft you're looking at is just a shuttle craft. Our main ship is in your planets orbit and has one hundred and forty eight other humans on board that have been rescued from a planet called Hope. They were all from my space station, the Darwin."

Calling back Ron said;

> "It's a nice story Justin but from where I am standing, I have every reason not to trust you! How do I know that you have not been brainwashed into saying all of this? Or maybe you are human clones? We have been isolated on this planet for a few years now and out of the blue you turn up in what looks like an alien space ship! Tell me truthfully Justin, how would you react?"

Justin nodded and replied;

> "Captain Walker, I would react exactly the same as you are. I knew this would not be easy for both sides, so how about you send a delegate or two with us. We will take them up to our main space craft and they can meet all the other humans that have been rescued?

Keeping a poker face, Captain Ron Walker thought about this for a few moments and said;

> "Justin, I will go but, I warn you, I will be armed! I also have another condition; I want you Captain Justin Harper to stay here on the surface and under guard. This is to ensure my safe return."

Justin smiled and raised his two thumbs up and jovially replied;

"Well as one captain to another captain in the old buccaneer terms, it looks like we have struck a deal for a parley."

Captain Justin Harper looked at his lifelong friend John McNally and said;

"While I am away, would you give Captain Walker the VIP tour of Notus One and the trilo-mother ship? You will also have to re-introduce him to Elaine. He may be a little surprised to see she has had an alien makeover"

John chuckled and then in true nautical terms, the first officer replied;

"Aye Aye captain."

Captain Ron Walker walked slowly over to the trilo-shuttle craft with his gun in his hand and greeted Captain Justin Harper and John McNally with a hand shake. He then looked at both of them and coldly said;

"If this is some kind of trap or trick, I will shoot first and ask questions later! My people also have the same orders!"

Both men acknowledged this with a nod and John McNally gestured and said;

"Captain, please come this way, the shuttle ride back to our space ship should only take ten minutes. In that time, you can have a chat with Doctor Elaine Laurence."

Surprised, Captain Walker inquired;

"Elaine is on this shuttle?"

Smiling, John McNally answered;

"She sure is, and she is the one who instigated the rescue mission!"

As Captain Walker entered the trilo-shuttle craft his poker face changed to one of shock as he looked at Elaine and the triloraptor next to her! Quickly he regained his composure, raised his gun, pointed it at Elaine and then said;

"Who the hell are you?"

Inwardly Elaine was extremely upset that Captain Walker had not recognised her but, she put on a brave face and replied;

"Captain Walker, it's me Elaine. I know I have no hair and my skin is blue but, it really is me!"

Narrowing his eyes, the Captain then pointed the gun at the triloraptor and in a derogative tone said;

"And what is that thing next to you?"

This question made Elaine angry and she snapped back;

"How dare you refer to another being as 'that thing'? Shame on you Captain Ron Walker! Since you have been on this planet, you seem to have lost your manners! Now lower that gun before you get hurt or you hurt someone else!"

Captain Walker burst out laughing, pointing his left finger at Elaine and through his laughter said;

"Oh my god, it is really you Elaine! Only you would get so fiery when you thought someone was wrong! What it the name of Jupiter has happened to you and who is this with you?"

Elaine calmed down and explained;

"The crew and passengers from both the space recreational stations Darwin and Stephen Hawking were abducted from earth's orbit and then left on various planets in this universe! I was left on a planet called Notus and the only way I could survive the atmosphere and climate was to adapt.

The person with me is a triloraptor; they are a spacial nomadic race. I will explain more about them later. Now, I believe you would like to meet some of the other rescued passengers and crew from the Recreational Space Station Darwin.

The Captain smiled, nodded and said;

"Can you really get this shuttle into space in ten minutes?"

To the surprise of the Captain, it was the triloraptor pilot who answered;

"Ten earth minutes is slow, take a hold of something and I will get you there in three earth minutes."

Not having a uni-net link with a built in language translator, Captain Walker could not understand a word the triloraptor said, so Elaine loosely translated;

"This is a triloraptor shuttle craft; its speed and technology will defy the laws of earthly physics!"

In less than three earth minutes, the trilo-shuttle craft docked in the triloraptors mother ship bay and Captain Ron Walker was greeted by one hundred and forty eight fellow humans. Captain Walker gathered everyone around him and over the next two and a half hours, he asked them questions about their abduction and what had happened since then.

When he exhausted his questions, Captain Walker then told his story and how over the last few years they had built a colony in an area they call Novus Inceptio, meaning, new beginning, on the planet Gladious which they now classed as their home. He told them that none of this would have happened without help of an intelligent species of mammal that they call the Kreios. He continued by saying that the Kreios are a warm friendly race and a lot of his people have adopted them and now the Kreios live with them as family members in their homes.

With all the talking over, Captain Walker was then taken for a tour of triloraptors part of their mother ship and then into Notus One's blue crystal command centre by John McNally. It was at this point of time that Captain Walker asked;

"Elaine, from the number of people you have already rescued and the ones down on the planet Gladious, I assume you still have to locate more human abductees?"

Replying, Elaine answered;

"That is correct, from the information I have, I know exactly where they are. They are on a planet called Arpeggio. It's an awful long way from here. All we have to do is go there, disarm the triloraptors spacial mines and planetary booby traps and then if they are OK, pick them up. The rescue mission will then be over and we can all head back to earth!"

Captain Walker looked concerned and Elaine asked him what was wrong, he replied;

"In the short period of time that I been on-board your space ship, I have realised that you have gone to extraordinary lengths to rescue us. But Elaine, I do not think a lot of the people on the planet Gladious will want to go back home to earth!"

It was something that Elaine had already come to terms with and said;

"Ron that's OK, I think it's great that they have new lives. I just wanted to let your people know that they were missed and if they wanted to, they could return to earth."

Smiling, Captain Walker walked over to Elaine and gave her a big hug. As he hugged her he said;

"Elaine, you are a good person, I and my people really appreciate what you have done."

Stepping back he continued;

"I have just had an idea. Why don't you bring everyone down to the surface? We would make them really welcome and if you wanted, they could stay on the planet Gladious until you pick up the other abductees?"

Elaine thought about this for a moment and then replied;

"Ron, this sounds like a good idea. It will certainly give everyone a chance to get some fresh air and stretch their legs. I do have one concern, do you have enough food?"

With a smile on his face Ron answered;

"If that's your only concern, then let me assure you that we have ample fresh food and water. And as a bonus, just a few kilometres away, we also have the sea. There are some real nice fish to be caught, and they taste fantastic."

Elaine then suggested;

"It might be a good idea if you go back in the trilo-shuttle craft and inform your people of your proposal. In the mean time, I will get everyone organised here and if your people are in agreement. We will follow you down to the planet's surface in a couple of earth hours."

With the plan set, Captain Walker headed back to the planet Gladious. Elaine then informed the triloraptors that they needed to take Notus One down to the planet's surface, as everyone was going there for a little rest and recreation. She knew the triloraptors did not need any rest or recreation but, she guessed that they might need a break from the humans on-board!

Elaine then had a virtual uni-net call from Captain Justin Harper, who appeared washed, shaven and with a long toga type robe on, said;

"Elaine, Captain Walker has returned safely and everyone down here is really enthusiastic to meet with you all. They are planning a reception in the towns square with a fire work display later this evening."

Elaine clapped her hands together in joy and replied;

"That's great Justin, we will be touching down in about one earth's hour. By the way you look very dapper in your toga."

Justin laughed out loud and said;

"See you soon." And then, Justin ended his uni-net call.

Elaine left it up to the triloraptors to navigate Notus One through the planet's atmosphere and to their landing point. As they touched down, the shuttle bay door opened and Elaine's rescued people poured out to a rapturous welcome. All the ladies were given a beautiful bunch of flowers and the men were given a mug of locally brewed strong ale.

To say Elaine was nervous was an understatement! She had decided to keep her trilo-combat uniform on as she felt embarrassed by the way she looked! As the last few people left the shuttle, Elaine followed and everyone cheered and clapped as she began to walk amongst them.

It was only then that she realised that her adaptive DNA had changed and she was human again! The moment overwhelmed her and Elaine began to cry with joy. Captain Walker came over and put his arm around her and said in a loud voice;

> "Captain Elaine Laurence, welcome to Novus Inceptio. It is a great honour to have you and these wonderful people here."

He then whispered in her ear;

> "Everyone was expecting the blue lady."

Elaine wiped her eyes, laughed and whispered back;

> "Its lucky it's not cold, you would have got the hairy polar woman!"

Captain Walker did not know what Elaine meant by the hairy polar woman but, he politely smiled and said;

> "Ladies and gentlemen from the star ship Notus One, I would now like to introduce you to our friends, the Kreios."

Tactfully and almost whispering, Captain Walker enquired;

> "Will the triloraptors be joining us today?"

Slowly shaking her head from side to side, Elaine replied;

> "No, they do not like social gatherings."

At that, the crowds made a path and over two thousand of the one metre tall Kreios came bounding in. They enthusiastically greeted Elaine and her party as if they were long lost friends. Elaine and her group could not help but stroke their long lustrous fur. And the Kreios responded by bowing their heads and purring with enjoyment.

Elaine could hear that the Kreios made a clicking noise with their mouths and asked Captain Walker if that was there way of communicating? Captain Walker replied;

> "Yes it is and they are saying 'welcome'. If you click back rapidly eight times, you can say 'thank you' back to them."

Elaine did this and then thought that she had really taken the uni-net for granted, as it made specie to specie communications so easy.

After chatting and exchanging stories, everyone then headed to the colonies main town square where further refreshments were provided. Captain Walker then asked for everyone's attention and said that the Kreios would like to play some music for them. A hushed silence then filled the town square as Kreios played the most beautiful country style piped music. Almost whispering, Elaine asked Captain Walker;

> "Have they always played music or did your people teach them?

Whispering back the captain said;

> "We made some wooden flutes and began playing them and the Kreios seemed enchanted with the sounds. So George, the man who made the flutes, ingeniously adapted them and gave them to the Kreios. Within days, they were not only playing them, they were composing their own music!"

Elaine whispered back;

> "That's absolutely fantastic!"

The Kreios were full of surprises; they then upped the tempo; rose up on their powerful hind legs and started dancing! And to everyone's amusement, Captain Harper and John McNally joined in. Elaine suspected that her two crew members had had a little too much of the local ale but, then everyone began to join in. Captain Walker took Elaine by the hand and said;

> "Captain Laurence, would you give me the honour of this dance?"

Elaine's feet had already been tapping to the beat of the music and laughing she said;

"Captain Walker, I thought you would never ask."

For the next hour, Elaine continued dancing and only stopped when Captain Walker announced it was time for the fireworks display.

The fireworks were spectacular and as each one went off; everyone gave a loud earthly cheer and clapped. Most mammals on the planet earth shy away from fireworks but, the Kreios of the planet Gladious loved them. And to show their appreciation, as each fire work went off, the Kreios mimicked the humans! They stood on their hind legs and clapped their front paws together!

As night began to fall, the crowds began to dwindle and the Novus Inceptio people headed for their homes with their new friends. Politely, Captain Walker tried to suppress a yawn and said;

"It's been a long eventful day Elaine. I don't know about you but, I think I am ready for my bed. I'll see you first thing in the morning."

He gave Elaine a hug and then retired to his home. Elaine, Captain Harper and John McNally slowly walked back to Notus One and Captain Harper said;

"Today has been a good day. When we get to the planet Arpeggio, let's hope it works out like today."

Elaine smiled and teasingly replied;

"Oh you're coming then? I thought you and Mr McNally were going to stay here and drink them dry of Novus Inceptio ale?"

Laughing and pretending to slightly slur his words, Captain Harper replied;

"The beer is good here but, we've heard its better on the planet Arpeggio!"

Just after dawn, Elaine left Notus One and meet up with Captain Walker. They spoke for a while of Elaine's next phase of her rescue mission and Captain Walker said;

> "Elaine while you are gone, you do not have to worry about your people, they will be looked after well. When you return, we will talk about who wants to go back to earth and who wants to stay here."

Elaine thanked Captain Ron Walker, kissed him on the cheek and then said goodbye. As Elaine began to walk back to Notus One an elderly man approached her and said;

> "Captain Laurence, my name is Dan Woverly. I was one of the people you rescued from the planet Hope. I was hoping that you might let me tag along and help for the next part of the rescue mission."

Elaine smiled, shook Dan's hand and replied;

> "Dan, you are more than welcome to come, we may need all the help we can get."

As they both walked back to Notus One, Dan told Elaine of his own story and that all he ever wanted was to go into space. He then told her, he couldn't believe that he now had the chance to see other planets and civilisations; this was beyond his wildest dreams! Laughing, Elaine said;

> "Dan, if you would have told me a few months ago that I was going to travel through the universe in a space craft made out of a diamond. I would have thought you were bonkers but, here we are."

Elaine and Dan boarded Notus One and within fifteen earth minutes, the space craft was outside the planet Gladious atmosphere and on its way to their next destination, the planet Arpeggio co-ordinates.

CHAPTER ELEVEN

Planet Arpeggio

The distance from the planet Gladious to the planet Arpeggio was vast! So Elaine asked Notus Ones super computer to go to maximum speed. The computer informed Elaine that Notus One had no speed restrictions but, with the triloraptors mother ship surrounding it; it would be safe to only accelerate to a maximum of twenty gravitons. The computer then informed Elaine that they could then hold that speed until they were ten light years away from the planet Arpeggio solar system and then they would have to begin to de-accelerate. Elaine said that was fine and then sat in her command chair, closed her eyes and telepathically asked Notus for any information on the planet Arpeggio. Notus replied;

"Elaine, first, please accept my sincere congratulations on your mission to Gladious. I am really pleased that everyone was safe and well, well done! I also think it was a good idea to leave your rescued passengers there while you travel to the planet, Arpeggio.

Now, the planet Arpeggio used to have a reasonably advanced civilisation on it but, as it does not have one of my species as its guardian, my knowledge is limited. What I can tell you is, a few hundreds of your earth years ago they developed a form of nuclear power. This is always dangerous and can have dire consequences! I also believe that to date, they have not sent out any space probes or attempted to explore space for themselves."

Elaine inquired;

"If they had nuclear power a few hundred years ago, then logically they must have some form of energy for industry, lights and heating? If they have all this, then do you think they would have also developed high tech weapons?

Notus instantly answered;

"Elaine it's all possible but, the best people to ask are the triloraptors. They went there shortly after they dropped you off."

In all of the haste and rushing from one rescue to another, Elaine had forgotten this. She thanked Notus and then called the triloraptors and said she needed to talk to them urgently. Within a few earth minutes the four triloraptors joined Elaine in Notus Ones command centre. She then asked them for details of the planet Arpeggio. The triloraptors spokesperson informed her;

"I have some good news for you and some bad news. First the good news, we did not have time to booby trap the planets solar system or indeed the planet.

Now the bad news, life at one time on this planet was in abundance. But now, it is a barren lifeless and in most places, a highly radioactive planet! This we believe was due to a reliance on atomic energy and not being able to contain it! We took the precautions of getting the trilo-bots to inject all one hundred and thirty four humans with an anti radioactive isotope to help boost their immune systems. But, this booster would only last for a few earth weeks!

Next, the pressure in the planet's atmosphere is greater than on earth and for humans this produces higher levels of nitrogen in the human blood stream. For the humans that we dropped off, the atmosphere would be uncomfortable but liveable!"

The alarm bells began to ring in Elaine's head! She could not believe what the triloraptor had just said. Angrily she replied;

"You're telling me that you dropped off families knowing that the planet was high in radiation and that everyone will be suffering from nitrogen narcosis and residual nitrogen effects! How the hell do you think they were going to survive that?"

By now the triloraptor spokesperson was more than familiar with Elaine's angry outbursts and calmly answered;

> "Captain Elaine Laurence, as you will recall, at the time we were dropping you off on the planet Notus, we were also dropping the rest of your people off. It was at that point of time that the planet Notus began developing strange electromagnetic storms and we had to abandon that planet and find another one. We also had news from our central command that the U.I.C had recently declared war on the triloraptors! On top of that, the U.I.C was going to use planet Notus as a staging area to try to trap us! With all of that going on, we were ordered to head back to our main fleet.
>
> The closest planet we could find to drop of the humans was planet Arpeggio. We had very little information about the planet and I agree its atmosphere was not ideal! Our trilo-super computer gave us two options! The first was to drop the humans off on Arpeggio or we could go for option two; kill them all and eject their bodies out of the trilo-air lock! We chose option one."

As always the triloraptors put forward a good case and Elaine knew she would not get anywhere arguing with them. So she dismissed the triloraptors and then began thinking of her options. They would clearly have to go down to the planet surface and see if there were any survivors. However, she could not take Justin, John or Dan with her as they would be exposed to the high levels of radiation and be overcome from the effects of high atmospheric pressure.

From the space stations crew, Elaine remembered that Doctor William Tulsar was amongst the one hundred and thirty four in this group. She had worked with this doctor onboard the Recreational Space Station, Stephen Hawking and knew he was a good doctor. William would know how to identify the symptoms of narcosis and residual nitrogen in the blood stream. The only problem with this was Doctor William Tulsar would also be suffering from narcosis and residual nitrogen symptoms. In the earlier stages, these symptoms are often displayed as euphoric behaviour. If this were the case, then the doctor's medical judgements would be highly questionable!

The next medical dilemma was even more worrying, radiation sickness! This was a killer and should be treated immediately! The problem was all one hundred and thirty four people had been exposed to this for nearly one and a half earth years! Doctor William Tulsar would not have any medical provisions to treat his patients. Elaine's mind then jumped to an even worse scenario, what if there are survivors? Notus One or the triloraptors did not have any radiation sickness treatments on-board! As a doctor, Elaine knew that even if some miraculously survived, they would, for the rest of their lives, have to be monitored for all types of cancers!

Elaine then thought of another option; contact the Universal interplanetary Congress for medical assistance. They had highly advanced medical nano technology. She then realised that this was a stupid thought because, the U.I.C had put a restriction on all space flights! Her last but what she classed as a serious option was, just travel back in time and rescue them all before they were exposed to the planet's atmosphere and radiation!

While Elaine was pondering on these problems and options, Notus telepathically said;

> "Elaine, your mind is in an absolute turmoil. You have analysed the problems, now just face them one at a time."

It was one of these moments where Elaine was pleased to have Notus inside her head and jokingly she telepathically replied;

> "Notus, you are wise beyond your years. I will go to the planet's surface first and then see what I need to do."

Even at the colossal speed Notus One was travelling at, it still took a few earth weeks to get to the planet Arpeggio's solar system. In that time Elaine had been studying all she could on human exposure to radiation and also narcosis and residual nitrogen symptoms. The U.I.C medical data base was extremely useful for this, as they had had to deal with both medical problems, time and time again. In all cases, numerous preventive measures were well documented but, irrespective of what species you were, prolonged over exposure to both medical conditions produced the same results, a long and often painful death!

One glimmer of hope was reconstructive cellular nano technology. It had been used successfully on several of the Universal Interplanetary Congress's species who had been exposed to high levels of radiation. But, obviously it had never been done on a human! By a uni-net link, Elaine contacted the U.I.C medical board, explained what she was facing and asked if they would begin clinical tests immediately. To Elaine's delight, they said they had human DNA on file and would prioritise this, and let her know of their finding as quickly as they could.

Elaine knew that Captain Harper, John and Dan desperately wanted to help in the rescue mission. But, she had to explain to them the dangers they would face if they were exposed to the high levels of radiation and the planet's atmosphere. Captain Harper asked Elaine if the triloraptors could fabricate biological hazard suits for the three men but as trilo-resources on-board were low, this was not an option.

As high levels of radiation exposure were her main concern, Elaine told all three that when they landed, they would have to stay on-board in a quarantined area. And as an extra safety measure, Elaine also got the trilo-bots to inject the three men with a short term anti radioactive isotope.

If there were survivors, Elaine needed somewhere to use as a re-pressurisation chamber and an area to quarantine and nurse the victims. So she got the triloraptors to convert a large cargo bay into a sterile sealed ward with a decontamination entrance and exit. Using trilo-technology, each bed inside the ward had its own re-pressurisation field and radiation containment field.

With the preparations ready, Notus One began to enter Arpeggio's solar system. Elaine asked the virtual reality unit to display Arpeggio's solar system and it instantly brought up what Elaine could only describe as a spectacular view. The solar system had forty two planets in it, thirty two were gas planets and five were made of gas, molten liquid and rock! Elaine could only guess that they would be classed as semi solid planets.

The remaining five were the inner planets and looked equally amazing as they had numerous multi coloured moons. The systems sun is a red giant and as Notus One super computer explained to Elaine, in this universe, it is a relatively old star. Its diameter is about 100 times bigger than it was originally and had become significantly cooler (the surface temperature is under 6,500 K). As a red giant, the sun gave off a radiant orange glow. This orange luminosity emanated out into the far reaches of the solar system and as its warming light touched the planets, it made the spacial solar views spectacular.

Fortunately for the planet Arpeggio, it is the fifth planet from its red sun and as its sun began expanding in size, it had very little effect on Arpeggio atmosphere. However, the overall planetary temperature dropped by two degrees Celsius and that caused its ice caps to expand and many regions close to its Northern and Southern hemisphere went into a prolonged ice age!

Before landing at the co-ordinates that the triloraptors provided, Elaine got Notus One super computer to do a bio scan sweep of the area for life forms. Sadly the scans came back negative. The area Notus One touched down in was on the top of a hill, approximately one thousand five hundred kilometres above the planets equator and the air temperature was an acceptable twelve degrees. Elaine had put on her full trilo-combat uniform and even before she had got a foot on the surface of the planet, her adaptive DNA kicked in and she was 'silver woman'.

As Elaine looked around, she could see skeleton evidence that this area at one time had trees! Now all that was left was a radioactive waste land! In the distance, Elaine could see the crumbling remains of what looked like domed structures. She could only guess that this was once a town or even a city but she thought, if she had been stranded here, that's the first place she would head for.

While Elaine continued on foot, the triloraptors had taken to the air and it was not long before Elaine got a trilo-call saying that they had seen the trilo-survival round black containers at the opening of a cave! Without delay, Elaine created an anti-gravity field around her body and flew to the opening of the cave. When she arrived, the triloraptors were already leaving the cave. The triloraptor spokesperson came over to her and said;

"Captain Elaine Laurence, we have found the humans, they are all dead!

Although Elaine had half expected this, the triloraptors words still shocked her. Without really thinking she replied;

"Are you sure their dead, did you check for life signs? How many are in there?"

Confidently the triloraptor answered;

"They are all there, one hundred and thirty four dead bodies!"

Bracing herself, Elaine walked past the triloraptor and into the cave. The cave was dark and had the distinct smell of decomposing bodies! Looking through her trilo-visor menu, Elaine found an icon that showed her trilo-combat suit illuminated. She mentally clicked on this and instantly the cave lit up with white light. As a doctor, Elaine had seen her fair share of dead bodies but, she had never seen a mass open grave before! The sight made her physically shudder, the decomposing skeletons of men, women and children lay across the caves uneven floor. The cause of their deaths was obvious; they had initially been exposed to planetary narcosis and then high levels of radiation.

Out of respect, Elaine did not disturb any of the bodies as some lay in what looked like family groups with husbands and wives holding hands, and the parents embracing their children. It was a sad sight and tears began to fill Elaine's eyes. As she turned and began to slowly walk out of the cave, out of the corner of her tear filled eyes, Elaine saw a glimpse of a shadowy light towards the rear of the cave. She immediately stopped, turned around and to her utter surprise; a large translucent light began to approach her!

The translucent light then stopped about a metre from Elaine and slowly began to circle around her? Once it completed its circle, it darted off! Elaine was not disturbed by this, she immediately thought it was some form of life but, from her initial encounter, she could not tell if it was an intelligent life form. Notus had picked up Elaine's mental thoughts and telepathically said;

> "Elaine, what you just came across, was a radioactive life form! There are several species across the radioactive spectrum and range from, alpha, beta, gamma, X ray and neutron. The one you just meet was probably an alpha radioactive life form."

Elaine instantly had several questions to ask, but before she could, Notus has read Elaine's mind and continued saying;

> "Elaine, they are not hostile, most live in space and in their own way, they are extremely intelligent."

That quick summary answered some of Elaine's questions but, she still had one that Notus had not answered and mentally inquired;

"What was that one doing in this cave, with all those dead human people?"

Notus knew this question was coming and answered;

"This is just a guess but, I think it was guarding the dead. It must have seen the alien triloraptors go into the cave followed by you. It must have then thought you were going in to desecrate their graves!

This answer really confused Elaine, so she asked;

"Why would it think that and why would it care?"

Notus knew that the answer would surprise Elaine and said;

"Please sit down for a moment, I have a story to tell you and you might find it hard to believe."

For the short time that Elaine had known Notus, she knew that when Notus had a big revelation to make, it was normally a stunner. So preparing herself, she sat on a rock in the cave and said;

"Ok, I'm ready, please begin."

For once Notus left the humorous 'Once upon a time' headings out and commenced to tell the story of radioactive life forms.

"Elaine, radioactive life forms have been in this and other universes since their creation. Each universe is full of radiation and that's what nourishes these beings. One radioactive dietary thing they like is the miniscule radioactive particles that are left after a planet is formed. They go to the planets and forage for the radioactive particles; I suppose to them, this is a culinary delicacy.

Over time, the planets radiation levels deplete and on certain planets, various types of biological life forms begin to develop and the radioactive life forms out of curiosity begin to take an interest in them. The best way I can describe the initial interest is, the way you humans have cold, tropical and marine fish and corals in various tanks or animals in a zoo. In this case, the planet is the proverbial atmospheric tank or zoo. This initial interest is then taken over by the development of evolving intelligent life forms.

What happens next is truly amazing. The radioactive life forms develop a fondness not just for the species but, for an individual life form! Unbeknown to that person, they are unofficially adopted by the radioactive life form for that person's life time! I can only guess, but, this must sound similar to what you class on the planet Earth as having a guardian angel."

Still sitting on her rock, Elaine could not decide if Notus was winding her up. Playing along, she asked;

"If and I say 'if' this is true, wouldn't the radioactive life form radioactively contaminate its adopted biological adoptee?"

Since they first meet on the planet Notus, Notus the being could see into Elaine's mind and knew she was sceptical and answered;

"That would depend on who your guardian angel is. In the case of the humans on this planet, the radioactive life form here is probably an ionizing alpha. To understand this being and other radioactive life forms you must first understand a little about radiation. The word radiation is often used in reference to ionizing radiation that would be gamma, alpha, beta and so on. But the term radiation also refers to non-ionizing radiation, like light, heat and radio waves.

Both ionizing and non-ionizing radiation can be harmful to biological organisms and can result in changes to their natural environments. In general, ionizing radiation is far more harmful to living organisms per unit of energy deposited than non-ionizing radiation and over exposure to ionizing radiation can destroy the biological organisms DNA and that can lead to cancerous growths and death!

All radioactive life forms have elements of heat and light and various forms of radiation that make up their primary formation. From this basic foundation, they then fall into various radioactive life forms such as; Alpha, Beta, Gamma and X-ray and finally Neutron.

Elaine, I know you have studied physics at college and university but, I want to break these radiation forms down further. That way you will be able to understand each radioactive life form. I will begin with Alpha.

Alpha radiation is a heavy, very short-range particle and is actually an ejected helium nucleus. Fortunately, most forms of alpha radiation are not able to penetrate human skin. So contact with humans would be a very low to moderate risk. Even if an alpha radioactive life form touched you, you would only get a slight marking of the skin.

Beta radioactive life forms are a little more dangerous as beta radiation is a light, short-range particle and is actually an ejected electron. If beta radioactive life forms came into contact with humans, the beta radiation can penetrate the germinal layer and prolonged exposure would cause serious skin injury or cancer.

The next ones are Gamma and X-ray radioactive life forms, they are more dangerous and they know it! Gamma and X-ray radiation is sometimes called 'penetrating' radiation and even dense shielding will not stop its penetrating power. So when possible, Gamma and X-ray radioactive life forms try to avoid contact with biological life forms.

By far the deadliest for most universal life forms is a Neutron radioactive life form! Neutron radiation is the radiation that had been released from the nuclear reactors on this planet and is responsible for killing every life form on this planet! In mythological terms on most planets, a Neutron radioactive life form is also known as the 'angel of death'!

Elaine sat for a few moments and let this information sink in. She then asked;

"I know this sounds really stupid but, have radioactive life forms visited the planet Earth?"

Without hesitation, Notus answered;

"Yes, they were there at its birth and they will be their when it dies. I dare say that in your planets mythology there are numerous accounts of humans seeing apparitions of them. Their even written accounts of humans speaking to them and also taking advise from them. Furthermore if you think about it, earths and other planets religions are not far out when they say angels come from the heavens. They certainly come from open space!"

While Notus was answering Elaine's last question, Elaine's mind was still taking in this information and then two other important questions popped up. As soon as Notus finished speaking, Elaine eagerly asked the next questions;

"Would it be fair to say that these radioactive life forms actually help clean a planet up of waste radiation and my next question is; are they related to your species?"

It was two good questions and Notus answered;

"Radioactive life forms do indeed contribute to helping reduce the levels of harmful radiation that are left when a planet's atmosphere is formed. They then continue for that planets life to absorb harmful radioactive particles. This radiation reduction process is obviously beneficial, as without it most biological life forms would never exist! Think of it this way, on earth you have a honey bee. The bee goes from flower to flower collecting nectar but it also helps pollinate the flowers. The radioactive life forms do a similar thing by absorbing radiation.

Now, to answer your second question; radioactive life forms are not related to my species but, I can see where you are coming from. I and my species are made of pure energy. Alpha, Beta, Gamma and X ray and Neutron are completely different life forms as they are made up of radioactive energy."

Standing up, Elaine began to walk slowly to the caves exit and telepathically said;

"Wow and double wow, so what you have just told me was for real. Angels are real, wow! OK Notus, I have said enough wows, I have to move on. How do they communicate with each other and more importantly, how can they communicate with me?"

The one thing Notus liked about Elaine was her tenacity. Replying Notus said;

"They communicate by sending mental images to each other and that's how they would also communicate with you. When you get these mental images, you might find them hard to decipher as they are snap shots of what they think, see and recall."

Elaine telepathically thanked Notus and exited the cave. As she stood at its entrance, she decided it would be appropriate to seal her fellow human's tomb. Looking around, Elaine could see several large boulders; she then created an anti-gravity field around each one and mentally lifted them and placed them so the cave entrance was sealed. From her trilo-visor menu, Elaine then summoned her trilo-tron and used it to carve the letter's R.I.P into one of the mains boulders. With that done, as Elaine headed back to Notus One, all she had on her mind was time travel!

One of Elaine's first jobs was to decontaminate herself before briefing Captain Harper, John and Don on her sad findings; however, she thought it wise to leave out the radioactive life forms 'angels' for the time being. All three men seemed genuinely upset at what Elaine told them but, when Elaine told them of her plan to travel back in time and rescue the one hundred and thirty four people, they were ecstatic.

To put the time travel plan into action, Elaine got the triloraptors to calculate the exact time and date they dropped off the humans on the planet Arpeggio. This information was then feed into Notus One super computer and within a few trilo-minutes Notus One had left the planet's surface and was heading for its planetary alignment position in readiness for the extrapolation of energy time from the planets warped time vortex.

Next, Elaine wanted the virtual display unit moved into the large cargo bay that was now the sterile sealed ward. What she was planning was to get the time portal to open directly in the sterile ward and that way she would reduce the risk of radioactive contamination to her crew members. Elaine called the triloraptors and asked for their assistance but there was no reply? She then called Captain Harper by his uni-net link and again there was no reply? She immediately left Notus One's command centre to find out what was happening and as she walked down the trilo-corridor, to her absolute horror, she came across Dan Woverly's body; he had been cut clean in two! Dan's blood was still flowing from the two halves of his body! So Elaine guessed that whatever had happened had only been done a few earth seconds ago!

Instinctively, Elaine called as loud as she could;

"Justin, John come quickly! Dan is dead, he's been killed!"

But Notus One was filled with an eerie silence and there was no reply! Elaine carefully stepped over Dan's body and continued to the quarantine area where Justin and John were staying. Before she got there, to Elaine's horror, she came across another body! This time it was, Captain Justin Harper, he had been decapitated! Holding back the tears, Elaine knelt down by the side of Justin's and held his hand for a moment and then whispered;

"Justin, oh Justin, what's happened? I am so, so sorry!"

This by now, had turn into Elaine's worst nightmare! Her heart was pounding and she still had to find John McNally and the four triloraptors! Her thoughts then instantly went to the triloraptors. Were they responsible for these murders? Then a moment of panic set in as Elaine realised that she had taken off her trilo-combat uniform but, it was too late!

The blast from a pulse energy gun hit her in the back with so much force that it thrust her almost twelve metres down the trilo-corridor! Before Elaine hit the floor, another volley from the pulse energy gun slammed into her body, sending her crashing into the trilo-corridor walls!

Because Elaine's adaptive DNA had not had time to kick in, she could feel and hear her own bones breaking from the impact! She slowly slumped down onto the floor, only to be hit again by another volley! This volley sent Elaine tumbling across the corridor floor and again more bones made a crunching sound as they were crushed and broken!

Totally stunned from what had just happened, Elaine lay face down in the corridor and was not able to move. Pain filled her body and mind and she could hear someone groaning and whimpering. Elaine tried to open her eyes and then realised the groaning and whimpering had stopped, what she had heard was, her own voice!

From a distance, Elaine could hear footsteps approaching her! In desperation, she tried to crawl away but, her shattered limbs would not function! In an attempt to further mutilate or kill her, whoever it was, then stamped as hard as they could several times on Elaine's head! Elaine's one leg was then seized and she was unceremoniously dragged back down the corridor. As Elaine was dragged past Justin Harper's decapitated body, she could feel a sticky wetness on her own body! Although she was still only semi conscious, with repulsion, Elaine realised it was Captain Justin Harper's blood! After that, Elaine must have blacked out.

As she began to regain consciousness, Elaine could hear muffled voices, but she could not make out what was being said! She tried to open her mouth to call out but, the injuries she had prevented her from doing this! Elaine forced her one eye to open just a little and to her horror, she found that right next to her was John McNally pulverised body! The right side of Johns head had been completely smashed in and Elaine thought that John must have also been shot several times with the pulse energy gun!

Slowly, with her one eye, Elaine began to scan where she was. It was the trilo-shuttle bay and to her far left she could see the four triloraptors! One walked over and looked down at Elaine and said;

> "Captain Elaine Laurence, you are a hard person to kill but, I might have a remedy for that!"

Using its powerful talons, it grabbed Elaine by the throat and dragged her across the floor towards an open phonon torpedo launch hatch. The triloraptor then flung Elaine's battered body on top of Justin Harper and Dan Woverly and then, one by one it stuffed all three bodies in the empty launch hatch. Looking at Elaine, it callously said;

> "Captain Elaine Laurence, please don't go away, I have one more passenger!"

The triloraptor then went and collected John McNally's body and stuffed him into the torpedo hatch as well! With a tone of complete contempt, it finally said;

> "Captain Elaine Laurence, we have taken back control of our trilo-mother ship and we now have control of Notus One! Since doing this, we have changed course and are now just over ten light years

away from the planet Arpeggio! Let's see if you, the 'famous' Captain Elaine Laurence can survive in open space!"

The triloraptor then closed the torpedo launch bay hatch and activated the launch switch. With a loud whoosh, Elaine's body and her dead colleagues were then blasted into outer space!

CHAPTER TWELVE

Return to Gladious

While Elaine had been gone, the people and Kreios of the Novus Inceptio region on the planet Gladious had been getting along fantastically with their new human friends. So when they saw the trilo-mother ship fly above their settlement, they all ran out into the town square and streets and began cheering and clapping with excitement. Hearing the commotion, Captain Ron Walker left his home and looked to the sky, seeing the obsidian black spaceship, he called out;

"Elaine is back, let give her and her rescued people a big Novus Inceptio welcome."

Everyone waited patiently for the craft to land but to their absolute bewilderment, the trilo-mother ship began firing its pulse cannons at the Novus Inceptio bridges, security tunnels and trenches! In a few earth seconds they were all pulverised! Captain Ron Walker had no way of communicating with the space ship but, he did what all humans do. He automatically called out shouting;

"Elaine, have you gone mad? What the hell are you doing?"

Captain Walker then realised what the trilo-mother ship was doing, it was blocking their chances of escaping! Immediately, Captain Walker called out to sound the alarm that they were under attack! This call to arms caused confusion not only for the Novus Inceptio humans but also for the rescued humans from the planet Hope! Why was Elaine doing this? She had done so much to help everyone.

Despite their confusion, within a few earth minutes, Captain Walker's militia were manning there field artillery weapons and giant catapults. Additionally, every able bodied person had some kind of weapon; they then nervously waited for their order's.

To everyone's surprise, the trilo-mother ship made another pass over head and then, as if nothing had happened. It set down just to the west of the Novus Inceptio settlement? Captain Walker was taking no chances! He immediately gave the order to train all weapons on the trilo-mother ship!

What Captain Walker had forgotten was the trilo-mother ship was actually two ships! Notus One was being operated remotely from the triloraptors mother ship and was heading in silently from the East at 338 kph (approximately 750 Mph), that is just under the speed of sound. The triloraptors had put Notus One into attack mode two and that activated the hydrogen and helium fusion weapon!

Now Notus One's central band of facets were now glowing white and from its centre. A deadly mixture of hydrogen and helium had fused together forming a glowing band that expanded out twenty five times the circumference of Notice one! The band was designed so that it narrowed down to a white hot, sharp razors edge!

As Notus One approached the Novus Inceptio settlement, it flipped onto its side so that the sharp glowing hydrogen and helium fused band was pointing to the sky and the ground! It then instantly accelerated to 676 Kph (1.500 Mph)! Instantly a sonic boom was created, its blast shook every building and house in the Novus Inceptio settlement and terrified the inhabitants! This however was not its sole purpose. What was planned was the sonic boom would shatter every piece of glass in the settlement! This turned every window into a deadly weapon! Razor sharp shards of glass flew everywhere and countless humans and Kreios were badly injured!

Before anyone could react, Notus One dropped its altitude and its sharp, circular, white hot band was now slicing through the land like a hot knife through butter! At an incredible speed; Notus One then shot through the Novus Inceptio settlement with its hydrogen and helium bladed weapon acting like a giant circular saw! Within seconds, it tore a twenty meter deep rift straight through the settlement! The devastation it caused was horrendous, countless lives were lost and building and homes were destroyed!

Notus One then swung around again and this time, Captain Walker's militia were ready! They bravely blasted their field guns at Notus One but, it was to no avail! At the speed Notus One was travelling, they could not hit it. Also even by some miracle, if they did, their artillery shells were as useless as throwing ice cream at the sun, they would have just melted!

Out of fear, the people and Kreios in the Novus Inceptio settlement were now running for their lives as Notus One then tore another twenty meter deep rift to the far left of their settlement! Those victims who could not get out of the way were either pulverised by the blade or roasted alive by the immense heat it gave out!

While the chaos continued, the trilo mother ship then began to send a bombardment of hydrochloric acid mortar air shells into the settlement! They were designed to explode three metres above the ground and scatter the lethal acid indiscriminately over a large area! Those who were caught by the acid attack had no defences as the acid burnt straight through clothing and fur and melted the skin and bones in seconds!

Captain Ron Walker was at his wits end! His people and the Kreios were being slaughtered and his defences were useless against the trilo mother ship and Notus One! But then he noticed that the surviving Kreios in the settlement had re-grouped and were digging frantically at the foot of one of the rifts Notus One had cut. He ran over to see what they were doing and realised they were digging small shelters for themselves and their human friends. Calling to everyone, Captain Walker said;

> "Quick everyone help the Kreios, dig deep into the side of these rifts and make shelters for yourselves and the Kreios."

People and Kreios grabbed what they could use, slid down the rift walls and began digging for their lives! But this was exactly what was planned! Notus One had headed to the East of the Novus Inceptio settlement and was now over the sea. It dropped its altitude and let its white hot blade slice through the sea bed and continued cutting until its new rift meet the one that ran straight through the Novus Inceptio settlement!

Within seconds, a roar could be heard as the sea water gushed down the rift, there was no escape! The force of the water smashed into humans and Kreios and crushed their bodies against the rifts tall walls. Those who were not killed instantly soon drowned as parts of the rift walls collapsed and trapped them under tonnes of water, mud and rubble!

Notus One then headed inland, and turned to the same co-ordinates the second rift and then dropped to almost ground level. Those who had scurried into this rift for safety now faced Notus Ones blade of death! Captain Ron Walker wept as he watched more people and Kreios die as Notus One tore through the rifted landscape. Then out of the corner of his eye, Captain Ron Walker noticed that the triloraptors were just about to leave the triloraptor mother ship. He quickly bent down and picked up a high powered sniper rifle, the fifty calibre bullet was already in the chamber!

Captain Ron Walker looked down the large metal sights, chose his prey and gently squeezed the trigger! The bullet hit the one triloraptor in the central mass of its body but, its trilo-combat uniform deflected the fifty calibre bullet as if it were nothing! Out of frustration, Ron re-loaded and fired again but this allowed the triloraptor to lock on to Ron's exact co-ordinates. Though its trilo-visor, the triloraptor returned fire with its razor sharp bladed trilo-tron. Captain Ron Walker never knew what hit him, as the trilo-tron sliced through him, cutting him and his gun in exactly two halves! The triloraptors response time and kill happened in less than point five of an earth second!

It was now time for the four triloraptors to take to the air. All four had their trilo-trons by their sides and their prey was anything that moved! The trilo-super computer had divided the Novus Inceptio settlement into four areas and each triloraptor had its own area to hunt and kill in!

A small group of humans and Kreios had huddled into a small dwelling, just on the outskirts of the settlement. Unfortunately for them the first triloraptor had honed in on this through its heat sensors in its trilo-visor! The triloraptor swooped down and landed quietly on the dwelling roof. Through its heightened senses, it could smell the fear of the humans and Kreios! However, its trilo-detector also picked up that most humans were armed! This pleased the triloraptor as it knew that through fear they would attempt to fight back. Using its trilo-tron in the blade mode, it cut a perfectly round hole in the roof and it fell in! The triloraptor jumped through the hole and landed in the middle of the fearful group!

This particular group were made up of women, children and Kreios. However, the women were all mothers, and they were determined at all costs to protect their young! From all corners of the room, gun fire rained out as the mothers repeatedly shot the triloraptor. What they and the other people of the Novus Inceptio settlement did not know was, the triloraptors trilo-combat uniform is made from R.I.T.S (robomatic inter transdimensional substance). And in the correct mode, they could almost withstand the blast of a four mega tonne hydrogen bomb, so their ineffective bullets just bounced off it!

In seconds, the protective mothers ran out of bullets but, they could see through the thick cloud of gun smoke that the triloraptor was just still standing there, unharmed! Fearing the worse, they clutched their children close to them but, the triloraptor did not retaliate? It looked around the smoke filled room and then flew out of the hole it had created in the roof!

At first, they were all jubilant. Until they noticed a small metallic device lying on the floor, it was an old fashioned phosphorous grenade! The grenade then exploded sending shrapnel and white hot phosphorous around the room! Instantly the people, Kreios and room caught fire, and those who were able, instinctively ran outside! But, that was what the triloraptor had planned, and it was waiting for them!

Mother's, children and Kreios were screaming in pain as they exited the inferno! But a worse fate was waiting for them! They were then cut down by the triloraptors razor sharp trilo-tron! The triloraptor had set the trilo-tron, so that it surgically removed the arms and legs of the humans! And the front and rear legs of the Kreios! The survivors were then left lying in pools of their own blood, to die an excruciatingly painful death!

Novus Inceptio militia's steam powered tank lay hidden and camouflaged with netting and shrubbery close to the centre of the settlement. Its powerful 75 mm gun was trained on one of the triloraptors and they were ready to fire when they heard a heavy clunk outside? Puzzled, the front gunner slowly opened the front viewing port and to his amazement, he found that that the four metre long cannon barrel had been cleanly cut off!

Before he had a chance to report this, he was killed by the triloraptors trilo-tron! Its shape was a needle pointed javelin, which had been fired with extreme trilo-accuracy. Before the man could blink his eye, the javelin shot through the open viewing port and went straight through the man's right eye and into his brain! The man sat motionless as the trilo-tron silently withdrew its needled point. Without giving that one single kill another thought, the triloraptor then changed its command mode in its trilo-visor's menu and the trilo-tron change shape to a large battering ram!

With tremendous speed, the trilo-tron ram then flew forward and began smashing into the tank! Its powerful strikes easily dented and crumpled the tanks metal exterior but, then it stopped? Within a trilo-second, it had changed its shape again. This time it was a large flat plate! The trilo-tron plate sped to the front of the tank and started pushing the tank backwards! The crew fired up their steam engine and with full power to their tracks, they dug in and gradually moved forward. However, with the damage to the exterior, they could not open any of the hatches to see where they were heading but; they were determined to try to stand their ground!

Seeing what was happening, the triloraptors withdrew the trilo-tron and commanded it to fly around the back of the tank and now push the tank forward. To further assist in the forward motion of the tank, the triloraptor jumped onto the rear of the tank, spread its four meter wide wings and began to flap them vigorously!

With all this power, the tank was trust forward, faster and faster! Confused by what was happening, the tanks crew tried to engage the tracks reverse gear but, it was too late. The tank was now close to the edge of the settlements central rift and under the weight of the tank, the ground began to subside and crumble away! The triloraptor then stopped pushing, flew into the air and watched as the tank and occupants toppled slowly into the rifts twenty metre deep muddied water!

When Kreios are afraid, they naturally huddle together in a group; these groups or herds can be some times as big as several hundred Kreios! The females and young are always in the centre of the group and the male's face outward, growling and baring their teeth!

One of the triloraptors saw a group of about two hundred and fifty Kreios trying to escape the settlements mayhem. Seeing the triloraptor, the Kreios immediately formed their defensive position and the males growled louder and louder as a triloraptor flew in circles around the terrified group! Randomly, the triloraptor would swoop in and grab a young Kreios that was close to the centre of the group! The young captured Kreios would scream out but, the others knew they could not save it. All they could do is watch in horror as the triloraptor tore the poor juvenile creature apart, limb by limb with its powerful talons!

Within a few trilo-minutes, ten young Kreios were dead on the ground but courageously the Kreios group stood fast. However, the triloraptor had something that would test this resolve! It swooped in again and grabbed a small Kreios but, as it was leaving, it dropped a plasma fire cracker into the centre of the group! The plasma fire cracker went off immediately and as it exploded with loud cracks and bangs. It also shot out streams of hot plasma! The plasma streams ripped massive holes straight through those Kreios closest to it! It then continued to fatally injure and maim other Kreios that were in its destructive range!

In sheer terror, the group began to scatter but, they did not get far! The triloraptors trilo-bots were waiting for them! Using percussion grenades, the trilo-bots herded the fleeing Kreios into a large portable electrified enclosure! Once captured, the trilo-bots then proceeded to kill each Kreios by shooting each one with a powerful neurological exterminator gun! With almost two hundred dead Kreios bodies, the trilo-bots then set to work skinning and de-boning them and then transporting their meat to the trilo-mother ship refrigeration chamber! Kreios meat is an excellent source of protein, and was just what was needed for the triloraptors onward journey!

With almost all of the human and Kreios dead in the Novus Inceptio settlement, it was now time for the triloraptors to leave the planet Gladious. But before they did, the triloraptors had one more task, and this task was left for the trilo-bots to do. The trilo-bots went around and collected as many of the Novus Inceptio militia's weapons as they could find and then load them into one of the spare cargo bays on-board the trilo-mother ship. The four triloraptors had already flown back to their mother ship and were busy making preparations for their final farewell for this planet. With the arrangements completed, they took off and joined

Notus One in space 1,609.3 Kilometres (one thousand miles) outside the planet's atmosphere.

One of the triloraptors turned on their own holographic display unit and said;

"All of the data has now been loaded into Notus One's super computer, it is now in attack mode one. Firing will commence in ten trilo-seconds!"

All four triloraptors then watched the holographic display unit as Notus One flipped onto its side and began drawing dark matter from space and then super compressing it. As the countdown continued, three, two, one, Notus One fired the super compressed dark matter at its co-ordinates; the Novus Inceptio settlement!

The invisible blast was so powerful that it initially punched a 321868.8 kilometres (two hundred mile) wide hole in the planets ozone layer and within half a nano second, the planet's atmosphere began to vent out into space! Within another nano second, the colossal wave of super compressed dark matter hit the land, its force instantly smashed clean through the planets mantle! Right away, dust, debris and plumes of molten lava shot out into the planet's now weak atmosphere to heights of over 4.828032 kilometres (three miles)! Again within a few nano seconds, the massive shock wave spread throughout the whole planet, causing massive tsunamis and rupturing the planets tectonic plates! As the triloraptors watched, the injured planet could not take any more destruction and slowly, it began to fall apart!

Satisfied with what they had done, the triloraptors re-joined their mother ship with Notus One and headed for their next destination, the planet Earth!

CHAPTER THIRTEEN

The awakening

Universally, the scientific understanding of sleep in all species is still an open book. Some speculate that when we go into this semi-conscious state, it helps our bodies and minds to repair. But what if you had no body? After being in open space for weeks and without the protection of her adaptive DNA, Elaine's broken body had been destroyed by cosmic radiation! It had also been ravished by the extreme cold of space to the extent that her body froze and crumbled into atomic particles! All that was left was the remains of her pure energy atoms. What's more to put it into an unscientific way, they were in a higgly piggly way!

Notus the being had tried numerous times to communicate with her but, her scattered pure energy atoms had no way of understanding any messages. So Notus did the same as with Olotinium, its dead offspring. It quickly drew Elaine's pure energy atoms back to the planet Notus. Once there, Notus put a tight gravitational field around Elaine's pure energy atoms and set them down on the beach where Elaine had first meet with Notus the being after arriving on the planet Notus. Notus then left Elaine's atoms cocooned in a gravity field sleep for a while, and hoped that in time they would slowly recover.

At dawn each day, Notus would spend time just telepathically talking to Elaine but, after two earth weeks, the response was negative. That's when Notus decided to bring in some additional help; the help came in the form of an alpha radioactive energy being. An alpha radioactive energy being can communicate at a different level of consciousness and it can do it with multiple images. So Notus asked the A.R.E.B to try to communicate with Elaine's conscious atoms with simple single framed images of objects from her own planet Earth and see if she could respond.

This again proved negative but, the A.R.E.B did not give up and after several days the A.R.E.B thought there was some small progress. It reported to Notus that it could see spasmodically, small unrelated images in Elaine's conscious atoms. Excited by this, Notus asked the A.R.E.B to capture the mental images it could see and then play them back to Elaine.

For Elaine, mentally the last month never existed, but now she was beginning to see images? But they would come and go so fast that she could not remember them until the next time she saw them. The process kept repeating itself until she mentally tried to hold onto an image. The first image she managed to capture was that of a young child. Her mind asked, "Who is this child?" But then the image was gone and darkness returned. The child's image returned again and the same question was asked, "Who is this child?" But then another small breakthrough happened. Mentally Elaine asked another question was asked; "What is the child's name?" But before an answer came, the darkness returned. Time and time again this process was repeated until gradually the image stayed a little longer.

After another week of repetition, Elaine's mind was now beginning to hold onto the image and then recall short dream like events about her own childhood. Her childhood dreams began to bring in other people. At times in her dreams, she was playing with school friends and other times, she was with her mom and dad. Over the next few days, the dream cycle began to develop and in Elaine's dream she was now a teenager with the name Elaine. Elaine liked music, college and she now had a boy friend named Gareth.

It was at this point of time that Elaine's dreams started to become confused and sometimes terrifying! Elaine would be enjoying time with her college friends and then a dark strange creature would appear and chase her! She would run and run but, the creature would catch her and start beating and pounding on her! She could hear her bones breaking and see blood everywhere! In a panic, Elaine would try to defend herself but it was useless, the creature was too strong. Thankfully, the dream suddenly stopped, and the safety and comfort of darkness returned!

As Elaine's dreams changed from being a teenager to becoming a young woman, the nightmare of being chased kept repeating itself! Elaine was mentally now trying to control her dreams so that the dark strange creature was not part of the dream story but it kept creeping in! While Elaine was having one of these dreams, she kept hearing a far-off muffled voice but, she could not make out what was being said. While she was running from the dark creature, she called out;

"I can't hear you properly. Your voice is muffled."

Before she could understand who was calling to her, the dark strange creature had caught up with her and was beating on her again! In all the other dreams the only way of fighting back for Elaine was kicking and punching! Except, in this dream she had an idea, and used an anti-gravity force field around herself for protection. From inside her anti-gravity force field, she could see the dark creature flailing out but, this time it in her nightmare it was not hurting her! The dream then ended and the comfort of darkness fell again.

From out of the darkness, Elaine could hear sounds and slowly she began to focus on one individual sound. She recognised it as the sound of waves crashing on a shore. She then noticed a distinctive smell; it was the smell of the sea air. Curious, Elaine tried to open her eyes but they would not open. She thought of the last moments she was on Notus One and remembered her head being stamped on! Now she rationalised that she was still injured and that's why her eyes would not open.

Slowly the darkness returned and after a while Elaine began to dream again, this time she was on-board Notus One. She was in a corridor and she was being chased by the dark strange creature! As she ran down the corridor, she mentally tried to take control of the dream and her adaptive DNA kicked in! Instantly, she turned into trilo-woman and was now wearing her full trilo-combat suit! In her dream, Elaine stopped, faced her potential attacker and then using her trilo-tron she commanded it to slice the creature in two! The trilo-tron shot forward and to Elaine's relief it cut the creature clean in two! Slowly, she then walked over to the dark strange creature and looked down at its dead body. To her utter surprise, it was someone she recognised! It was her travel companion and the one who had tried to kill her before, it was a triloraptor!

Shocked, Elaine staggered back and all the bad memories of what had previously happened on Notus One flooded back. To escape this nightmare, Elaine forced opened what she believed to be her eyes and found she was on a beach. The surroundings all looked very familiar; she was on the planet Notus! At this point of time Elaine did not know if this was a dream or not but, then a familiar voice came into her head, it was Notus. Notus inquired;

> "Elaine, how are you? You have been unconscious for quite some time. I have been trying for ages to talk to you."

Elaine tried to answer verbally but, her mouth was not working. So she telepathically replied;

> "All I can remember is being torpedoed out of the triloraptors mother ship and then having lots of strange dreams. This too must be a dream, as I don't remember travelling here?"

Notus knew that what Elaine was about to hear was going to come as a shock to her but, there was no easy way to say it. So Notus said;

> "Elaine, this is not a dream, you really are on the planet Notus. When you were torpedoed out of the triloraptors mother ship, your earthly body was severely injured and your adaptive DNA could not function. Elaine, I am terribly sorry, your earth body died and all that was left was your pure energy atoms. I gathered them up and brought you back to the planet Notus to heal. Elaine, you are now like me, a pure energy being!"

Elaine didn't know whether or not to believe Notus. She looked down to see her own body but, there was nothing there? In Elaine's mind's eye, she still had arms and legs but, when she tried to move them nothing happened. She could even sense her human heart pounding faster but, again there was nothing there! Elaine took a few moments for this to sink in and then telepathically said to Notus;

> "If this is a joke then it is in extremely poor taste but, Notus if this is for real, then thank you for saving me!"

Notus replied straight away saying;

"Elaine this is no joke, I have been so worried about you. For a while, I genuinely thought I had lost you. You are home with me and I will help you adjust to your new out of body life."

Elaine felt a little emotional but, she suspected that a pure energy being could not cry. She said;

"Notus, what has happened to my space ship, Notus One?"

Notus gave out a mental sigh and answered;

"The triloraptors have stolen it but, let's not worry about that for now. The first thing we need to do is get you mentally mobile and then I have someone who you might want to meet."

Elaine said "OK", but she mentally felt tired and asked if it was alright to have a sleep for a while. Notus laughed and said;

"Elaine, of course it is, I am just so pleased to have you back. Elaine, you and I are immortal; we do not have to worry about time. Rest and sleep all you want and we will begin your mental training later, but only when you are ready."

At that, the darkness closed in on Elaine and for the first time in weeks, she slept without having a nightmare about the dark strange creature. Her sleep however was not restful; her mind played over and over again about Captain Justin Harpers, John McNally and Don's deaths and the triloraptors despicable treachery! She woke with a start and mentally called out to Notus;

"Let's start my mental training immediately, I have a new mission. The triloraptors are up to no good and I am going to stop them!"

From the tenacious Elaine, this response was exactly what Notus expecting and said;

"Do you know you were asleep for only two earth hours and that is probably the longest you are ever going to sleep again."

Elaine coldly replied;

"That's good, the triloraptors need sleep and while they are asleep, I will be hunting them down!"

Laughing Notus said;

"That's my girl; you always see the bigger picture. Now let's reel you in a little and begin putting things into prospective. You no longer have eyes, so do you understand how you can see?

There was only one answer Elaine could come up with and replied;

"I guess it is through my mind's eye."

Notus began to sound like a school teacher and enthusiastically said;

"Good girl, your right! Your mind and your pure energy atoms are bonded together. However, it is your mind that controls your ability to see, hear, and communicate. It will also control any movements you make.

Because you are a newly formed pure energy being, I had to create a gravitational field around you. This gravitational field helped your healing process by containing your pure energy atoms. In a few moments I am going to release the gravitational field around you but, I want you to create a field inside my one. Are you ready for this?"

Mentally Elaine nodded but, as she no longer had a head, she thought it was better to telepathically answer and said;

"I am ready, but what would happen if I did not have a gravitational field around me?"

Sounding a tad serious Notus said;

"At this stage, your atoms would possibly disperse and you float away! OK, putting that aside let's do this in, three, two, one."

Elaine did as she was told and formed a new gravitational field around herself. As to the dispersing and floating away, she did not know if Notus was being a little melodramatic but, thankfully she felt no different and then asked;

"That was pretty easy, so how do I walk or move around? Come to think of it, where is the top, bottom, front and back of my new energy body?"

The last thing Elaine said amused Notus and with laughter in Notus's voice, Notus answered;

"Elaine you are thinking like a human being, at this time, there is no top, bottom, front or back! You are a whole energy being and you can see, hear and move in all directions! Let's try this, look forward, then back, right and left and then up and down as quick as you can."

Elaine was astonished; although she was a little disorientated, she could see three hundred and sixty degrees in any angle almost instantly! Excitedly, Elaine did this several times and then said;

"That is absolutely amazing! Would I be right in guessing that I can also move in exactly the same way?"

Notus could sense Elaine's excitement and said;

"You can but to start with, you have to be very careful! The normal laws of physics that governed your earthly body do not apply any more. Elaine, you can now travel at extremely fast speeds."

To move, you need to mentally focus on where you want to go and then it will just happen. Look to your left, there is a large rock about a little over two kilometres away. Try mentally focusing and move to the rock and then back here."

Elaine looked at the rock and to her utter astonishment she was by it! She had travel just over two kilometres in less than one earth second! She looked back down the beach and almost instantly, she was back where she had started.

"Wow," She said, "this is amazing. I do have a question however, how come I did not make a sonic boom as I must have travelled faster than the speed of sound?"

This question again amused Notus and chuckling Notus answered;

"As you are now pure energy, you cause no atmospheric resistance and air can pass straight through you.

Elaine, you will also be interested to know, that once you are more atomically stable, you will be able to turn off the gravitational field around you and then you will be able to pass through certain objects."

The thought of being able to pass through objects appealed to Elaine, especially when she encounters the triloraptors again. Now she was ready for her next question;

"Ok Notus that sounds real cool. Now, as you are aware, I no longer have arms and hands. How do I pick things up and touch things?"

Notus answer was partly what Elaine was expecting but, she was also surprised when Notus added;

"Elaine, all that you could do before with gravity fields you can still do. The difference is picking things up and touching things. Everything will now feel very different. When you had human hands, your hands had nerves that would transmit a sensation to your brain of what you were holding. Let me give you an example; as a human being, if someone placed a piece of ice in your hands with your eyes closed, you knew instinctively that it was ice! Why, because your hands would feel the cold of the ice and the wetness of the water as it began to melt.

Now, when you pick something up or touch something, you will feel its texture and energy but, you will also see its life force! Look at the sand below you and with your mind, pick up a single grain and then mentally explore it"

Without question, Elaine mentally focused and picked up a single grain of sand. Suddenly her mind went into overload! She could feel the heat from the grain of sand and its texture but, she could also begin to see its life's journey! The longer she held it, the more this minuscule grain of sand told her. This tiny grain of sand was once part of a larger boulder and that boulder had been worn down by the ocean on the planet Notus over hundreds of thousands of years! And before that, the boulder was once part of a large rocky comet that was orbiting the sun at the same time that the planet Notus was being formed!

Elaine dropped the grain of sand, looked around and picked up a little ant that was scurrying across the hot sand. Elaine could feel its movements and its life force. But what was surprising was she could also feel its extreme indignation at being stopped from doing its important duties! So Elaine carefully placed the little ant back on the sand and said to Notus;

"That was amazing, I felt as if I were able to understand the origin of the grain of sand and the purpose of the ants life!"

Agreeing Notus answered;

"Yes that is exactly what you should sense. As a human being your body evolved on a planet and was perfectly suited to that planetary environment. Now that you are a pure energy being, you are not tied to a planet, you are a universal creature!"

What Notus said took a few moments to comprehend and then Elaine inquired;

"From what you just said, am I right in assuming that I can now travel and explore the universe without a space ship?"

Notus loved Elaine's presumptions, even though they were sometimes a little extreme and answered;

"The universe is yours to explore but, you have to realise space is infinite. Although you can travel at vast speeds, you cannot travel faster than the speed of light and that could restrict your exploration plans. However, as your power and skills develop, you will be able to bend and fold space and that will allow you to travel vast distances quickly! In the mean time; the use of a space craft that can travel faster than ten gravitons would certainly help."

Elaine knew everything Notus said was factual. However, if she still had a human heart; it would be now pounding with excitement! She had read on earth about 'string theories' and of being able to fold space but on earth, these were just theories! Now for Elaine, with her new abilities, this form of space travel would soon be an actual reality! But this euphoria only lasted a few moments as a sobering thought came into Elaine's head. Notus One was now in the hands of those double crossing, murderous triloraptors! They had stolen it for a reason. What were they up to? Notus picked up on Elaine's thoughts and knew that it was time to tell Elaine about the loss of her friends and the fate of the planet Gladious!

Although Notus did not know all of the gory details! Notus knew that the planet Gladious had been destroyed, and the logical assumption from that was that all of its inhabitants were also killed! That's what Notus portrayed to Elaine. Hearing this tragic news, Elaine was devastated! All the people and her friends rescued from the planet Hope were dead! Captain Ron Walker and all from the Novus Inceptio settlement dead! Sadly every living thing including the adorable Kreios on the planet Gladious had been killed by the triloraptors but why? What had the triloraptors got to gain from this barbaric act?

It was at this time that Elaine wished she was still human. She felt that she needed to shed some human tears of sorrow, but, to her frustration, her new pure energy structure did not have tear ducts! She felt mentally upset and wanted to scream but, she had no vocal cords! Notus could feel Elaine's sorrow, anguish and frustration and said;

> "Elaine, I know how you feel. You are understandably upset and you feel you need to mourn the loss of your friends. All energy beings have feelings and we too feel sorrow at the loss of our loved ones. I am still morning the loss of Olotinium, my dead offspring. Nearly all species in this and every other universe feels grief, we just have different ways of portraying it. If you concentrate and open your mind, you will be in touch with the alliance of all pure energy being's. We join together to share our problems and grief."

The feeling of pent up grief was beginning to overwhelm Elaine, so what Notus had said was something she had to try! Concentrating, Elaine tried to mentally open her mind but, no matter how many times she tried, her mind was clouded by grief! In anger, Elaine looked down the beach and using an anti-gravity field she picked up a massive boulder and threw it out to sea. Just as the boulder was about to hit the water, Elaine stopped it as she had realised this action would only hurt the aquatic creatures it landed on. Gently, Elaine drew the boulder back and placed it back on the beach. Feeling a little calmer, she tried once more to open her mind. To her astonishment a mental doorway seemed to open and instantaneously a flood of warmth and comfort flooded in. This was a strange experience for Elaine, it was an emotional comforting feeling without words or physical hugs but, whatever it was, it certainly felt good.

It was Notus who broke Elaine's pure energy alliance's link, when Notus telepathically said;

"I can mentally see you were able to open your mind, Elaine, how do you feel?"

Elaine really did not have to reply as Notus could read Elaine's thoughts but, out of politeness Elaine replied;

"Wow, that's quite an experience, Notus I truly do not know how to explain it?"

In an understanding tone Notus telepathically said;

"You do not have to explain it; I already know how it feels. Except what I want to really know is, honestly, how are you?"

Elaine answered truthfully and said;

"What has happened will never be erased from my mind! Plus I still feel a great sadness but, I also feel angry and used!

I suppose I will be OK but, I know one thing. I desperately want to get back Notus One and stop those treacherous triloraptors!"

Notus knew that Elaine had, to use an earth saying, 'been through the mill and back.' So what Notus was about to say, wasn't what Elaine wanted to hear;

"Elaine, I understand your anger but, we are on a planet at the far end of this universe and we do not have a space ship like Notus One to catch the triloraptors. Realistically, the chances of stopping them without help are very slim!"

This was the first time that Elaine had heard Notus concede to being defeated and with a little scorn in her voice she said;

"I cannot believe that the great Notus is giving up so easily! Do you realise that they know how to time travel and I believe they are going to take full advantage of that! Can't you just build another space ship like Notus One?"

This was a typical response from Elaine and Notus admired her for her gutsy attitude. So Notus calmly replied;

> "Elaine, I do not have enough pure energy atoms left from Olotinium to build another space ship. If I had, this would be the first thing I would have done. I also agree that the triloraptors stole Notus One for the purpose of time travel! That is why we need to enlist some help but, you are going to have to find this being to help! And I should point out, that I really do not know if this legendary being exists!"

This statement got Elaine really curious and she also felt a little guilty for snapping at Notus. So she replied;

> "Notus please accept my apologies for being so disrespectful in my attitude; I know you are on my side and equally upset at all that has happened. So who is this mythological being and where do I have to go to find them.?"

Laughing Notus answered;

> "Elaine you do not have to apologise. You are understandably upset and have been betrayed by the triloraptors. That gives you an infinite number of 'get out of jail free cards' in my universal monopoly book.
>
> Now, as for our help, this is one mythological being in the history of this universe that will really stretch your imagination. But, before I go into this, I want you to meet someone who has already helped you and would be willing to go with you on your next quest."

Elaine looked around and from across the beach an alpha radioactive energy being came into view. With some pride, Notus announced;

> "This is Alpha, a radioactive energy being. You meet one when you were on the planet Arpeggio. I asked Alpha to help when I could not telepathically communicate with you. Furthermore I have given Alpha some human images to help mentally communicate with you now."

The radioactive energy being came close to Elaine and in her mind she could see an image of two human people shaking hands. Elaine guessed that Alpha the radioactive energy being was saying hello earth style and to acknowledge this, Elaine sent the image back to Alpha. She then tried to conjure up an image of 'thank you for your help' but, all she could come up with was two people hugging, so she sent that image. To reinforce this, she also asked Notus to thank Alpha for its help. With that done, Elaine enquired telepathically to Notus, saying;

> "I don't believe for one moment that Alpha is the real name for this being. Who came up with the name for Alpha?"

Notus knew where this was heading and modestly said;

> "It was me. Now, I bet your going to tell me that I did not use much imagination, just the same way I did not use much imagination when I named this planet after me and the space ship Notus One after me."

Laughing, Elaine replied;

> "Get out of my head and stop reading my mind.

Changing the tone of the conversation, Elaine continued;

> "Now let's get down to the serious business of whom and where can we go to, to seek help in stopping the triloraptors."

Replying Notus answered;

> "As I said earlier, this is one being that is almost legendary to all beings in this and other universes. But I do have some evidence that this being exists and has been in this universe longer than I have. Many different species in this universe and other universes know of this being through their own mythology. I believe on earth you have the Greek name KRONOS meaning 'time'. In your mythology KRONOS is the Titan father of Zeus and is the founder and defender of time.

Notus paused, so Elaine could take this in, but when she had no questions Notus continued;

> "As you are aware, the planet Earth has one of my offspring's as its guardian. Earth has told me that in its ancient past, some of these mythological creatures actually visited the planet Earth and that's where you get your Greek mythology from.

I now suspect that the being KRONOS has been monitoring your time travel! And even prior to this, KRONOS may have already put measures in place to stop any universal temporal changes."

While Elaine was surprised by what Notus had said, Elaine had no reason to dispute any of this and asked;

"Do you think the being KRONOS is responsible for the missing graviton engines and the disappearance of the twelve space craft?"

Grimly, Notus answered;

"I would go further than that! Some force or being has placed that gravitational field around the planet Hope's solar system! Elaine, that kind of intervention can only come from a being as powerful as the legendary KRONOS!"

Elaine thought about this for a few moments and then said;

"OK, if this all powerful creature KRONOS is getting involved! Why don't we just leave it up to KRONOS to sort out the triloraptors and their time travel?"

For once, Elaine was not looking at the big universal picture and Notus pointed out;

"Elaine, I suspect the triloraptors are heading for the planet Earth! And if they interfere with earth's time line and KRONOS gets involved, earth might end up in the same situation as the planet Hope!"

This revelation shocked Elaine and puzzled she asked;

"Out of the whole universe, why would the triloraptors want to go to earth to change its time line?"

Notus replied candidly;

"Elaine, I really do not know but, knowing the triloraptors. I will bet my last Olotinium atom that they will be up to no good!"

Although Elaine was now a pure energy being, she could feel her 'human' stomach tighten and churn at this thought. She then asked Notus;

"How do we contact the being, KRONOS?"

Notus answered;

"I and all my kind are going to try to telepathically communicate with KRONOS. Also, once you have fully recovered, you and Alpha are going into open space and all of the radioactive energy beings are going to try to communicate with KRONOS through imagery. We will all have one message, and that is to ask KRONOS to meet with you!"

CHAPTER FOURTEEN

A time to kill

Back on the triloraptors mother ship, the final plans were being fine tuned for their arrival at the planet Earth's solar system. On the instructions of the triloraptors, Notus One's super computer had been researching the history of Elaine's family history! With its super speed, it rapidly found that one of Elaine's ancestors in the year 1607 was one of the earliest British settlers in an area known as Jamestown, Virginia America! That was where the triloraptors aimed to go on their first time mission!

Notus One's computer also came up with some interesting information concerning the resident American Indians and their reverence of the eagle. This was something the triloraptors wanted to investigate, as there was a two percent chance that they could have already visited America in this or another time line! And it could also indicate that they had possibly failed in their temporal mission!

As the triloraptors mother ship approached the dark side of earth's moon. It split and allowed Notus One to take its position in earth own vortex of warped time. Spacial detection wasn't a problem; on a previous visit the triloraptors had destroyed all of earth ground and space telescopes and satellites. To date, with all the political and military wrangling, earth had not been able to build or launch any new telescopes and spacial satellites of any real significance!

Uninterrupted, Notus One began gathering data from the planets energy time vortex but, this process was extremely difficult as earth had had millions if not trillions of events that were recorded in the energy time part of the vortex. To help speed up this process, the triloraptors linked their own super computer to Notus One's. But, even then, the going was incredibly slow! This was due to the energy time signal being extremely weak!

After almost two earth weeks, the two super computers had isolated the exact energy time information for the earth year 1607. That information was immediately directed into the space craft, Notus One and its pure energy atoms began to boost the signal! This process again took time, but the triloraptors did not mind. They were meticulous in there planning and while this was going on, they ran multiple simulations of their overall plans. The preliminary part of the plan was, as soon as the time portal opened; two of the triloraptors were ready to go through the time portal and the other two would stay, one to man Notus One and other their mother ship. The two time travelling triloraptors would then stealthily seek out any local American Indian People and begin the next phase of the plan.

From the early onset of the war with the Universal Interplanetary Congress, the uniqueness of Notus One had been admired by the triloraptors. Since capturing it, trilo-central command had tried to replicate it but, even if they had an abundance of pure energy atoms, they could not even come close to its basic abilities, let alone its ability to boost energy time. Within two earth days, Notus One had worked its magic and the time portal opened in Notus One's command centre!

Both triloraptors stepped through the time portal and found the sun had just risen and they were on a vast open prairie. Using their trilo-visors they did a comprehensive scan of the area for life forms and then majestically they took to the air. As they looked down, they could see vast herds of a species called buffalo grazing on the tall grasses. Their natural urge to hunt and kill these beasts had to be restrained for now, and both triloraptors headed North to a resident American Indians encampment they had spotted.

One triloraptor landed to the North of the encampment and the other to the South, and then wearing their full trilo-combat uniforms, they both just walked into the Indians camp! It was still very early in the morning and the triloraptors were first greeted with dogs that began barking and snarling at them! The noise of the barking stirred the occupants of the twelve tents, who had up to this time been sleeping and one or two of them called out to quieten the noisy dogs! However when the dogs carried on barking and growling, the males of the tents came out to investigate the disturbance. To say they were stunned at what they saw would be an understatement! That's all they saw, the propofol gas that the triloraptors had released as they walked forward now took its effect! Within a few earth seconds every man, dog and beast in well over a mile radius, fell unconscious!

The two triloraptors then went from tent to tent gathering up the local American Indians weaponry. They piled them up outside and through their trilo-visors they scanned each weapon and then got their trilo-tron programme to replicate them. Once they were finished, the triloraptors pulled all the local American humans out into the open. Then using their trilo-tron bladed weapons, they sliced the top off of every human's head in the encampment! Each scalp was then hung on the camps totem pole! In earth's 'new' history, this would be the first mass human scalping and its blame would be placed on the British settlers!

Ironically, before the triloraptors left the encampment, one of the triloraptors undid part of its trilo-combat uniform and using its trilo-beak; it plucked out a small feather and placed it on the totem pole. The triloraptor had read that to be given an eagle's feather was the highest honour that could be awarded to a local American tribe. While the triloraptor felt no guilt or remorse for what it had just done, it respected this indigenous culture for its high opinion of one of its distant ancestors, the eagle.

It had been just over an earth week since the sailing ships the Susan Constant, Godspeed and Discovery had dropped of its one hundred and four colonists on the Southern shores of the James River at Chesapeake Bay. In that short period of time, the colonists had worked diligently on building shelters and securing the area. Expectations were high from the Virginia Company of London who sponsored this expedition that this venture would turn a high profit with local gold mining. Colonists were easily recruited as every man and boy who had braved the year long voyage also expected to become independently wealthy.

The Virginian Colonists knew of the 14,000 strong Algonquian speaking Indians that lived in the Virginian area. It was the colonists hopes that they would be able to convince their powerful leader named, Powhatan that they had a lot to offer this area, and that it would be highly beneficial to both parties to begin trading with each other.

Just after mid-day, two of the men who were cutting lumber looked up and saw what they could only describe as a massive flying metal eagle! The eagle swooped in and with its powerful talons, snatched one of the men and threw him high into the air. Before the man hit the floor a spear shot out of nowhere and went straight through his chest!

Seeing this, in sheer panic, the other man began to run and shouted at the top of his voice;

"Indians, we are under attack from Powhatan Indians!"

The triloraptor had 'graciously' allowed this fellow to live long enough to raise the alarm but, now it was time for him to die! Using its trilo-visor, the triloraptor instantly change the trilo-trons shape from a spear to an Indian tomahawk and then threw the super sharp weapon at the man. The weapon whirled through the air, hitting the man on the back of his head with a loud clunk! Amazingly, the man continued to run for a few more paces and then, with blood gushing from his head, he fell to the floor! For the triloraptor, this had been a good kill, as the rear of the man's head had been split clean in two by this ancient weapon!

Although the trilo-tron software had been able to replicate the local American Indians weaponry, the bow and arrow was something a triloraptor as a bird species, could not fire. To compensate for this, the software modified the trilo-tron to look like a single large arrow but, when it was launched by the triloraptor through its command centre in it trilo-visor, the weapon split into ten independently guided razor pointed arrows!

With the alarm raised, every one of the colonists had armed themselves and was bracing themselves for the imminent Powhatan Indian attack. What they were not expecting was an airborne attack! Both triloraptors swooped in and with there trilo-trons set in arrow mode they both unleashed their multi directional weapons. The colonists had nowhere to hide; each small but deadly arrow could easily pass through wood and other barricaded items used to shield the colonists. The deadly weapon would then continue on its appointed trajectory, swiftly killing its targeted victims! In the first few earth seconds, twenty colonists died and before a full earth minute were up all one hundred and two colonists were slain! Historically, under the old time line, over the next two years nearly all of the colonists would have perished, but it was the male 'John

Smith' explorer, soldier and writer that started Elaine's ancestry, and now with this massacre, that time line had 'almost' been eliminated!

With the colonist's killing over, twenty trilo-bots entered the time portal and began unloading the weaponry that they had taken from the Novus Inceptio militia. The trilo-bots then made their way to the Jamestown settlement and collected all one hundred and four dead bodies and placed their mutilated corpses on wooden stakes around the Chesapeake Bay! This ploy by the triloraptors would make it look as if the Powhatan Indians would not tolerate any expeditions into their lands! The triloraptors and their trilo-bots then moved on to the next phase of their plan.

In addition to bringing the colonists to Jamestown, the head of this expedition, Captain Christopher Newport was asked to seek out a new route to the South Seas. However, due to the slow pace of the James River and low winds, the three sailing ships the Susan Constant, Godspeed and Discovery had covered only forty two miles when they encountered a large wooden blockade across the river! Captain Christopher Newport was a highly experienced sailor and had dealt with high seas piracy before but, this was different. It was a clever trap; the three ships could not move forward or backward. Consequently all three ships were hemmed in by the close proximity of the rivers banks!

The only option Captain Christopher Newport could see was to bring some of the main cannons forward and blast their way through the wooden blockade, but this would leave the lead ship vulnerable to attacks from either side. In that moment's hesitation, several loud startling booms were heard from both shores and all three wooden ships literally burst apart, killing everyone on board! The triloraptors had ingeniously modified the captured Novus Inceptio militia's seventy five millimetre field guns and now the seventy five millimetre shells were packed with multi directional pulse grenades that exploded on impact! These small but powerful grenades could punch their way through over twenty centimetres (about seven point eight inches) of armour plating! So a wooden sailing ship stood no chance! All three vessels were instantly blown apart and a plume of blood, guts, water and debris shot well over four hundred metres into the sky and then all this fragmented matter fell back to the river and its banks.

The two triloraptors flew over the scene of nautical carnage and were reasonably content with their work. They then turned off the three dimensional holographic unit that was set to look like a wooden blockade and then patiently waited for the local Powhatan Indians reaction to the explosions that disrupted this normally peaceful area. While they waited, they updated the main trilo-computer with all that had transpired and were pleased that the super computer reached the same conclusions they did.

Killing all the colonists in Jamestown gave a ninety nine percent chance that this would destroy Captain Elaine Laurence's time line but, that still left a one percent chance that John Smith might survive! The triloraptors and the trilo-computer came up with a scenario that John Smith could as an explorer, have ventured on to one of the three ships and therefore, it was necessary to destroy them as well.

Within one trilo-hour, the Powhatan Indians were scouting the James River's banks in search of what had caused the mighty bangs they had heard. All they could find was parts of the river had turned red with blood and the splintered wreckage of the sailing ships! One of the Indians happened to look up and spotted two great black metallic eagles soaring above them! He called out to the others to look up and to their astonishment; the two eagles swooped down and landed close to the shore line!

As this was an investigation, the tribal, medicine man had accompanied the search party and he was the first to gingerly approach the two, two metre tall black metallic eagles with their spears by their sides. The triloraptors stood perfectly still as this wise elder approach them and then they slowly turned and gestured with their heads that the medicine man should follow them. All three walked briskly for just over a kilometre and the rest of the Indian search party followed some distance behind in deadly silence. The triloraptors took the group into the open prairie and there, they showed the medicine man the arsenal of weapons they had taken from the Novus Inceptio militia!

Some Powhatan Indians had seen the muskets and cannons the white skins had brought to their lands, but to the average Indian, the only weapon they knew were the bow and arrow and hunting spear. So looking at these seventy five millimetre field guns, fifty calibre sniper rifles, machine guns and numerous types of hand guns that were on display, was mind boggling. Although the medicine man pretended to know what he was looking at, the triloraptors knew the weaponry was beyond his comprehension, so using a language translator, one of the triloraptors said;

"We are from the stars and these fine weapons are presents for you. We need to speak with your Chief Powhatan. We will wait here while you get him!"

Without saying a word, the medicine man ran off as fast as he could and within two trilo hours he had returned with several hundred male Powhatan Indians! The main party were on horseback, while the others ran alongside with ease. As the party came closer, they immediately halted and those on horseback dismounted and stood breathlessly as they looked at the two majestic eagles.

Their leader, Chief Powhatan slowly walked over to the two eagles and said;

"I am Chief Powhatan; it is a great honour to have two great sky eagles visit our lands. My medicine man told me you wanted to talk to me?"

The one triloraptor addressed everyone and in a loud confident voice replied;

"Chief Powhatan, yours and other national American Indian tribes have shown great respect for the sky eagle. We have a high regard for your culture and want this culture to continue long into the future. Others from far off lands want to change the national American Indians and have dishonoured your tribe by killing and scalping all of the inhabitants of a small encampment not far from here. We have restored your honour and have killed all these foreigners and destroyed their sailing ships. Regretfully they will be back with vast armies that have muskets and cannons! Their incursions onto your lands will not be tolerated and to ensure that the great national American Indian culture survives for many years to come, we have brought you weapons that will keep these foreigners away!"

To attempt to communicate with a sky eagle in local American Indian culture, the males of the tribe would have had to enter a dream tent. Then with the aid of a medicine man and 'his potions' the men would go into a trance like condition. It this trance, they would then seek out the sky eagle and other spirits for guidance. But, for the Powhatan tribe's men, the situation was surreal. They had actually seen two sky eagles and also heard one of them speak their Algonquian language in broad daylight and, they were truly overwhelmed and did not know how to respond! There was a few moments silence as they waited for their leader's reaction. Chief Powhatan coolly looked around at his braves, smiled and raised his arms into the air and began to whoop out loud. With that endorsement, they all joined in.

While the Powhatan tribe's men were still making their whooping noises, one of the triloraptors walked over to the arsenal of weapons and picked up a bolt action fifty calibre rifle that was mounted on a monopod and then presented it to Chief Powhatan. Silence then fell over the group as Powhatan meticulously inspected the rifle. The Powhatan chief had never seen such a weapon and the triloraptor knew this and said;

> "Great Chief Powhatan, with the power of this gun, you will be able to kill your enemy at a great range. Place the gun on the ground, lie on your stomach and tuck the butt of the gun into your shoulder."

Eagerly, Chief Powhatan did as he was told and then waited for his next instructions. Seeing that the chief was in the correct position, the triloraptor continued;

> "Pull back that bolt and place this bullet into the chamber."

It took the chief a few goes to get this right but, when he had done it correctly the triloraptor said;

> "Now, push the bolt forward again and that will load the bullet into the chamber."

Again the chief followed his instructions and looked up at the triloraptor and said;

> "Is the fire stick ready?"

Nodding, the triloraptor called out to everyone to clear the firing area and then said to the chief;

"On the horizon there are several great buffalo grazing, choose one. Now look down the metal sight of the gun, aim for its head and then gently squeeze the trigger."

Chief Powhatan was a great hunter and he patiently lined up the sights of the gun and as if he had fired this gun many times before, he then gently squeezed the trigger! The gun fired with a loud bang that startled the Indian tribe's men but, they soon got over that when they saw the buffalo lying dead in the distance! Once again they whooped with excitement but, Chief Powhatan remained calm and asked the triloraptor;

"If this gun as you call it can do that, what can those mighty cannons do?"

The chief was referring to the seventy five millimetre field guns and the triloraptor answered;

"Chief Powhatan, they can completely destroy the foreigner's wooden sailing ships and settlements!"

Those answers pleased Chief Powhatan and he humbly said;

"Great sky eagles, you have given us so much. We do not have much but, if there is anything you desire, we would gladly give it to you."

Answering, one of the triloraptor replied;

"All we ask is that you preserve your culture and keep this land safe."

This to Chief Powhatan and the all national American Indians was all that they had wanted but, sadly they had been used! They did not know that the sky eagles 'triloraptors' had another agenda! Over the next few earth hours, the triloraptors instructed the Powhatan tribe's men in the usage of all of the weapons and then gave Chief Powhatan a scroll. Printed on the scroll were the blueprints for the manufacturing of further weapons! With their final task complete, the triloraptors headed back to the time portal and then as if by magic, they disappeared!

CHAPTER FIFTEEN

Chronological time changes

As soon as the triloraptors walked back through the time portal, Notus One closed it. With the portal closed the energy time within earth's gravitational vortex slowly began to change. The changes started in the year 1607 but, the changes were not just in Jamestown, Virginia America, they were happening all around the world! At first it was just minor things like, the people in the North American Indian encampment dyeing before they were supposed to. Then it went to the North American Indian children that were never borne and the achievements they never accomplished! The same happened with Elaine's ancestor. Historically, Captain John Smith should in the year 1608 have become the leader of the Jamestown settlement. In the same year, Captain John Smith should have also got an agreement to open trading with the Powhatan Indians for food but, that part of history had now been re-written. Again in the year 1609, after an accident, Captain John Smith should have returned to England and that was where he should have met his wife but, through the new time lines, this event was never going to happen!

Time was also slowly being re-written back in the British Isles. The three ships, the Susan Constant, Godspeed and Discovery should have returned with their captains and crew! The leader of the Jamestown expedition, Captain Christopher Newport should have gone on to achieve many other notable accomplishments and each ship should have had many other memorable voyages! When they did not return, the Virginia Company of London counted its losses and did not send any more colonists for several years! When they did return to Jamestown Virginia, they were met with a hostile reception that cost many, many more lives!

Back in America in the year 1620, the Pilgrim Fathers should have landed at Plymouth in Massachusetts but, their ships were destroyed by the advanced weaponry of the resident American Indians and consequently this affected the very foundation of America's culture, beliefs and aspirations. As time passed, the national American Indians dominated every corner of America and in the year 1787, the American Constitution should have been formulated and adopted. This historical and important piece of legislation never happened!

With America clearly belonging to the North American Indians, America never took part in the industrial revolution. Consequently the American car industry was never borne. This meant that the time line that recorded the birth of the Model T Ford in 1908 had been erased along with all other American industrial achievements for that time.

The energy time in the earth's gravitational vortex was now re-writing history at an extraordinary rate. Some who had lived and had achieved greatness were now expunged from time. Battles that had historical significance like the Little Bighorn River in the year 1876, never happened! However, when earth's time line hit the year 1914, the date of the First World War! With some significant changes, this event in the time line was sustained! It was when the Second World War that started in the earth year 1939, that earth's time line drastically changed!

Adolf Hitler knew that for his war efforts to succeed not just in Europe but also globally, he would have to have extraordinary resources. America had all the natural untapped resources he needed. Consequently a massive offensive was mounted in 1940 and within three months, America fell to the Nazi regime! At the same time, Japan allied itself with Germany in September 1940 and they were given parts of America to govern, one of those areas was the state of Virginia! All surviving national American Indians were made to work under threat of death in appalling conditions. They worked in mines for twelve hours a day and dug for metals, coal and gold. Under these harsh conditions, many died of malnutrition and disease! The more fortunate ones were shipped to work camps; they too were forced to worked long hours for little food in foundries and munitions factories. Adolf Hitler also took advantage of America's rich oil fields and with all of these resources, the Second World War continued until 1951 when Germany and its close partner Japan had gained world dominance!

With the worldly time changes, in 1963, Russia's scientists had been secretly developing a portable nuclear bomb and in the same year, Russian freedom fighters exploded their nuclear bombs in Berlin and Hamburg! The same faction aided by their allies also nuclear bombed, Hiroshima and Nagasaki in Japan and Rome, Italy! Italy was targeted because of its collaboration with Germany. These bombings sparked off the earth's third and bloodiest World War! This world war lasted a little over two years with Russia leading the offensive!

Within a year, numerous German held countries were liberated, the first being Poland, England, France, America Africa, Australia and China. The rest soon followed but, like all wars, the casualty rates were high! When Germany and Japan finally unconditionally surrendered in November 1965, the human death toll globally was estimated to be over two billion, four hundred thousand!

At this point of time, the four triloraptors on board their trilo-mother ship had no way of knowing how many deaths they had caused. But in the new universal history of the triloraptors, this was the largest planetary kill ever made by only four of them! That achievement would please every triloraptor, no matter what time line they came from!

Earth's time lines were now in turmoil, and this temporal disorder began to spill out into earth's solar system! Yuri Alekseyevich Gagarin should have been the first human to journey into outer space on the 12th April 1961. In the new time line, this event never happened! Eight years later on the 20th July 1969, at 2:56 UTC the American, Neil Armstrong from Apollo mission eleven should have been the first human to walk on the moon, again this historical event never happened! Because of world war three, earths's space programme never really got started until 1996, when Russia launched their first man and president of the USSR, Vladimir Putin into space!

With the military devastation on earth, it was taking earth's government's all its time and resources to rebuild the cities, towns and infrastructure that had been destroyed in the last world war. So launching military, communications satellites and space recreational stations had not happened when the triloraptors first came to the earth to abduct the human's hostages. This is where time began to change for the whole universe!

Instead of abducting Elaine Laurence and her colleagues from the space recreational stations Darwin and Stephen Hawking, they had to capture groups of humans not just from the planet's surface, but also from public places! As this would be a daylight abduction; the small but reasonably well populated Island known as Britain was chosen. Four hundred young, fit people were targeted from two universities, one in London England and the other in Edinburgh, Scotland.

Under the directions of the overlord, the Universal Interplanetary Congress had sent a small fleet of battleships to conquer the planet Earth! This first U.I.C invasion fleet had been foiled by the triloraptors, who in 'both time lines' destroyed their whole invasion fleet! However, before destroying the U.I.C's invasion fleet, the triloraptors boarded the Universal Interplanetary Congresses battleships and looted their arsenal of weapons!

One weapon they found that would be extremely useful was a large portion of propofol gas. This gas had been used universally as an anaesthetic but, it had been modified to be used as a weapon that could leave all air breathing species unconscious! The U.I.C had intended to bombard the earth's atmosphere with this gas and render all of earth's life forms unconscious. Then, while the earth's humans were unconscious, they would invade the planet, immobilise earth's armies and conquer the planet Earth in the name of the overlord! With the propofol gas on-board, the triloraptors plan was to shower each university campuses with the propofol gas and then using trilo-bots, they would move in and indiscriminately grab four hundred young fit human beings.

The abduction went off without a hitch and all four hundred humans were taken to a planet on the outskirts of this universe known as Notus. However, just as the triloraptors arrived on the planet Notus, they had news from their trilo-central command that they had to abort their mission and return to the main triloraptors fleet! Ironically in both time lines, the Universal interplanetary Congress had deployed its fleet and intended to use the planet Notus as its main theatre of operations and herd the triloraptor fleet towards Notus's solar system!

The triloraptors had two options, one was to drop the human hostages off at the closest habitable planet and the other was to kill them all. Being triloraptors, this decision put them in a bit of a dilemma, they had gone to great lengths to capture the humans but, holding hostages was against everything the triloraptors stood for! Instinctively they chose the second option and killed all four hundred humans. It was at this exact point of time that the universes time lines changed drastically and temporal chaos began!

With Doctor Elaine Laurence not being dropped off on the Planet Notus, she never got to meet Notus the being and as a result of this, Notus One the space craft was never created! All that had happened since that point of time onwards through Elaine's, Notus's and Notus One's interventions never happened!

The consequences of this temporal disarray was now being felt on every U.I.C planet, as new time lines were being created! One of the first things to happen was, from just outside earth's warped gravity time vortex, Notus One along with its two 'time pilot' triloraptors, just disappeared! The two triloraptors on their Notus One look alike mother ship watched this happen and were helpless to stop what was about to happen, their trilo-mother ship space craft also vanished! Both space craft were erased from the universes time line!

In the old time line, Notus, Elaine and the space craft Notus One had battled with the triloraptors in and around Notus's solar system. In this battle, the triloraptors main fleet along with their original mother ship were destroyed by Notus the being and Captain Elaine Laurence. In the new order of time, this battle never took place and therefore the triloraptors fleet were free to engage the Universal Interplanetary Congresses fleet in a ferocious battle. Both parties suffered great losses and ultimately, with the aid of the overlord, the U.I.C Congress won the day. After this, at the orders of the overlord, the triloraptors trilo-crafts were then singularly hunted down by the U.I.C and over a period of one decade, they were eradicated from this universe!

Universal time continued to unravel and the next chaotic temporal elimination came not from our universe but, from the evil overlord's micro universe! Back in old time, after the overlord had been defeated in this universe, the U.I.C and triloraptors formed an alliance with Captain Elaine Laurence. They then conjured up a plan to go to the overlord's universe and if possible, bring him to justice!

This plan was marred by the fact that they would have to micro engineer a fleet of space craft and weaponry. The triloraptors stepped in and with their advanced trilo-space skills they built a micro fleet that could travel through the micro wormholes that led to the overlord's universe. Once there, with the assistance of Captain Elaine Laurence and Notus, they hunted down the evil overlord and after a massive battle, they managed not only to kill him but also all of his tyrannical lords!

Now, back in this new temporal arrangement, these monumental events never took place and that left the tyrant, the overlord alive! As time re-wrote itself, the overlord began a new era in which he dominated both universes! What was even more shocking was, through a human symbiotic host, he was now ruling his and our universe from the conquered planet Earth!

For almost two earth weeks Elaine had been steadily recovering from her ordeal. She had ventured further and further away from the beach and when she felt confident, she and Alpha went into space around the planet Notus. Today however was a bizarre day! She had been exploring the planet Notus on her own when suddenly things all around her began to change! She could not comprehend what was happening and instantly she thought she was relapsing!

Panicking a little, she telepathically tried to communicate with Notus but, she could not get any response? She then tried sending a mental image to Alpha but again, she could not get any response? Concentrating hard, Elaine focused her thoughts on her beach and in less than a second, she travelled five hundred kilometres and found the beach barren! Heavy clouds of sand dust filled the air and through the dust she could see huge deep craters dotted all around the beach. She was really confused, this beach normally looked beautiful? As she looked out to sea, the water was full of debris and rotted aquatic bodies! As far as Elaine could see, the planet Notus looked like a battle zone? Once again, she telepathically tried to reach Notus and Alpha but, again she had no reply.

Suddenly every atom in her body began to tingle and then the tingling became a harsh vibration. Instinctively, Elaine created a tight gravitational field around herself and out of panic she flew as fast as she could into open space. From space, Elaine could see the outline of planet Notus and other planets in the solar system but, everything visually was a blur? Slowly, over what seemed like hours things began to calm down and everything in Notus's solar system return to normal. Elaine knew as a pure energy being she had not got a human heart anymore but, while this frightening episode was going on, she could in the silence of space actually hear her phantom heart pounding!

Once again she telepathically called out to Notus and to her delight she got a reply. But, it was not the reply she was expecting! Notus said;

"Greeting's fellow pure energy being, I am the guardian of this planet, my name is Notus. It is nice that you have chosen to visit this solar system. Please tell me, what is your name?"

Elaine had experienced Notus's wicked sense of humour before but, with what had just happened, she was not in the mood for Notus's humorous games and replied;

"Notus, it's me Elaine, stop messing around! What just happened in this solar system? I have to say, it frightened the hell out of me!"

Completely puzzled by Elaine's reply, Notus said;

"Truthfully Elaine, I have no idea what you are talking about."

This response really worried Elaine; given her circumstances and all that had recently transpired, she knew that Notus would not wind her up, so after a moment's thought, she telepathically asked;

"Notus, has the planet Olotinium been destroyed?"

With a sad tone in Notus's voice, Notus answered;

"Yes, this happened recently, it was the first major attack from a being known as the overlord. After that, a war started throughout this universe between two forces, the overlord's Universal Interplanetary Congress and the nomadic triloraptors. It has only been a few of my planets months since the universal war ceased.

Continuing, Notus said;

"Now Elaine, I also have a few questions. I find it strange that you asked about Olotinium? Olotinium was one of my offspring's and all pure energy beings would be aware by now that Olotinium is now dead! Did you know Olotinium? And my second question is, your pure energy atoms are made up from my offspring Olotinium, how did you get them?"

As bizarre as Notus's questions were, Elaine's instincts told her that something was seriously wrong and over the next few earth hours, Elaine told Notus everything that had previously transpired. Notus listened without saying a word and after Elaine finished, Notus telepathically contacted as many of the planet guardians as possible and then replied;

"Elaine, I and all of my species that I have been able to contact have no recollection of what has happened in your other time line. What is also puzzling all of us is; how you are the only pure energy being in this times current line that has any recollection of what had previously happened? This question will wait to be answered, so please do not worry about it for now. I also want to assure you that I and the rest of the planet guardians believe every word you have said. Now, from what you have told me, I would hazard a guess and say that the triloraptors are the key to this. When they stole your space craft, Notus One, they must have used it to travel back in time! Once there, they must have sparked off some immense temporal changes that have altered this universes time lines!

Now Elaine, I have to bring you up to date on the temporal changes. Sadly, the planet Notus and its solar system have been used as a massive battle ground. The battle that raged here has left the planet Notus solar system in a critical state. Sadly, the planet Notus is dying and has only a few hundred earth years left! I tried my best to dissuade both the U.I.C and the triloraptors forces but, their forces were immense and too strong for me!"

This situation for Notus was extremely distressing and Notus had to pause. After a few moments Notus continued but, this time the tone was one of complete sadness;

"Elaine I failed and my beautiful planet is dying! With the war over, the victory went to the overlord! He defeated the Universal Interplanetary Congress! After that, he then defeated the triloraptors and now, the overlord rules this and his own universe!

Elaine, I am also sorry to have to inform you that, your home planet Earth has also been conquered! This is now where the overlord resides and rules both universes from!

Elaine, taking all of this into account, your old time line sounds way better than this new time line. The planet guardian Notus in old time and I are in agreement that we need help! Further, my previous time line idea of attempting to contact the being your earth people call KRONOS still stands!"

The news of all these time changes came as a complete shock to Elaine! But what really shook Elaine to her pure energy core was the thought that the evil overlord was now dominating this universe from earth and it could have been her fault! Angry at all of this, Elaine said to Notus;

"Notus, we have to change time back to how it was! The triloraptors are not the only one to blame, it was me who wanted to go back in time and bring back my abducted friends and colleagues. We and this universe really do need help from KRONOS but, if we cannot get this help, then I am going to earth to destroy the overlord and restore order in your time line!

In my old time line, you got an Alpha radioactive life form to help me; is there any chance that we can do the same?"

Still sounding very sombre, Notus replied;

"Elaine, the Alpha's, and a few other energy beings are already on their way.

Now Elaine, you cannot blame yourself for the temporal changes, all of this stemmed from the overlords invasion of this universe. I truly believe you were acting in the best interests of your friends and fellow colleagues. Since that point in time, the triloraptors in your old time line have really screwed things up, but, they really have paid the price in this time line!

As for re-setting time, my species and all the radio active life forms will try through our various means to contact KRONOS. But if plan A does not work, then we will begin plan B and return order to this universe! Irrespective of plan A, as I said earlier my planet is dying and

I will have to leave my dearly loved planet Notus. I really feel bitter about this as it should not have happened for about another four billion years! I cannot stress how angry I am at the overlord! Through his actions, my offspring Olotinium is dead, and my other offspring earth is his prisoner and my planet Notus is dying! Elaine, I will be at your side and jointly, we will destroy this evil cruel being!"

Notus the being had joined as its guardian with the planet Notus several billion years ago. Elaine and all other pure energy beings knew that this separation was going to be utterly heart-breaking for Notus. Elaine also recalled that this happened to Notus once before in another universe and that parting really saddened Notus. Compassionately she said;

"Notus, take all the time you need in separating from your planet, I can always carry on and you can join me later."

Replying, Notus said;

"It's OK Elaine, the longer I leave it, the harder the separation will be! Elaine, I will re-iterate, after my planetary separation, it is going to be my life's ambition to stop the overlord! He has mined the planet Earth's core with several thousand atom sized nuclear bombs and has stated that he will detonate them if he does not get total compliance from the human race! I don't know if you know this but, that's what he has done to thousands of other planets! I know he will not hesitate in doing this, as that was how he destroyed the planet Olotinium, and killed my offspring!"

Elaine was shaken at the news that her planet Earth had become another victim of this evil maniac. However, she knew this was the normal tactic of the overlord and Elaine recalled that he had also planted several thousand atom sized nuclear bombs around the cores of numerous planets in his own micro universe! As for the fate of Olotinium, she just simply replied;

"Notus, I did know that, sadly, this outcome also happened in my old time line."

Suddenly mentally, Elaine began to feel a great sadness, and realised she was feeling what all pure energy beings in this universe were feeling collectively. She also realised that her telepathic conversations with Notus were now been shared with all of her new universal family. The nice part was, through this collective universal mind, she knew exactly what to say to Notus;

"Notus, we the pure energy beings are all united with you in your time of need. Now Notus guardian of the planet Notus, it's time to let go."

While Elaine knew what to say, she had no idea what was involved in the separation of a guardian from a planet. Unexpectedly through the planets murky atmosphere, Elaine thought she could see movement in a large 0.804672 kilometres (half a mile) tall, dormant volcano situated on a small island close to the planet Notus's equator!

From its base, rocks, trees, shrubbery and debris fell away as the volcano began to rise slowly! But, surprisingly, there were no volcanic eruptions? As this massive volcano which must have weighed several millions of tonnes reached about 1.609344 kilometres (one mile) above the ground, a soft golden light began to emerge from below the ground where the volcano bowels reached deep down into the planets core.

Elaine watched in awe as the soft golden light rose higher and higher. As it reached the base of the floating volcano, it split into several veins and continued upwards for some forty eight kilometres (thirty miles) until it was almost touching the planets stratosphere. At this stage, the soft golden light from the planets core began to fade! Notus the being had successfully detached itself from its host planet!

From space, Elaine was astounded by Notus's overall size, at forty eight kilometres (thirty miles) long and 1.609344 kilometres (one mile) wide, Notus looked majestic! Notus then began to slowly fly in a large circle and retract its pure energy tail, so that its appearance was that of a 16.09344 kilometres (ten miles) in diameter luminous golden ball. Once this shape was completely formed, Notus return to the floating volcano and controlling the anti-gravity field around it, Notus slowly lowered it back down to its original place. As the volcano began to touch down, Elaine could see small but controlled lava eruptions around the volcano's base! Elaine guessed that Notus was doing this as a way of re-sealing the volcano to its base.

Once the volcano was sealed, Notus telepathically said;

"Elaine, as you can see, I have just separated from the planet Notus. If it's OK, I would like to join you in space and together we can fly around the planet. I have never seen my planet from space and it would be nice to do this before it dies."

Elaine felt quite emotional. If she had still been human, she knew by now, floods of tears would be cascading down her face, and to be honest, she really did miss this emotional release. With extreme sadness in her voice she telepathically replied;

"Notus, it would be an honour to accompany you."

For the next few earth hours, Notus and Elaine slowly flew in space just outside the planet Notus's dying atmosphere. As Elaine looked down at the devastation caused by the warring triloraptors and the Universal Interplanetary Congress, her empathy went out to Notus. Through the dense clouds that continually rumbled with thunder so loud that it could be heard in space, Elaine could see massive electrical storms that were raging constantly throughout the planet! Where gaps appeared in the clouds, Elaine was shocked to see that whole continents had been repeatedly pummelled with high intensity pulse missiles and other weapons of mass destruction. These horrendous weapons had not only flattened vast mountainous and hilly areas; their immense fire power had also multi-fractured the planets crust! In the aftermath, massive earthquakes were now erupting globally and the deep fissures were throwing red hot lava and volumes of dust high into the planet's atmosphere!

Along every coastline Elaine witnessed colossal tsunami damage that spread inland for several thousand kilometres! Further inland, vast forests that acted as the lungs of the planet had been systematically destroyed. All that was left were a few smouldering embers that were once forests of majestic of trees, oceans of shrubbery and kilometre after kilometre of exotic plants!

Elaine could only hazard a guess that the loss of animal, marine and insect lives taken in this planetary mayhem that is called war, must go into the trillions! Ironically, this destruction should have been a triloraptors dream. But, the reality of this living nightmare was, they, through their own callous actions had caused this and their own temporal extinction!

Throughout their heart-rending farewell flight, Notus never telepathically spoke a word and Elaine just couldn't come up with any words to consol her grief-stricken friend! As they ended their spacial viewing of the planet Notus, Notus telepathically said;

> "Elaine, please accept my sincere thanks for accompanying me. I have lived a very long life but, this is one of the saddest days I have experienced! Sadly, without me being inside the planet, Notus will die within a few of your earth weeks!"

Almost choking for words, telepathically Notus continued;

> "Elaine, it's time to go! We have some serious work to do!"

As the sadden pair flew away in silence, their minds were filled with love and support from every other pure energy being in the universe.

CHAPTER SIXTEEN

Space

Although Elaine had experienced space travel inside the space ship Notus One, being able to travel in space under her own steam was something quite else! She could sense that Notus was allowing her plenty of time to develop her spacial wings. Elaine's first spacial task was to fly from just outside the planet Notus's atmosphere to Notus's closest moon, Callebradis! That was an incredible distance of 363,104 km (225,622 miles) at its closest point, known as the perigee. And at its most distant point, called apogee, the moon Callebradis gets to a distance away from the planet Notus of 406,696 km (252,088 miles).

The actual distance and facts seemed daunting to Elaine but, Notus telepathically said;

> "Elaine, you are now a pure energy being, do not concern yourself with the distance in kilometres or miles. Just focus your mind on travelling to the other side of Callebradis and it will happen."

Elaine looked at the moon and then mentally chose a point in space just past Callebradis and willed herself to be there. Without any sensation of speed or sense of motion, Elaine found herself at the place she mentally envisaged! She looked back and could see the planet Notus some 406,696 km (252,088 miles) away and inwardly she felt excited. As she looked around, Notus was close by her and she telepathically said;

> "Notus, that was incredible, I have just travelled over 406,696 km (252,088 miles) in less than an earth second! What is our next destination?

Notus began to laugh and said;

"Well, as you are aware, our ultimate destination is your planet earth. But, let's lower our sights for the time being and try for the other side of the next planet in this solar system named Hemerald. I know your mind is still thinking in human terms so here are a few facts. When Hemerald and the moon Callebradis are closest, they are 390,682,810 miles (628,743,036 km) apart. At their most distant, they are 576,682,810 miles (928,081,020 km) apart. Those figures are when the planet and moon are on opposite sides of the systems sun, Saulė Majoris.

The Saulė Majoris solar system is gigantic compared with your earth's solar system. It has ten planets, five inner terrestrial planets and then five super gas giants that make up the outer planets. It also has an assortment of comets composed largely of metals and volatile ices. Just to break free of this solar system, we are going to have to travel over thirty six trillion earth miles!

Now, if you look at that large bright light in between that cluster of stars that are shaped like a three dimensional triangle, that is where we are heading."

In her other time line, Elaine had travelled well beyond Saulė Majoris solar system and into the vastness of space in her space craft Notus One. Now life was different, as inter-planetary spacial navigation was now totally down to her. Elaine mentally acknowledged Notus's information and began to scan the starry open space. After a few moments, she mentally fixed her mind on the brightest point she could see in the cluster of stars that were shaped like a three dimensional triangle. Then mentally laughing, she asked Notus;

"Have I got the right place? It would be a bit of a disaster if I got lost, even before we leave this solar system!"

Notus began to laugh and said;

"Elaine, your mental universal planetary compass is spot on, and even if you go wrong, you do not have to worry. We are linked by our pure energy atoms, so no matter where you go in the universe, I will be able to find you."

Despite Notus's reassurances, Elaine felt a little nervous but she knew she had to just go for it. So she mentally concentrated and to her surprise, she was transported to the other side of the planet Hemerald with ease! She could sense Notus's pride at her modest achievement and enthusiastically said;

"Wow Notus, that was pretty easy, what's the next planet on the list?

At this stage in Elaine's spacial flight training the reply she got was one that she was not expecting, as Notus said;

"We are now going to travel just over thirty trillion earth miles!"

Flabbergasted at this, Elaine nervously inquired;

"How am I going to do that, at that distance I have nothing to mentally focus on?"

In a calm almost parental voice, Notus answered;

"Elaine, up to now you have done well in travelling from the planet Notus to its first moon and then onto the planet Hemerald. However we have an appointment with a group of radioactive beings. They are waiting for the both of us on the outskirts of the solar system, so I am going to give you a pure energy lift."

Notus's answer intrigued Elaine. She also sensed that Notus was waiting for her to ask the all-important question, so she jumped in and asked;

"How does a pure energy lift work?"

It was now Notus's turn to sound excited and replied;

"Well Elaine, I have never done this before but I guess all I have to do is wrap myself around you and then focus on our destination, and within a few earth minutes, we should be there."

Elaine began to laugh and jovially said;

"So this will be our real first hug, along with a pure energy maiden flight! You know that sounds really cool. I do have a small problem, me! I am tiny compared with you, how do I know you won't smother me?

That made Notus laugh and in an equally jovial tone, Notus replied;

"Are you trying to say I am a little overweight? You know I have been stuck inside a planet for the last few billion years. To be honest, it's been a little compact inside there, so I have not been able to do much physical exercise!

Now Elaine, just keep still and I will begin to smother you with my fat body!"

Although Elaine was joking about Notus's mass, Notus's 16.09344 kilometres (ten miles) in diameter golden form began to encompass Elaine's 'tiny' human sized pure energy shape. The manoeuvre only took a few moments and to Elaine's surprise as the move took place Elaine could feel Notus's awesome power surrounding her! She also felt strangely comforted by Notus's embrace as it reminded her of the feeling she had when her mom or dad would give her a hug when she was a child. Notus could sense what Elaine was feeling and for a moment they both enjoyed the experience. Notus then telepathically said;

"Elaine. I believe we are ready, all you have to do now is just mentally relax and enjoy the ride."

Elaine did as she was told and Notus began to accelerate. Surprisingly, the acceleration did not feel very fast! But, from within Notus's transparent pure energy form, Elaine could see a high speed blur as the passed their first planet! After that, Notus's speed increased dramatically and all Elaine could see was a haze of colours and lights as they shot passed each planet in the Saulé Majoris solar system. As Notus had predicted, the pair of pure energy beings were transported to the outer regions of Saulé Majoris solar system in less than fifteen earth minutes!

As Notus slowed to a full stop, Elaine tried to calculate the speed they had travelled at but, she was instantly distracted by the reception waiting for them. Thousands of alpha, beta, gamma, X ray and neutron radioactive beings had come along with other energy forms that Elaine did not recognise. Taken aback by this reception, Elaine telepathically asked Notus;

"I thought you said there were a few Alphas going to meet us, this looks like a small army! Surely they aren't all here to help us?"

Before answering, Notus began to unfold its massive pure energy body allowing Elaine to fly out into open space. Notus then answered;

"Elaine, telepathic word had spread to every corner of this universe of your quest to make corrections to the time line and if that fails, to defeat the overlord. Without exception, every energy being in this universe is prepared to help! What you see now is only a small portion of those who are coming to join in this important mission!"

Elaine was absolutely flabbergasted, her plan initially was to seek help from the mythological being KRONOS. In her wildest dreams she never envisaged help from all these energy beings. However, she now had a new problem. All these beings had come to help, and she had no plan of action to defeat the overlord! Notus had picked up on Elaine's thoughts and telepathically said;

"Elaine you do not have to worry about any master plans just yet. We need to gather as much intelligence as we can first. After that, we can go and tackle the overlord. Now it's time for you to say hello to all your new friends."

From her previous experience, Elaine knew that radioactive beings communicate with mental images. So she mentally formed an image of her human self waving and smiling and then sent that image out to all the radioactive beings. As soon as she did this, Elaine had instant doubts that they would understand this earth gesture but, Notus intervened and said;

"Elaine, I think your greeting imagery is perfect. When I telepathically sent out the invites, I informed everyone that you were once human. Some of these energy beings have never heard of or seen a human being? So I tapped into your mind and also sent out lots of earthy images. From now on, all of your mental communications with all of the radio active life forms and energy beings should be fairly easy.

As you can see, we also have quite a few other types of energy beings and the good news is they all communicate through telepathy or mental imagery."

Inspired by this, using telepathy, Elaine politely said "hello" to all the other energy beings and once again, Notus's previous comments had fired up Elaine's curiosity and she enquired;

"Notus, you say there are other energy beings here, what kind of energy beings are they?"

Replying, Notus said;

"Elaine as you are aware, energy life forms on the universal 'energy scale' cover a wide spectrum. So like us, there are several pure energy life forms. There are also quite a few dark energy life forms, numerous microwave energy life forms, plasma energy beings that total a few hundreds and also few dozen gravity energy beings.

Other energy forms and life forms will be joining us as we get a little closer to the planet Earth. They will include, electromagnetic and their relatives, photon life forms. I also believe several thousand electrical energy life forms are congregating on the outskirts of the star Proxima Centauri. They will join us as we pass by."

Hearing this, Elaine felt both excited and nervous at the same time. At that, a question popped into her mind and she asked Notus;

"In the history of the universe, have all of these energy beings joined forces before to defeat another life form?"

In a serious tone, Notus answered;

"No! Most of the energy life forms are space dwellers. On the whole they keep away and avoid any planetary life forms. This however is different; the universe is now dominated by one individual, the overlord! They feel that if they do not intervene, this universe will end up like the overlords micro universe, desolate of any planetary or spacial life forms! Furthermore, every one of these life forms would prefer to have the timeline that you once lived in!"

That was all the information and support Elaine needed, she was now determine to either correct the time line or once again, defeat the villainous overlord. She then said to Notus;

"We are at the far end of this universe, how are we all going to get to earth, we do not have a space ship and as you are aware, earth is trillions and trillions of light years away?"

Notus knew this was a serious question and answered;

"We are energy beings, by combining our energy, we are going to bend space, create small worm holes and travel through them! It may take several of your earth weeks but, this way, we can travel faster through space more rapidly than any known space craft."

Once again, Elaine was more than interested in what had been said, and telepathically asked Notus;

"Have you ever travelled this way before?"

Notus promptly replied and said;

"Yes I have. I and my species have been travelling this way for billions and billions of your earth years. This however is not true of all energy beings. Take for example the Alpha's and Beta's, they have limited energy and power and normally reside in one galaxy. If they want to move from one planet to another, they travel in real space time and do it in high energy radioactive bursts that follow the normal flow of spacial radiation.

But as a planet guardian and pure energy being, I have enough power to bend space, and then open a small worm hole in which I can then travel through to my destination. What I plan for our trip to the planet earth is all the pure energy beings will jointly combine our powers. Now putting this into an earthly term, Elaine, this trip should be, just like a walk in the park."

Elaine could recall some of her college physics and what Einstein had theorised on about bending space. Notus made it sound as if Einstein's theories were correct but, the way Notus had explained how to travel vast distances by bending space stirred up a few more unanswered questions, and out of interest Elaine enquired;

"Notus, surely you cannot bend just one piece of space, create a worm hole and then travel all the way to earth. Also, what happens if you bend space close to a solar system, as we have already established, space is already curved around each planet?"

These questions were worthy of a good answer and Notus replied;

"Bending space is a delicate process! If you bend it to much, it can cause some serious spacial distortions that in turn can have a calamitous influence on the space around that area for literally millions of earth miles!

Also, you can actually tear space if you bend it too much! This can lead to the formulation of a large, out of control, one ended worm hole! If you were drawn into this cataclysmic worm hole, you could be trapped in spacial oblivion or it could possibly throw you into another time line or spacial dimension!

When bending space, we also have to choose a safe spacial region to do this. The primary rules of bending space are; always choose a point in space that is not close to the outer limits of a galaxy, black hole or other spacial anomaly, and definitely not close to a solar system! I would guess that if you tried to bend space close to a planet, planetary time and energy time would be thrown into temporal disarray!

Now, for all of us to travel to earth, with the vast distances we will have to cover, I estimate that we will have to bend space and create worm holes at least twenty times. Where we cannot bend space, those energy beings who have the ability to travel faster, will have to piggy back the slower ones."

Elaine was more than satisfied with Notus's answer and as she did not ask anything else. Notus then took the incentive and using telepathy and imagery the pure energy being informed everyone it was time to leave. Notus then began to open up its colossal body and Elaine and the radioactive beings flew in so that they could be piggy backed on the first leg of their epic journey. The other pure energy beings followed Notus's example and within a few earth minutes, Elaine's army was on the road to its major theatre of operations, Earth!

The group travelled at a speed of about ten gravitons into open space. At a safe spacial point, Notus began to de-accelerate to just the exact speed of light, 299,792,458 metres per second (186,282.4 miles per second). Notus then concentrated on creating a massive gravity field just in front of its self. At the same time, Notus also began to radiate a colossal amount of pure energy through the gravity field and the space in front of Notus began to slowly bend!

At first, space curved and rose to about ten metres but, as Notus increased the mass of the gravitational force, the fabric of space curved and rose higher and higher. Within a few earth seconds, space had swelled to a massive ten thousand metre curve! Seeing this, some of the other pure energy beings and gravitational beings began aiding this by moving to the right and left side of Notus. In unison they all began increasing the pure energy and gravitational pressure being applied to space, the overall force was colossal!

Within a few earth minutes, the space in front of Notus had yielded enough for Notus to carry out the next phase. Notus shot out a pure energy burst which hit the curved space with tremendous force and created the opening to a small worm hole. Before the worm hole collapsed in on its self, Notus and the other pure energy beings blasted it with several other pure energy bursts and this stabilised the worm hole.

Elaine had been observing this and instantly thought of Albert Einstein and if his theories on the equation $E = mc^2$ had any relevance to what had just happened? Before she could contemplate this any further, Notus used mental images and telepathy and with a sense of urgency said;

> "Attention everyone, we only have a short period of time before the worm hole begins collapsing and space resumes its original shape again. So we all need to pass through this as quickly as we can."

Hastily and in single file, all the energy beings passed through the worm hole. Safely on the other side, Elaine telepathically said to Notus;

> "Wow, that was amazing; in light years, how far do you think we just travelled?"

Notus was constantly amused at Elaine's human side and replied;

> "Well, I believe a light year in earth miles is 5,865,696,000,000 miles. So what we just did was that, times just over half a billion! Now Elaine, get your mental calculator working and do some serious maths. We

still have about nineteen worm holes to go and a good deal amount of open space in between this. So I recommend you just relax and enjoy the spacial scenery."

Elaine laughed; even in her head those numbers were incalculable. As for enjoying the spacial scenery, all she could see from inside Notus's embrace was a golden blur and the occasional vivid burst of bright cosmic light.

CHAPTER SEVENTEEN

Planet Earth

Since the overlord had conquered this universe, the planet Terra or as it is known to its indigenous species as Earth had become the headquarters for the mighty overlord. Now as the overlord sat in his new, highly fortified fortress, close to the top of Mount Everest, he pondered on his latest universal conquest and thought;

> "The Universal Interplanetary Congress folded with great ease!"

With mocking sincerity he then additionally thought;

> "That's because, when you have an easy target like the Universal Interplanetary Congresses uni-net and a bunch of spineless leaders who were supposed to govern the U.I.C, what could any adversarial conqueror do?"

The overlord laughed out loud and said;

> "You make them your uni-net and physical slaves!"

Standing up from his deep padded luxurious golden throne, he leisurely walked over to one of the four metre thick blast proof windows and surveyed the Mahalangur region of Himalayan area where his fortress was located. Snow was falling and it looked cold and bleak outside but, that's just how he liked it. His fortress was almost 8,000 metres above sea level and the fifth furthest point from the centre of the Earth. That meant this high, cold, hostile place was a veritable safe zone from his enemies. And no matter where the overlord went in this and his own micro universe, he had plenty of enemies, and all wanted him dead!

While billions, if not trillions wanted him dead, the overlord controlled their wretched lives through tyranny, fear and now using advanced technology, the uni-net! Every being in this universe was now linked into the uni-net through their neurological receptors and brains synaptic pathways. Now through a bit of brilliant technical ingenuity by the overlord, they all had an individual destruction codes built into their uni-net device that were controlled exclusively by the one who was also their god, the overlord! They, meaning every being in this and his micro universe, were simply there too serve him! And if they deviated even marginally from their subservient paths, he simply killed them and all of their families!

The overlord's 'calming' thoughts were disrupted by a uni-net call coming in from Madam Chair elect Zissiani of the Universal Interplanetary Congress. In an annoyed tone the overlord said;

> "Zissiani, as always your life hangs by a fine thread. I have told you before; you only contact me when you have something of importance to tell me. So your intrusion had better be of significant importance or I will vaporise your slimy snake like brain!"

Chair elect Zissiani had been dealing with the overlord's rude and abusive attitude ever since he took control of the U.I.C. He had threatened to kill her more times than she had scales on her snake like body but, she played the survival game well and respectfully responded;

> "Great Eminence, I only wish to report that the first galactic battleship made to your specifications is ready to leave the Quzzzuzzzian space dock and will be heading to earth on its maiden voyage. Would you like to do a virtual appearance at its launch?"

Zissiani waited patiently for the overlord to reply and after a few earth minutes, he coldly said;

> "Zissiani you are an absolute idiot, why would I want to make a virtual appearance? What I want is my battleship to be launched and you supply ten of the best U.I.C battleships fully manned, so that my galactic battleship can destroy them! And I want this event to be

179

broadcast in real time on the uni-net throughout this and my micro universe!"

At that, the overlord abruptly ended the uni-net call and thought;

"This will send a message to every planet in both universes that I, the overlord, am to be totally feared and no one's life is safe!"

With that thought put aside, he then glanced at his new body in one of the many mirrors that surrounded his throne room. Flexing his arms large biceps muscles, he smiled and said out loud;

"Sir, you are a powerfully built, handsome fellow, and even if I say so myself, this new body suits you well!"

From hundreds of live donor bodies, the overlord had carefully chosen this body. He selected the body of a strong Scandinavian male for his mind transfer. The overlord now stood two and a quarter metres tall and had a massive barrel chest. For his age, his twenty five year olds 'reluctant' donor had been a top power lifting athlete but, this handsome, rugged young man was also an excellent pentathlon competitor who had personally won several gold medals.

After quite a lot of trials and many, many errors the overlords mind transfer procedure had been perfected and it was then and only then, that the overlord underwent the twelve earth hour, highly complex operation under the supervision of some of the overlords 'trusted' lords. The actual operation was carried out by a virtual super computer that with immense precision removed neuron by neuron the donor's memories from the cerebral cortex and then replaced them with the overlord's own neural memories!

As the overlord was an extremely cautious and above all suspicious man. He also had an elaborate backup plan! Just on the off chance that anything went wrong in this universe. The overlord's old but powerful body that was still in his micro universe and had been preserved in a highly sophisticated cryogenic chamber. In the same chamber, he also had several backup copies of all his cerebral cortex and neural memories!

These highly valued items were then locked and stored in a hidden vault that was only known to the overlord. It was universally well known that the overlord was an absolute genius and in true form, he had devised a unique neurological signal that was built into his earthly brain that would be activated if his earthly body was dying. This signal would trigger a uni-net pulse that would travel back to his micro universe and the virtual super computer that was also locked in his secret vault would automatically start up and begin a complete neurological restoration programme!

After admiring his new body for a few lingering moments more, the overlord turned his attention to his virtual display unit; it was displaying the planet Earth and its atmospheric defence field that spread out as far as the planets exosphere. This area was heavily patrolled by armoured robotic cubed sentinels (A.R.C.S). A.R.C.S's are highly competent defence and offence mechanisms at low, mid-range and high altitudes, and if need be, in the far reaches of outer space! They also function extremely well on land and in the depths of any planetary sea.

These highly versatile weapons are the creation of the overlord and in size; each one is just a metre square cube. Their unique feature is; each face on the cube has been ingeniously designed so that it splits into nine equal segments, similar to an earths Rubik puzzle cube.

Each segment is attached to a pivot mechanism allowing each segment to turn independently. Plus each segment has a different weapon assigned to it! They are; Proton, Neutron, Graviton, Pulse, Sonic, Light, Laser, Chemical and Biological weapons. At any one time, any nine of these different weapons could be fired in one direction or nine to the front, nine to the rear, nine from the top, nine from either side and if airborne nine from the bottom.

That represents an amazing fifty four different weapons that could be fired simultaneously! When you begin to mix up the weapons fired from each face you could end up with a staggering 43,252,003,274,489,856,000 or about 4×10^{19} weapons combinations from a single cube!

If by chance anything got passed the sophisticated A.R.C.S, the next line of defence that had been recently installed was, a highly complex microwave controlled, rarefied plasma force field! This was situated 611.55072 kilometres (three hundred and eighty miles) in the gap between the exosphere and the mesosphere. Through nano-sensors, the plasma force field automatically detects if the planet is under attack or an unauthorised object has entered the zone and within less than a nano second it turns itself on and surrounds the entire planet Earth! Once activated, the rarefied plasma force field has enough power to destroy any object known to the overlord in this and his micro universe!

As the overlord was paranoid over security, the final spacial planetary defence system was an old fashioned but, highly effective micro laser grid that was just above the earth's stratosphere. Although the laser grid did not sound much, it was powerful enough to obliterate a large meteorite storm or numerous invading space ships!

Most fanatical cosmic tyrants would be contented with the external planetary spacial security but, the overlord's obsession for his personal safety had no planetary boundaries! Every single mountain top and elevated position on the planet Earth had an array of highly sophisticated ground to air or space missiles. Also in the depths of every ocean, sea bed and deep lake, there was an aquatic installation that was equipped with every conceivable weapon including thousands of A.R.C.S All were armed and ready and in less than a nano second they could blow any unauthorised ship, submersible, airborne or spacial object to kingdom come!

Satisfied that all the planetary defence systems were functioning correctly, the overlord walked back to his luxurious throne. Before sitting down, he paused and he activated his personnel protection device (P.P.D). This is a simple force field that can stop approaching objects such as, bullets used on earth, blasts from various pulse and photon firearms! It even has the capacity to stop people trying to personally attack the overlord!

All of this is done with high opposing kinetic force. The small display unit situated on his left arm showed the overlord that the personnel protection device was working with one hundred percent efficiency and that the sensors for auto activation were on. He then turned off his P.P.D and with his mind temporally at ease; he slumped into his comfortable chair and closed his eyes. His thoughts began to wonder to the harem of beautiful women he had when he was disturbed by a uni-net call! It was that slithering snake eyed Zissiani! With venom in his voice the overlord said;

"Zissiani, this is twice that you have disturbed me today! I'm warning you, this had better be extremely good. If not, today is yours and your family's day to die! And Zissiani, you scaly whore, I guaranty it will be a long drawn and excruciatingly painful death for all of you!"

Chair elect Admiral Zissiani chose her words carefully and meekly replied;

"Overlord, please accept my sincere apologies for this interruption. I only wanted to inform you that your galactic battle ship is ready and its crew are waiting for your command to engage ten of the best Universal Interplanetary Congress battleships!"

As his personal virtual reality unit lit up, the overlord could see his galactic battleship in all its splendour and for the time being, thoughts of killing Admiral Zissiani and her family went from his evil mind! In excitement, the overlord allowed his heart to beat exactly two beats a minute faster as he marvelled at the space ships proportions! The overall length of this galactic giant was 8.04672 kilometres (five miles) long and its width was an impressive 4.828032 kilometres (three Miles) wide! It had been made to the overlord's exact specifications and was an identical replica of to the one's he had back in his micro universe. This is with one exception; this one was several billion times larger!

The exterior of the galactic battle ship had been plated with material from collapsed dark star matter. This made the galactic battle ship extremely heavy but in space, a space craft's weight is not of major importance. What is important is, because of its extreme density; the dark star matter plated onto the battleships exterior acts as excellent exterior body armour. This cosmic armour can easily withstand most conventional proton, neutron, graviton, pulse, sonic, light, laser, nano and biological spacial weaponry attacks.

To further intimidate any 'naive' opposition, the shape of the battleship had been designed to resemble the overlords overall 'old' physical shape. The body of this ugly galactic giant resembled that of an ancient robot. It had a barrelled shaped chest on its front, while the back and both sides were completely flat. At the bottom of the battleships upper body were two short legs that could independently move in a one hundred and eighty degree angles in a forward and backward motion. These stumpy legs housed the two massive graviton engines. The mobility of these legs allowed the battleship to do manoeuvres that would be impossible for other large space craft. Attached at the base of each leg were two rectangular shaped feet that jutted out 1.609344 kilometres (one mile) in size! The frontage of these monstrous feet housed the space shuttle and small space fighter bays, while the bottom of the huge feet housed the main graviton engines thrusters.

Attached at either side of the battleships bodies were two massive rectangular shaped arms, with what looked like a large balled fist at each end. These huge limbs extended the full length of the battleship body, legs and feet. Each arm could independently rotate three hundred and sixty degrees clockwise and anti-clockwise, raise up and down a full one hundred and eighty degrees and were the battleships main armaments. And at the top of each battleship's enormous body was a large translucent half globed head; this was the battleships gyroscopic command centre.

Communicating through his uni-net device, the overlord ordered Admiral Zissiani to commence the battle demonstration. Without any delay Admiral Zissiani ordered her ten Universal Interplanetary Congress battleships to take up offensive positions and attempt to destroy the overlord's battleship!

In reality, the captains of each Universal Interplanetary Congress battleship and thousands of crew members knew this was a charade and that they were all about to die! But they had to put on a good display or all of their families, friends and associates would be publically executed!

Each of the Universal Interplanetary Congress battleships positioned themselves in a typical attack formation. They surrounded the overlord's battleship and then began firing every weapon they could muster at the overlord's new battleship. It was not surprising that the proton, neutron, graviton, pulse, sonic, light and laser weapon had no effect on the exterior of this galactic giant.

Suddenly and to the utter surprise of the overlord, all ten Universal Interplanetary Congress battleships began to retreat and two other Universal Interplanetary Congress battleships uncloaked. They were the latest in the fleet of Quzzzuzzz battleships and Admiral Zissiani's pride and joy, the cobrasant and viperious. Both of these splendid space craft's were fitted with the latest graviton engines and were armed with the new G.R.I.M (gravitational rotation inversion missile) weaponry. A G.R.I.M is a super-fast missile that can travel at almost the speed of light and when it is fired at its designated target, it explodes in less than a nano second! As the G.R.I.M explodes; a powerful gravitation field envelopes the chosen target. The gravitation field accelerates the selected target so fast that, the matter it's made of inverses in on itself. The collapsed matter becomes so dense that atoms collide and become destroyed; this in turn triggers multiple atomic explosions.

G.R.I.M's have successfully been able to destroy every target they have been fired at, including the triloraptors space craft's made of R.I.T.E.S! But they have never been tested on the overlord's battleship with its unique armour! Without hesitation, Admiral Zissiani gave the order to fire the G.R.I.M's but, before the word 'fire' left her mouth, the overlord's battleship reacted. The battleship pointed its giant balled fists directly at the cobrasant and viperious and fired its F.O.D (Fist of destruction) weapons. For a fraction of a nano second, each balled fist lit up like a small sun and then without a spacial sound, the F.O.D weapons smashed into the cobrasant and viperious driving them almost ten thousand kilometres backwards!

In less than a blink of a human eye, a fission process in which the heavy atomic nucleuses are split into two more-or-less equal fragments accompanied by the release of large amounts of atomic energy happened. This caused each spaceship and atom within it to light up like a miniature star! At the exact same time, the F.O.D weapons dimentialiser kicked in! And in less than a nano second, all the split atoms from both space vessels and their crews were thrown in and out of the fourth dimension! As the fragmented atoms regrouped and stabilised in this dimension, all that could be been seen of what was left of the cobrasant and viperious were, tangled and indistinguishable messes of highly radioactive merged matter! As for the crew members, they were just vaporised!

In his excitement, the overlord stood up, cheered out loud and vigorously clapped his large hands together. This was a human trait he had picked up and for the time being, he tolerated it. He was still connected to his virtual uni-net link when he looked at the large Quzzzuzzz snake, Admiral Zissiani, and said;

"Admiral Zissiani, you are sly and devious but, today your scheming has pleased me! This small demonstration has satisfied me. Now to show my appreciation, I will spare the other ten Universal Interplanetary Congress battleships and their crews."

Once again, the chair elect Admiral Zissiani had played a very dangerous game, but it had paid off and with a certain amount of reserve, she replied;

"Thank you for your generosity, the crew members and their families will be forever grateful to you. As for me and the Universal Interplanetary Congress, we are only here to do your bidding and serve you, your eminence."

The overlord could only stand a certain amount of grovelling from Admiral Zissiani and the sycophantic snake had just pushed her daily limit. He instantly turned off his uni-net link and began to re-examine his earthly planetary defence systems!

CHAPTER EIGHTEEN

Convergence

Despite not being human anymore, Elaine could not help imagining her heart was pounding with both excitement and trepidation as she, Notus and her ever growing army of energy beings exited their last worm hole. They were now well within earths Milky Way galaxy and in the star system Alpha Centauri. Their first objective was to converge on the outskirts of the star Proxima Centauri. From there; they would make their final plans to put an end to the universal tyranny of the overlord.

Notus gently released Elaine and all the other energy beings from its golden embrace and talking to Elaine, it telepathically said;

> "Elaine, as we are now only a few light years from your mother planet Earth. I think it is time for you to build upon your pure energy powers. I want you to concentrate on the star you know as Proxima Centauri; you can see it in the distance. Mentally lock onto this stars location and then will yourself to be just one light year away from it."

Elaine mentally said OK to Notus and to help with this task, she visualised that she had closed her eyes and then told herself to move close to Proxima Centauri. She felt no sensations or movement but when she mentally opened her eyes, she had travelled a little over three light years! What was even more surprising is she had done this in less than a second! While she was proud of her achievement, it was also comforting to know that Notus was right beside her. Again Notus spoke telepathically to her and laughingly said;

"Well done, you made that look easy. Now let's move to the other side of the star, I have a surprise for you!"

Within an earth second both pure energy beings had shot through space and without the restraints of having to de-accelerate they came to an abrupt halt just one light year away on the opposite side of Proxima Centauri! Elaine was knocked for six at what she saw; a vast army of energy beings were waiting for them! All Elaine could say repeatedly was;

"Oh my God! Oh my God! Oh my God!

Once she calmed down a little, with a small tremble in her voice, she telepathically asked Notus;

"Have all these come to help us, and how many of them are there?

Notus could sense and hear Elaine's excitement and also felling a little excited answered;

"Elaine, oh my God are the right words! I would estimate there are over two billion and possibly a few millions more, and the nice part is they are all here to help you!"

At that, all the other energy beings that had been travelling across the universe with Elaine and Notus began to arrive. There were now well over three billion energy beings! Elaine could feel her human emotions kicking in; all she wanted to do is cry with joy! But, energy beings do not have biological bodies or biological functions. So she did what all energy beings can do; she swiftly darted from one energy being too another and mentally gave them a big hug! Obviously she could not get around them all, and for all those she could not reach, she telepathically shouted as loud as she could;

"Thank you, thank you so much!'

While this was going on, Notus met with some of the Alpha scouts who had been able to go to the planet Earth and survey its defences. From their observations, the planet Earth was extremely well fortified for any attack from corporeal life forms. But, the overlord had not taken into account an attack from an army of energy beings!

Despite that, Notus knew that the overlord was a callous, cruel man and had rigged the planet Earth's core with several thousand atom sized nuclear bombs! Notus was also certain that the overlord would not hesitate to detonate these devices! Another important consideration was; each human had a coded uni-net disintegration device installed somewhere in their cerebral cortex and synaptic pathways. Furthermore the overlord will kill, without hesitation, every being on the planet Earth, if he thought he was under attack!

While Notus was pondering on these problems, Elaine had finished doing the 'hugging and thank you' rounds and returned to Notus's side. Instantly she could sense that Notus was perplexed and telepathically inquired;

"What's wrong? You seem extremely worried?"

Telepathically replying, Notus soberly answered;

"Elaine, despite our vast numbers, and the fact that we can get past the earth defences easily, the overlord has two aces up his sleeve. The first is, the several thousand atom sized nuclear bombs planted around earth core and the second is the uni-net disintegration device installed into the cerebral cortexes and synaptic pathways of every human! Once he knows he is under attack, he will kill the entire Human race and destroy the planet Earth!

Elaine took a few moments to mentally digest what Notus had said and then a few ideas popped into her head. She then thought about them for a few more earth minutes and then telepathically said to Notus;

"I think I might have the solution but, it would need impeccable timing and a bit of good old fashioned universal luck."

Notus resisted scanning Elaine's thoughts and in a bit of a more upbeat tone, Notus inquired;

"Would it be best if we all heard the idea? I could arrange this so we could do a collective mind broadcast."

That sounded like a good idea and Elaine asked Notus to set it up. Within a few earth minutes, over three billion energy beings were telepathically linked into Notus's mind and Notus then asked Elaine to begin. With an air of leadership quality, Elaine began;

> "The task ahead is going to be difficult but, I have come up with a plan that might work and I have to say, it will take every one of us to pull this off!"

Elaine paused for a reaction but, as she all she got was a wall of mental silence, so unperturbed she continued;

> "I personally intend to take the overlord out! To do this, I will have get close to him, render him unconscious and then trap him in a gravitational field. Once he is unconscious, I will then transport him to a secured area. This area will have to be lined with material that does not allow the transmission of any uni-net frequencies.
>
> At exactly the same time as I render the overlord unconscious, a group of electrical energy beings will be split into three. One group will disable the uni-net on the planet Earth, the second group will disable the uni-net satellites in earths its solar systems and the third group will disable all other spacial uni-net links!
>
> While this is going on, another group of energy beings can have the task of capturing the overlord's, lords on the planet Earth. They can also transport them to a secure holding area.
>
> Finally the rest of you will have the unpleasant task of disabling or removing the several thousand atom sized nuclear bombs planted around earth core!"

Within seconds, questions were being asked from every quarter and Notus intervened called everyone to order and said;

> "Elaine's outlining plan is a good one; however I do a few reservations about you taking on the overlord alone. The Alphas have informed me that he has a powerful personal protection device (P.P.D) that can fend off earthly weapons and certain energy attacks! Elaine, even if you could get close to him, the chances are he could still activate the atom sized nuclear bombs and the uni-net destruction devices!"

Elaine had to concede that the overlord's personal protection device (P.P.D) was something she had not considered! She remained silent for a for earth minutes, revised her plan and then said to everyone;

"We do have one advantage. To humans, I and some of the energy beings are invisible. What I now plan is still going to be a massive big gamble. Unlike us, humans need sleep, so we wait until the overlord is asleep. Then I and a small task force of energy beings covertly enter his bedroom; surround him and then blast slumbering overlord and his personal protection device with pure energy from every conservable angle! At exactly the same time, everyone else will have to do their jobs and instantly disarm the atom sized nuclear bombs, disable all uni-net communication sites and capture his lords!"

The overlord's personal protection device may protect him, but I am hoping that in the confusion, the rest of you will be able to disarm the atom sized nuclear bombs and the uni-net destruction devices! As a further precaution, my task force will jointly restrain the overlord in multiple gravity fields and if this works, we can transport him to the safe area and deal with him later.

Those detailed to capturing the overlord's lords will also have restrain them in multiple gravity fields and then convey them to the safe holding area.

As timing is critical for this operation to succeed, I would like Notus to be in charge of co-ordinating the whole event!"

The general consensus of opinion from Elaine's vast army was this was a good plan and when everyone had had their say, Notus said;

"As we are all in agreement on this plan of action, I would suggest that we run through a few simulations before we head for earth. We can use a planet known as Gliese 581 for this; it is only twenty lights years away from earth but has similar internal features. The planet Gliese also has a massive uni-net communications satellite in orbit, so while we are there, we can set up a team ready to disable it!

While we do this, I would also like to get a large team of alpha's to do some more earthly reconnaissance. That way we will know exactly how to find all the uni-net communications sites and get a more detailed plan of the overlord's fortress. The alpha team will also have to locate all of the overlord's lords and determine if any of these have access to any or all of the detonation devices!

My offspring Earth has given me details of deep caves, caverns and fissures that will help our teams through earth's mantle. Once they navigate their way through this, they can then head for earth's core in readiness for operation code name, time!"

Earth had also come up with a large cavern that is deep in its bowels, this cavern is thickly lined with lead and other heavy metals! With a few modifications, it might be a good area to hold the captured overlord and his lords."

Elaine and the other energy beings liked Notus's preliminary planning and the code name, time. Over the next few earth days, these introductory plans were put into effect and after lots of practice the plans seemed to work well. The alpha teams did their job and surveyed and mapped every uni-net installation on the planet Earth and the uni-net satellites in earth's solar system. For the Alphas and anyone else looking, it was easy to locate the overlord's lords. These brash, pompous men had been given control of large densely populated areas of the planet Earth and they made their presence known on a daily basis. The only spanner in the works was the Alphas had found that the overlord slept in a two metre thick vaulted chamber, buried deep in the rocky base of Mount Everest.

On hearing of this vaulted sleeping chamber, Elaine had the Alphas do a detailed analysis of what it was made of and how uni-net communications could be picked up through its mountainous rocky exterior and two metre thick walls. After some further investigations, the Alphas determined that the vaulted sleeping chamber was indeed a nuclear, pulse and numerous other types of bomb proof shelter! Its outer walls had one metre of re-enforced carbon steel concrete on it and the inner layer was made of one meter thick high grade titanium alloy that had been crisscrossed with high tensile carbon steel for extra strength. The Alphas also determined that the chamber also had its own emergency power and air supply that was vented through a complex, but highly secure filtration system. The same filtration system also housed some powerful but tiny two way microprocessors that boosted the uni-net signal and allowed a strong uni-net communications signal for the overlord!

Now that she was aware of these micro uni-net communications processors, Elaine knew that her first priority would be to destroy them before she attempted to capture the overlord. After thinking about this for a while, she calculated that she and the other energy beings could overload the emergency electrical supply with a blast of pure energy and hopefully, that would also fry the micro uni-net communications processors! She knew that this was another gamble but her options were limited!

Notus knew Elaine was deep in thought and concerned about her side of their plan, but Notus had a few important issues to run by Elaine. So trying to be courteous, Notus telepathically said;

Elaine, sorry to disturbed you but, I need to talk to you about a few issues we have not yet covered."

Elaine knew instantly that Notus had something of value to say and replied;

"You're not disturbing me; if we have missed anything, then we will fail, so please continue."

Notus began;

"There are two issues that we have not yet discussed but, I think you will agree they are important. The first is about the planet Earth. Have you considered what will happen to the humans once we overthrow the overlord?"

Elaine felt a little embarrassed, as she still classed herself as a 'kind of human' but, all she had thought about since leaving the planet Notus was, defeating the overlord. She coyly replied;

"To be honest Notus, I had not given this a thought. But now that you have mentioned it, they will have to completely restructure their lives!

Then another more important thought hit Elaine;

"Oh my god, they will also have to take on the overlords armies!"

Notus mentally nodded and added;

"Most of earth's armed forces have been conscripted from the Universal Interplanetary Congress. Do you have any contacts there that we can trust and possibly tip off?"

The only thing Elaine could feel at this point of time was her imaginary human stomach tense and tighten as she replied;

"As you are aware, the U.I.C is under the tight grip of the overlord and his lords. Regretfully, there are only two people I know from the other time line. One is the current Chair elect of the U.I.C and the overlord's Universal Interplanetary Congress chief military commander, Admiral Zissiani! She is a Quzzzuzzzian, most of this species are extremely honourable. But, Zissiani on the other hand, can definitely not be trusted!" The other one I know is the new chair elect for my time line. She is an aquatic from the oceanic planet named Ramlindos but, I do not think at this point of time that she is in a strong enough position to help us."

Elaine's reply did not surprise Notus and in a strong powerful voice said;

"Well it looks as if we are on our own and for the first time in the history of this universe, energy beings are going to be fighting alongside human beings in order to free earth and liberate the Universal Interplanetary Congress!"

As soon as Notus's words entered Elaine's mind, she realised that this was going to be a massive campaign. Before responding, Elaine took a few moments to try to visualise an overall battle plan but before she could formulate anything constructive, Notus mentally intervened and said;

"I know what you are thinking but, let's just stick to our original plan. If we succeed with that, we can go for plan B, that is, we can help the humans. While that is going on, I along with some of my species will implement plan C, destroy the overlord's new battleship and liberate the Universal Interplanetary Congress."

For some reason this simple A, B, C plan appealed to Elaine and she responded to Notus by telepathically saying;

"Did I ever tell you, you are a genius?"

Laughing Notus replied;

"Aren't all parents' geniuses."

Elaine laughed and then inquired;

"OK brain box that was the first issue you wanted to bring up, what was the second?"

Without hesitation, Notus said just one word;

"KRONOS."

That one word sent a shiver down Elaine's imaginary human spine. Once again she had to acknowledge that since leaving the planet Notus, she hadn't given KRONOS a second thought. Mentally she reasoned with herself, it was simply because KRONOS did not exist. Elaine also knew Notus was listening to her thoughts and telepathically said;

"I think if KRONOS was real entity. The lord, lady or both of time would have intervened or got in contact with me by now."

Notus was not so dismissive of KRONOS and wittingly replied;

"Elaine, only time will tell"

CHAPTER NINETEEN

And so it begins

One thing was puzzling Elaine as she and seven other pure energy beings began to descend through earth's atmosphere was; do energy beings actually feel nervous tension? One thing was for sure, she did and what made it worse was her imaginary human stomach had a massive swarm of butterflies doing all kind of manoeuvres in it!

As Elaine and her team broke through some high cloud cover, Mount Everest appeared directly below them. To Elaine it looked stunning and as she and her team continued to slowly descend, she thought how lucky she was to be able to see this mountain from this magnificent view. She also felt good to be back on earth but sadly, this was definitely not the earth she remembered. Thousands of menacing A.R.C's hovered around the overlord's mountainous fortress and numerous automated gun turrets speckled Mount Everest's rocky and snow covered slopes!

The Alphas had done a great reconnaissance job and had sent Elaine and her team hundreds of mental images of this mountainous stronghold and that made it easy for them to locate a side service entrance at the foot of the mountain. Using their invisibility, all they had to do was patiently wait for a delivery, slip past the A.R.C.'s security check point and timed plasma force field and then make their way to the overlords sleeping chamber!

What was highly noticeable to Elaine and her team as they made their way through a labyrinth of internal roadways and brightly lit corridors was the overlord's obsession with security! Armed miniature A.R.C's that were fitted with highly advanced C.C.T.V cameras patrolled every ten metres or so of this mountainous fortress. And at every four hundred metres; there was an armed robotic check point with its own security force field! This made the going slow, but after approximately four earth hours, Elaine and her team located the overlords sleeping chamber. From the outside, the vaulted door made it look like a safe worthy of protecting all the gold at Fort Knox!

As this imposing door was securely closed with numerous security devices and an alien coded timed entry, Elaine and her team had to wait for the overlord to arrive! This seemed to take forever and when the overlord finally arrived, he took Elaine by surprise! He was surrounded by thirty winged, one metre long armed ants! Elaine had never seen this species before but, with their scorpion like tales and pulse cannons, they looked ferocious! From the centre of his flying security team the overlord emerged and Elaine was once again bowled over! The overlord was only in his mid-twenties, tall, muscular and stunningly good looking! The overlord also had another surprise for Elaine and her team; he had brought three scantily dressed females from his harem with him!

While the overlord's females and security team moved back, the overlord went through the extensive procedure of unlocking the vaulted door. Elaine thought it prudent to observe this and made a mental note of everything the overlord did just in case they needed it later. The overlord then took a few paces back and the two metre thick door slowly opened outward. Elaine could now see inside the large vaulted chamber. The room looked extremely lavish with expensive bedroom furniture. However the centre of the room was dominated by an extremely large round bed that made any king size bed look miniature! The bed was adorned with sumptuous pillows and silk sheets and Elaine guessed that the mattress would be a high tech air or gravity one. To the rear of the bedroom chamber, there was another doorway and Elaine knew from the Alphas intelligence images, that this lead to the toilet and luxurious bathing area.

As the overlord and his female entourage made themselves comfortable, Elaine and six of her invisible team silently positioned themselves around the inner perimeter of the bedroom chamber. Now they had to wait for the overlord to fall asleep but, before that happened, they all had to witness the overlord's manly prowess as he took advantage of his female companions! As a trained medical doctor Elaine had witnessed births and deaths but invisible or not, she was uncomfortable at being in a room when sexual activity with four in a bed was going on! In between time and trying to block out the giggles, grunts and ecstatic groans. Elaine telepathically communicated with her team and began to plan on how to subdue the three females and the thirty guards waiting outside the vaulted chamber!

The plan that emerged was simple; at exactly the same time that the overlord was being subdued, the four energy beings outside would have to deal with the flying ant guards and the three 'concubine' women would be restrained in gravity fields. When things had settled down, the women would then be locked inside the bathroom.

To everyone's surprise, the overlord then unwittingly solved the 'concubine' situation by dismissing all three ladies and sending them back to their quarters. However this only happened after he had had his sexual gratification! For Elaine and her team this made the job at hand a bit easier but, Elaine realised that they missed a golden opportunity and they could have seized the overlord a little earlier! When the overlord was cavorting with his three female companions, he had actually turned off his personnel protection device (P.P.D) off! However, it was too late now and Elaine decided it was now best to stick to the original plan.

As Elaine and her invisible team watched, the overlord seemed to be in good spirits and decided to take a long hot shower. After what seem like a life time, the overlord emerged from his luxurious shower room dressed in black silk pyjamas and then settled down for a well-earned, good night's sleep. Within a few earth minutes the overlord closed his eyes and fell asleep. But, Elaine had advised everyone to hold back. As a medical doctor, she knew that the overlord had only just begun stage one of a five stage human sleep cycle.

At stage one, the brain begins to relax and slow down and slower brain waves known as alpha waves are produced. During this time, a human being is not quite asleep. What they needed was for the overlord to get to stage five and this would take about ninety earth minutes! During this time, Elaine carefully monitored the overlord for rapid eye movement (REM). REM sleep is characterized by eye movement, increased respiration rate and increased brain activity. REM sleep is also referred to as paradoxical sleep because, while the brain and other body systems become more active, body muscles become more relaxed. At this stage, dreaming occurs due to increased brain activity. Elaine was aware that the first cycle of REM sleep might last only a short amount of time and that was her window of opportunity to strike!

Typically, the overlord overshot the normal ninety minute slot and it wasn't until one hundred and twenty two tense earth minutes had passed, that the overlord went into (REM) stage. To be extra cautious, Elaine left it a few minutes longer and then telepathically called out to Notus the code word "Time".

Notus was on the ball and instantly, every being in Elaine's army went into action! On the border of Quzzzuzzzian space, two pure energy beings had been able to sneak inside the overlords battleship through a shuttle bay and were attacking its control and weapon systems!

At exactly the same time on earth, Elaine's team were bang on schedule with their plans. The tiny two way microprocessors hidden in the air ventilation system that boosted the uni-net signal had been melted by a targeted blast of pure energy. The overlords own uni-net link in his brain had also been targeted and disabled. What was more remarkable was, as Elaine looked at the overlord, he had been successfully stunned by several controlled blasts of pure energy before his (P.P.D) could react and was now unconscious on his bed!

Seeing this, Elaine and the other six energy beings hurriedly placed seven multi gravitational fields around the overlord. Elaine then checked the status of the overlord's ant guards outside the vaulted chamber. The four energy beings outside reported the ant guards had been successfully subdued and it was safe to exit the vaulted chamber. Acting as quickly as she could, Elaine instructed the energy beings to jointly raise the overlord's unconscious body off the bed and move him towards the vaulted door. It was then that Elaine was completely taken by surprise! A flash of bright white light filed the bed chamber and miraculously the overlord regained consciousness! The overlord then jumped up and as if the seven multi gravity fields surrounding him were nothing, he walked through them! Smiling he looked directly at Elaine and in a calm voice said;

"Hello Doctor or should I say Captain Elaine Laurence, I have been looking forward to meeting you!"

To say that Elaine was flabbergasted was an understatement, she thought she was invisible! Out of shock and sheer panic, she telepathically called out to Notus and the other energy beings for help, but for some unknown reason she could not get through? She quickly looked around the chamber and was surprised to see that the other six energy being had disappeared! She was alone with the overlord!

Although she was shocked by what had happened, Elaine's next reaction was to shoot a pure energy blast straight at the overlord. However to her disappointment and horror, it had absolutely no affect! She could only guess that his personnel protection device (P.P.D) was way better than anyone expected!

Once again the overlord smiled and shaking a finger at Elaine, he said;

> "Now Doctor Elaine Laurence, that's not a friendly way too make my acquaintance, is it?

Being an energy being, Elaine could not verbally reply, so she tried to communicate telepathically and almost fumbling for words she replied;

> "Can you hear me?"

To her utter surprise, the overlord telepathically answered;

> "Of course I can! If I could not, how do you think we were going to communicate?"

Elaine's mind was now in turmoil, how could this be? Trying to compose herself mentally, she inquired;

> "When did you become a telepath and how can you see me, I am an energy being and invisible to most breathing life forms?"

Laughing the overlord telepathically replied;

> "My poor confused energy girl! You are confusing me for the overlord; I am the one you and all the energy beings have been seeking, I am the one you like to call KRONOS!

For the time being, I thought it prudent for our first meeting to borrow this human body. Now, I will give you a moment for this to sink in and then it's down to some serious business!"

Elaine was gobsmacked, she never envisaged KRONOS the guardian of time as a being that could 'borrow a body'. She had seen several movies on earth like 'Clash of the Titans' and so on and each movie KRONOS was always portrayed as a forty metre tall fire breathing monster! KRONOS had picked up on Elaine's line of thought and with some laughter in his voice, he telepathically said;

"You know Elaine, that's exactly how numerous rising 'intelligent' life forms around this and other universes see me, as some kind of massive fire spewing monster! As you can see, I am not."

While Elaine listened, he continued on to say;

"In all fairness to them, I can appear to be anything I want but, in all the billions and billions of years that I have been alive, I have never been a forty metre tall fire breathing monster! Now let's get down to business. Since you and your associates began meddling in time, this and the overlords universe have become a catastrophe or should I say time-tastrophe."

He then laughed out loud and said;

"You know Elaine; I think I have just invented a new earthly word. Perhaps this should be included in all the universe dictionaries?"

Frowning and looking very serious his jovial tone changed and he added;

"Now before you say anything, on a 'time' level, things are only going to get worse! That's why I am intervening and between the two of us, we have to start and put all that is wrong with time right!"

Elaine felt like going on the defensive and putting forward her case about rescuing her fellow abducted humans. But before she could mentally utter a word, KRONOS waggled one of his fingers from side to side and said;

"Now Elaine, let's not go down that path. We are both adults, and we both know things have gone drastically wrong and I think you will agree, it's 'time' to try and put things right."

In that short sentence, Elaine had to concede that KRONOS was right. So she saved her 'saving the abducted humans' speech for later and replied with a question;

"Why didn't you intervene earlier, it would have saved an awful lot of grief?"

KRONOS walked over to the overlord's wardrobe and started sorting out some clothes and casually replied;

"Would you agree that there is a right or wrong time for everything, just like me getting dressed into my day clothes?"

Elaine thought she could see where this was heading but, she allowed KRONOS the courtesy of explaining and simply answered;

"Yes."

By this time KRONOS had put on some black trousers and was sorting through some of the overlords very expensive fine silk shirts. He then asked Elaine;

"What do you think looks better, the white or pale blue one?"

Before Elaine could even think of replying, KRONOS continued;

"Today I will go with the pale blue one. The reason I did not let you choose is, I am KRONOS and for billions and billions of your earth years, I have had to make my own decisions. Those decisions affect the delicate balance of time in this and other universes.

Today, I decided that Doctor Elaine Laurence was ready to help restore that delicate time balance. Yesterday and all the earth days prior to that you were simply not ready! I hope that answers your question."

To answer KRONOS, all Elaine had to do was mentally nod. However, she had more questions and she before she asked them, she politely thanked KRONOS for his answer. She then inquired;

"Now would you please tell me what has happened to everyone else, there were six other energy beings in this vaulted chamber and they have disappeared?"

KRONOS put on a pair of fine black leather shoes, smiled at Elaine and replied;

"Please do not worry about them, they are all still here but, I have frozen them in their time line. You and I are exactly five nano seconds outside of that same time line and that's why you cannot see them."

KRONOS answer tied in nicely with Elaine's own theory about the missing space ships and graviton engines and Notus's theory about a powerful being placing that gravitational field around the planet Hope's solar system. But once again, before Elaine could telepathically ask KRONOS about this, he threw both hands in the air and called out;

"Guilty as charged, yes it was me to all of that! Now let's move on and try to unravel this temporal mess! What we are going to do is go back in time to where all of this started."

Elaine thought for a moment and then commented with a twofold question;

"Would that be going back in time to the planet Hopes solar system or back in time on this planet, Earth?"

Putting on a long black trench coat, KRONOS replied;

"It's back to earth in the year 1607. Did you know you had an ancestor who was one of the earliest British settlers in Jamestown, Virginia America?"

This was news to Elaine and with some anger in her voice she answered;

"No, but I guess the triloraptors knew this and they went there to kill my ancestor!"

Nodding KRONOS said;

"Your guess is correct; those triloraptors are both devious and extremely clever. Now I have to warn you that this time journey is going to be perilous. As time has already been re-written, the new energy time vortex around the planet Earth is extremely delicate. If we fail, the fabric of time will disintegrate and whole of this and the overlord's universe is going to go into a temporal meltdown!

Elaine, I don't want you to worry about this right now, I will explain all the temporal intricacies and dangers as we proceed. Now let's get you ready. The first thing you need is access to a human body. I guess you would like a female one! Shall we pop up to the overlord's harem and do a bit of body shopping?"

By now, Elaine had gotten used of being told that what she was about to embark on was going to be extremely dangerous! However at this point of time though, her thoughts were being occupied by something KRONOS would possibly find trivial. As Elaine looked at KRONOS, the thought of occupying and using someone else's body just didn't appeal to Elaine one little bit!

Almost instantly, KRONOS felt Elaine's repugnance at this idea and he sympathetically came up with another, more agreeable solution. In a friendly way, he told Elaine to scrub the body snatching idea and suggested that she imagine a live image of her human self in her mind. Elaine like this idea better and did as she was told. After forming the image, KRONOS gave her mind a mental energy boost and then he told her that she should project that live image outwards.

Once again Elaine did as she was told, and slowly the live image in her mind began to form around her pure energy body into the shape and texture of Elaine's human body. Within a few seconds, Elaine had her 'old' human form again! She jumped up and down with joy and as she opened her mouth, the sounds of cheers and laughter came out! Laughing at Elaine's antics, KRONOS then telepathically said;

"OK Doctor Elaine Laurence, how about you pop on my dressing gown and we head up to the ladies quarters and find you some suitable clothing!"

Elaine had not realised she was naked and felt her cheeks flushing red. She then grabbed KRONOS's silk dressing gown, slipped it on and with a little embarrassment in her voice Elaine asked;

> "Can I do the same and project the image of clothing onto my human body?"

Nodding KRONOS replied;

> "There is no reason why you cannot, just focus as before and think of some nice female clothing."

Only one image came into Elaine's mind, her trilo-combat uniform! And within less than one earth second, that's what she was wearing! She slipped off the silk dressing gown and twirling around, she asked KRONOS;

> "What do you think?"

The guardian of time laughed out loud and said;

> "It isn't exactly what they are wearing on the catwalks in any universal fashion show but, I have to say, for the job at hand, it's absolutely perfect! I suppose now that you have set a criterion, I will need to get rid of this hansom human body?"

It was clear to KRONOS that Elaine liked this male human form. So before she could answer, he answered for her saying;

> "Maybe that would be a bit drastic! I guess I will do exactly the same as you and just project a live human image."

Elaine smiled and nodded and within a nano second KRONOS had given the unconscious overlord his body back and was now wearing an exact clothed replica. Smiling he did a twirl and then said to Elaine,

> "Now the earth year 1607 awaits you. But first, let's go and meet with your triloraptor friend's on-board Notus One!"

CHAPTER TWENTY

Intervention!

Within the blink of Elaine's 'new' human eye, Elaine was transported from the overlord's lair through time and into a cargo bay on her own space ship, Notus One! Standing next to her and smiling was the guardian of time KRONOS! KRONOS lifted his one finger to his lips and quietly said;

> "Shush, we are not alone; all four triloraptors are on the command deck and are just about to open the time portal to the earth year 1607. When the two triloraptors enter the portal, I want you to follow them, capture them and bring them back to Notus One. Do not allow them to make any time changes as this will destroy our mission and the fabric of time will tear!"

Whispering back, Elaine inquired;

> "Firstly, why can't we just stop them before they go through the time portal? And if that cannot be done, why don't you go through the portal and stop them, you are more powerful than me and the guardian of time?"

Using telepathy, KRONOS answered;

> "They are both reasonable questions, so in the first instance. The initial temporal changes happened on the planet Earth. The surface of the planet Earth is the epicentre for this time-tastrophe. So logically, that's where we need to start repairing time. Secondly, I KRONOS, guardian of all time have too much power to enter the fragile time

portal. If I did, I would definitely cause a temporal rupture in this delicate time line that I will not be able to repair!"

Nodding at those answers, Elaine telepathically then asked;

"OK, how do I get past the other two triloraptors who will still be on the command deck?"

Whispering KRONOS replied;

"I will deal with them! Now on the count of three, I will transport us both on to the command deck and you must enter the time portal immediately."

Elaine nodded and then KRONOS then did the count;

"One, two, three!

Instantly, Elaine and KRONOS were on Notus One's command deck. Elaine could see the portal was open and leapt through its opening! She found herself in a vast open grassy plane, and a few yards ahead of her where the two triloraptors.

Being universal hunters, triloraptors instincts are very finely tuned and simultaneously they turned around and saw Captain Elaine Laurence behind them! In a split second, their razor sharp trilo-trons shot towards Elaine but to their amazement, the two trilo-trons went straight through her! Before they could react again, Elaine fired two pure energy bolts that knocked the triloraptors who were fully clad in their trilo-combat uniforms several metres backward! With lightning speed, Elaine then followed that up with two gravitational fields that totally encompassed the two triloraptors in two sphere-shaped gravitational fields! Now slightly panicking, the triloraptors tried to escape but, Elaine's gravitational fields were to strong! As she slowly drew them toward her, she could hear the one say;

"Captain Elaine Laurence, we killed you, we saw your body perish in space!"

As Elaine thrust the two triloraptors back through the time portal, her emotions got the better of her and she yelled;

"You pretended to be my friends; I and my people trusted you and then, you callously slaughtered them! However once again, you underestimated me and that will be your final mistake!"

Without glancing back, Elaine walked back through the time portal and KRONOS closed it after her. The four triloraptors were all detained in a force field created by KRONOS and were suspended in the centre of Notus One's command centre. Elaine then looked at KRONOS and said;

"What shall we do with them now?"

With an ice-cold look in his eyes he replied;

"Elaine, I know they have wronged you but, I am KRONOS guardian of time and their actions have severely damaged this universes time line. That in turn has affected billions and billions of life forms. They will have to face my justice!" In this time line, I am going to imprison them in the centre of a moon I know where there is no escape, little air, no water or food. They are triloraptors, their natural instincts will kick in and they will turn on each other. Eventually in desperation, they will devour each other!"

As universal justice comes, Elaine thought KRONOS's justice was good. She thought back to the callous slaughter of her friend's, Captain Harper and John McNally on-board Notus One. The site of their blood and limp bodies was still fresh in her mind!

She then recalled how the triloraptors had heartlessly killed all the human people she had rescued from the planet Hope and the people and Kreios from the Novus Inceptio region on the Planet Gladious! These human people had done no wrong; they had been abducted by the triloraptors and against all odds they had survived and thanks to the leadership and insight of Captain Ron Walker they had even built a fantastic settlement. All of this had been needlessly wiped out by the triloraptors in a trilo-planetary killing frenzy! My god, now Elaine felt really angry! Rightly or wrongly, she hoped that the four triloraptors would suffer prolonged and painful deaths! With that, all four triloraptors disappeared. Elaine looked at KRONOS and asked;

"What of all the other triloraptors, they instigated this plan and I am confident that they will try to replicate the procedures devised in Notus One for other time travel?"

KRONOS walked over and put his arm around Elaine's shoulder and answered;

"Elaine, I cannot destroy a whole species. That would be wrong. Ironically Elaine, by reverting time back to its original time line, this will actually save the triloraptor species! But do not worry; I will stop them from repeating what has happened. Sadly to do this, I will now have to destroy Notus One!

KRONOS could see the tears forming in Elaine's eyes and trying to console her; he put both arms around her, hugged her gently and almost whispering he said;

"Elaine, I'm sorry, if I left Notus One in its current time line, the triloraptors would use it again and I believe they would do this or even worse, over and over again!"

She had been through so much and her human emotions had been pent up for so long, Elaine began to weep uncontrollably. The thought of Notus One being destroyed and the triloraptors walking away scot free, just tipped her emotional scales! KRONOS held her tightly and said;

"Elaine, I know you have been through so much but you must remember that you have achieved more than any being in this universe! It's OK to weep."

Elaine looked up at KRONOS and still crying asked;

"It's not over yet, is it?"

KRONOS looked down at this brave individual, pulled out a silk handkerchief from his pocket, wiped Elaine's tearful eyes and said;

"No, but once we sort out Notus One, earths planetary time from the year 1607 will have to be re-written and that gives us a few earth centuries before our next temporal action."

Still holding Elaine tightly, KRONOS continued;

> "Would you like me to sort out Notus One and leave you alone for a while?"

Elaine was enjoying the embrace and comforting words that KRONOS was giving her; it made her feel strangely human again. Also, she truly did not want to be alone, and if Notus One had to be destroyed, as sad as it was, she wanted to be there.

As always, KRONOS was perceptive of Elaine's thoughts, he gently let her go and said;

> "Come, Captain Elaine Laurence. Let's take Notus One on its last flight in this time line."

Elaine took the silk handkerchief out of KRONOS's hand, wiped away her tears and bravely smiling walked over to Notus One's controls and asked KRONOS;

> "Where are we heading?"

Half smiling back, KRONOS quietly answered;

> "Elaine, we need to head towards this solar systems sun."

Speaking softly, Elaine asked Notus One's super computer to make a heading for the earth's sun, she then took manual control and guided the space craft towards its final destination. Just after one million kilometres. Elaine gave the super computer the order to separate Notus One from its triloraptors mother ship shell. The two space craft parted for the last time and Elaine gave the order for the triloraptors mother ship to accelerate ahead, with a collision course of the centre of the sun!

Easing back on Notus Ones speed, Elaine took this magnificent space craft for one final spin around the sun before relinquishing control. She looked at KRONOS with sadness in her eyes and said;

> "We are both ready."

Both Elaine and KRONOS left Notus One's command centre and at just over forty nine million, six hundred thousand kilometres from earth's sun in open space, they both watched Notus One as it slowly fell towards the suns fiery surface. As this was happening, Elaine recalled her excitement and astonishment when she first saw Notus One as it rose majestically out of the sea on the planet Notus. She also remembered with fondness her maiden voyage and her excitement at actually flying her very own space ship! As a pilot, she had flown airplanes on earth before but, Notus One was the fastest and most unique space craft universally ever invented. Its crystal blue Marquise-Cut boat shaped diamond exterior and pure energy drive system made it that way!

Her thoughts then went to her mentor and friend, the being and guardian of the planet Notus, Notus. How was she going to tell Notus that the space craft that it made for her was now being destroyed? A terrible thought hit her; part of Notus One's atomic structure was made from Olotiniums atoms! Olotinium was deceased offspring of Notus! Using telepathy, she looked at KRONOS and said;

"I will have to let the being Notus know what has happened."

KRONOS began to slowly usher Elaine away from the sun and re-assuredly replied;

"Please do not worry about Notus, all planet guardians are atomically in touch with their offspring's, so Notus will instinctively know what is happening."

He then added a disturbing but also cautionary note;

"You must also remember that this point in universal time has yet to be re-written!"

Elaine could not help herself; she had to look back! And as she witnessed Notus One disappearing underneath the suns fiery surface, she too felt a small part of herself die!

CHAPTER TWENTY ONE

Time and Restoration

Within seconds of leaving Notus One, Elaine found herself only a few thousand kilometres from earth's moon. She wondered why KRONOS had brought her here. KRONOS glanced at her and said;

"Elaine, I will answer your thoughts. As you are aware, the planet Earth has undergone some radical changes in its time line. All of earth's time from the year 1607 is now being re-written and I have to make to certain that this part of the time line is not corrupted. To do this, I have to monitor key events in earth's history and make sure they are on the correct temporal track.

We are now looking at the planet Earth in the year 1607! I would like you to go to Jamestown, Virginia America and make sure a colonist named Captain John Smith, who is an explorer, soldier and writer is still alive."

Laughing, KRONOS knew that this had got Elaine's challenging inquisitive mind going and continued;

"Before you ask, Captain John Smith is one of your early ancestors and it is important that I establish that your own time line is on track."

This new challenged perked up Elaine's mood and after a few moments of thought she inquired;

"Do I go as a female human or as an invisible entity?

Seeing that Elaine was going to take her mission serious and wanting to give her a little more historic information. KRONOS answered;

"Elaine, As far as I am aware, there were no women on the first expedition to this area. It was probably deemed that it was far too dangerous for the fairer sex to travel to a land where what they classed as 'savage Indians' roamed! So it would be prudent to be an invisible entity and just make sure your ancestor is alive."

Before Elaine could ask any further questions, she found herself on the shores of the James River. Three large sailing ships had just put down anchor in the deep waters of the bay and were unloading large amounts of equipment and supplies. Elaine looked at the name plates on each ship and could see they were the Susan Constant, Godspeed, and the Discovery. Also disembarking were a group of men and as Elaine flew over and eavesdropped on their conversation, she found out that her ancestor, John Smith was on board ship and had just recently been appointed as a member of the governing Council! What she also found from the men's conversation shocked her!

During the voyage, Captain John Smith had been arrested for mutiny and had been incarcerated aboard one of the ships! What was even more shocking was he had been scheduled to be hanged upon arrival! Captain John Smith's destiny had changed when; one of the ships Captains, named Captain Christopher Newport opened upon their arrival sealed orders from the Virginia Company. The Virginia Company were the company who had sponsored this expensive expedition. To everyone's surprise, in those orders, Captain John Smith had been appointed as member of the governing Council! He was therefore released immediately!

As Elaine listened to the idle chatter of the men, she quickly learned that Captain John Smith was considered as rogue and hero by some, and a demon by others! He apparently had set of to sea at the age of sixteen! He had served as a mercenary in the army of Henry IV of France against the Spaniards, fought for independence from the Spanish King Phillip II, and then set off for the Mediterranean Sea. There he engaged in both trade and piracy, and later fought against the Ottoman Turks in the Long War!

John Smith was promoted to captain while fighting for the Austrian Habsburgs in Hungary, in the campaign of Michael the Brave in the year 1600 and 1601. After the death of Michael the Brave, he fought for Radu Șerban in Wallachia against the Ottoman vassal Ieremia Movilă.

John Smith is reputed to have defeated, killed and beheaded Turkish commanders in three duels! For which he was knighted by the Transylvanian Prince Sigismund Báthory and given a horse and coat of Arms showing three Turks' heads!

Elaine was astounded at Captain John Smith's rich history and as she flew over one of the row boats heading for the shore, she saw her ancestor! It was hard to tell his height as the heavily bearded man was sitting down but, she knew it was him as she heard one of the other men address him and say;

> "Captain Smith, it looks as if we have some hard times and hard work ahead of us."

Captain Smith looked sternly at the man and said;

> "We do indeed but, he, who works not, eats not"

After seeing Captain John Smith in the flesh, Elaine knew that she had completed her mission and before she knew it, she was back in space by KRONOS's side. KRONOS was smiling and said;

> "It would seem that you Captain Elaine Laurence and your ancestor, Captain John Smith have an awful lot in common!"

Elaine had no time to comment as KRONOS hurriedly said;

> "Now that we have the 'time ball rolling,' I have another time mission for you. I want you to go to Philadelphia, Pennsylvania in the year 1774. That's where the First Continental Congress met briefly. In earth's time line, this is a very important point in history and I want you to make sure all fifty six delegates are present."

Elaine wanted to get a few background details but, before she could she say anything, she found herself in an old grand hall filled with chattering men. They were all wearing clothing of that time and most were adorned with white floured 'judges' wigs! Thanks to KRONOS's timing, she was just in time for the assembly roll call.

On by one, each man called out his name and where they were from. It started; Samuel Adams from Massachusetts, John Dickinson from Pennsylvania and John Jay from New York's. As the list continued, Elaine felt a shudder down her imaginary spine as she heard the names and saw the faces of George Washington, Patrick Henry and John Adams!

As each man called out his name, Elaine counted each one and when she got to fifty six she was instantly transported to another time line! This time, she was at the second continental congress meeting on May 10th, 1775. And she was just in time to witness the adoption of the Declaration of Independence! She quickly glanced around the meeting hall and from old painting she had seen in art galleries many years ago, she recognised Benjamin Franklin, Thomas Jefferson and John Hancock!

Once again Elaine was whisked away and returned to the side of KRONOS. This time before KRONOS could speak, Elaine enthusiastically and speedily said;

> "Great lord of time, that was fantastic but KRONOS, what's with all this rushing?"

KRONOS realised he should have explained a few of the basic rules of temporal physics to Elaine and replied;

> "Please accept my sincere apologies; I have to stick with the laws of temporal physics. Let me explain, as time re-writes itself, its energy or fabric is extremely weak. Even your presence as a small energy being can UN-stabilise this energy time line and cause massive un-repairable rifts in earth's time!
>
> That is why I can only allow you to be there for a very short time. Also, all the events you attended are linked in time and should therefore flow from one event to another. I can monitor this natural time flow, by getting you to jump quickly from one time to another.
>
> I believe I mentioned earlier, that I cannot monitor these events myself as I am to powerful and I should have also pointed out that I am really lucky to have you with me to assist in this."

At that, KRONOS took Elaine completely by surprise as he reach over, put his big powerful arms around her and passionately kissed her on her lips!

Once she got over the initial, shook, she had to admit it was one hell of a great kiss! KRONOS then released her, smiled from ear to ear and said;

"Now let's send you on your next mission, and when you return their will be another one of those waiting for you!"

To say Elaine's mind was numb was an understatement! She could actually feel her hypothetical human heart pounding and her legs trembling! But, before she could analyse the kiss any further, she found herself in the city of Sarajevo in the Austro-Hungarian province of Bosnia-Herzegovina on June 28, 1914. She was standing by an old bridge when she recognised from her history lessons, Austria's Archduke Franz Ferdinand and his wife Sophie! As Elaine silently watched, they both entered the bridge were immediately shot down by a group of six assassins! Elaine realised this was the event that sparked of earth's First World War!

With KRONOS's explanation of time flowing from one event to another, Elaine guessed what was coming next, and she was kind of right. She expected to meet or see Adolf Hitler but she was transported into a street in Warsaw, Poland! The time date was 1st September 1939. Suddenly, the sound of air raid sirens began to wail and overhead German wars planes began bombing the City! This was the event that started the war to end all wars, World War Two! Before the first bomb landed, Elaine was speedily transported back into KRONOS's arms and once again he passionately kissed her! Smiling he said;

"I keep my promises."

While she enjoyed the kisses, Elaine tried to understand KRONOS's motive for doing this. Was he playing with her, or was he genuinely fond of her?

Still holding her close to him, KRONOS responded to her thoughts. Looking straight into her eyes he said with sincerity;

"Elaine, I am definitely not playing with you. I would not dare, you are the great Captain Elaine Laurence. No one messes with you!"

Embarrassingly, Elaine found herself giggling like a little school girl but, she was quietened down when KRONOS kissed her on the forehead and said;

"Now its back to temporal business, earth's energy time is healing well. The next time event is one we can both observe. Look down at the moon's surface."

Elaine could see that they were both above the sea of tranquillity and the lunar module that was carrying the Americans, Neil Armstrong and Buzz Aldrin had recently touchdown on the lunar surface! From her astronaut training Elaine knew that this was July 1969 and it was 2:56 UTC as the person in the space suit, Neil Armstrong was just about to step onto the lunar surface! She looked into KRONOS's smiling eyes and said;

"Wow, you certainly know how to show a girl the sites, don't you!"

KRONOS said nothing, he just kissed her again. It was Elaine who reluctantly pulled away, she needed time to think. As she did, she realised that they were now in another time zone. She could see orbiting the planet Earth, the Recreational Space Stations, Stephen Hawking and the Space Recreation Station, Darwin and just leaving the two Recreational Space Stations was a large obsidian black trilo-space craft! It was the exact time that she and four hundred and fifty nine guests and crew had been abducted from two recreational space stations!

KRONOS looked at Elaine and sympathetically said;

"I am sorry that you had to see this, I know it is painful but, we have to make sure that 'space time' is also re-writing itself correctly.

We have one more 'time jump' to do and then if you want to, we can spend a little leisure time together?"

With all that had been happening, Elaine's emotions were a bit topsy-turvy! But, she liked the idea of spending time with this extraordinary being that controls all time and enthusiastically answered;

"Yes, I would really like that."

Before Elaine could say any more, she found herself in the virtual great hall of the Universal Interplanetary Congress! A virtual hologram of Elaine was addressing the congress member's. In a loud clear and highly confident voice, Elaine's hologram announced;

"Both our universes are now safe!"

She instantly recognised the time event! It was her personal address to the Universal Interplanetary Congress. From just outside the wormholes that lead to the overlord's universe, Elaine informed the Universal Interplanetary Congress that she and the triloraptors had been to the overlord's micro universe, and after an immense battle, they had successfully defeated him!

That was all that KRONOS needed to know. He instantly transported Elaine by his side but when Elaine looked around, she was in an extremely tall forest, the likes she had never seen before! All the foliage was various shades of blue but, strangely there were no sounds of birds or insects! It took a few earth minutes for Elaine to take in this alien environment and when she was ready; she looked at KRONOS and asked;

"Where are we, this is definitely not earth and I guess nothing to do with the changes in time?"

Feeling quite happy with his choice of location, KRONOS nodded and replied;

"You are correct on both counts; we are on a planetary museum! A specie known as the Salminons actually build this and many other artificial planets. They then sectioned parts of the planetary surfaces off to re-create individual, beautiful wonders from around each universe!"

From time to time, I like to come to one of their planets as it is quiet, peaceful and figuratively speaking, it is almost 'time' free.

The blue foliage you see on all of the leaves is due to the way the leaves handle the extremely powerful sun light on their native planet. More interestingly, at night, their leaves glow florescent blue to help dissipate the extra energy they receive!"

Elaine was highly impressed but, KRONOS had an even more impressive site to show Elaine and continued;

"If you listen, you can hear water running. Come and I will show you a really wonderful planetary sight!

Enthusiastically, Elaine followed KRONOS through the tall blue forest. And almost immediately they came across a fast flowing river. KRONOS beckoned Elaine to follow him down stream and in next to no time, they were on the edge of a massive five hundred metre water fall! If Elaine had breath, the view would have taken it away! Stunned by what she was looking at, Elaine looked at KRONOS for an explanation. KRONOS was extremely pleased with Elaine's reaction and said;

"What you see is the most unique water fall in all the universes. The river bed and walls behind the water fall are made of various coloured crystals. They were formed over a billion years and released through volcanic eruptions. With the water cascading over it and the sun light hitting the crystals, it produces the most spectacular rainbows and natural light show effects ever!

KRONOS continued enthusiastically talking;

"Elaine, at night, these light effects change drastically. The lights given from the blue glow of the foliage and the different colours of each crystal make the whole place look like an enchanted area. Wait until you see it, its stunning!"

On their first day together, Elaine was still concerned that KRONOS was just 'stringing her along'. He certainly had a way of being charming and Elaine suspected that this charm had been used time and time again!

KRONOS sensed this and immediately re-assured that from the first time he saw her, she swept him off his preverbal feet! He explained that he had roamed through many universes and travel throughout time but, he had never come across anyone quite like Elaine! Elaine also had to admit that she had fallen head over heels for this incredible, charming and at times, gentle, dignified being of time!

Over the following few earth weeks, Elaine was really, really happy. She and KRONOS, walked, talked and flew over this incredible area. As they talked; Elaine told KRONOS her life story and explained in detail what had happened since she was abducted from the earth space recreational station. The one part that really caught KRONOS's attention was her account of how she woke up on a beach on the planet Notus and how she was saved by the planet guardian Notus. KRONOS asked Elaine to describe the beach and as she did KRONOS formed a highly detailed three dimensional mental image in his mind and then projected it in Elaine's mind. He then inquired;

"Is this what it looks like?"

Elaine examined the image and replied;

"Yes, it's perfect, right down to my little ant friends crawling on the sand."

They both laughed at that.

As the artificial sun set, they would both sit and watch the crystal falls light show. In this romantic, enchanted setting, they would embrace and in a human way, make passionate love. Late one evening on their third earth week, Elaine began to feel sleepy and as she huddled into KRONOS's arms, she said;

"Wow, all this excitement must be tiring me out. I did not think that energy beings got tired but, I hope you do not mind. I need to close my eyes for a while and sleep."

KRONOS did not say anything; he just held Elaine in his big powerful arms and let her drift into a deep sleep. Once she was asleep, he gently kissed her several times and ever so quietly said;

"Elaine, my love, please forgive me for what I am about to do! The time has come and I the one you know as KRONOS have to restore the last part of your time line!"

CHAPTER TWENTY TWO

Back in Time

Suddenly Elaine woke up! She was sitting in a trilo-shuttle craft and was wearing her trilo-combat uniform? Her trilo-visor was showing trilo-symbols on the inside of the screen and as far as she could tell each symbol was a numerical number. Her mind went into overdrive; she was confused, what just happened? And then she said out loud;

> "Oh my god, I must have just dozed off for a split second! I can't believe I have just done that, and I am about to try to deactivate a trilo-nuclear mine!"

Unbeknown to Elaine, her mind had been wiped clean of all future events and she was back on the outskirts of the planet Hopes solar system!

As Elaine got her act back together, she tried to understand the triloraptors numerical system. At the same time, the trilo-shuttle she was sitting in left Notus One's launch bay and began searching for the closest trilo-nuclear mine! The first problem was trying to identify them as they were individually camouflaged to look like chunks of space debris! Using both long and short range scanners, the triloraptor who was piloting the trilo-shuttle, calmly said;

> "I have located one; it is just twenty five thousand metres straight ahead! This one looks like a small piece of space ice about ten metres wide. Captain Elaine Laurence, are you ready for your space walk?"

Without saying a word, Elaine just nodded and walked over to the air lock and waited for the triloraptor to open the air lock door, she then walked in and the air lock door closed behind her. Depressurisation only took four earth seconds, and Elaine counted three, two, one. Then using her ability to manipulate gravity, she then mentally activated a spherical shaped anti-gravity force field around herself.

As the exterior doors opened, Elaine's visor showed her the exact location of the camouflaged nuclear mine. Concentrating hard, with her anti-gravity force field around her, Elaine drifted out of the air hatch and into open space. The triloraptors had assured her that the trilo-nuclear mines motion detection would only activate if it detected motion from something as bulky as a small shuttle or space craft. They also mentioned that, as she was less than two metres tall and now a pure energy being, the trilo-nuclear mine should not detect her motion, and she should be alright! That was not a comfort to Elaine; in the back of Elaine's mind she still did not trust the triloraptors! After all, they had already tried to kill her before!

Putting those thoughts aside, Elaine paused and made sure her trilo-combat uniform was not radiating any heat. She also set her trilo combat uniform so that it appeared to allow a laser beams light to go straight through it. Satisfied that everything was functioning correctly, Elaine moved slowly forward another two hundred and fifty metres and then stopped again. Through her trilo-visors communications, one of the triloraptors said;

> "When you get close to the trilo-nuclear mine, activate the icon now showing in your visors display, this will open the spacial mines control unit! Our trilo-super computer has narrowed the code down to fourteen thousand possibilities! However, you only get one chance, and if it is wrong, the mine will activate the tamper device and in one nano second, the trilo-nuclear mine will detonate!

Hearing that, Elaine's heart nearly jumped out of her trilo combat uniform! She took a few deep breaths to calm herself and then realising what she had just done. Elaine mentally laughed to herself and thought;

> "Old habits die hard, come on Elaine, you're immortal now. You don't need air!"

But then a horrible thought jumped into her head;

"You may be immortal but, remember what killed Notus's offspring Olotinium who was a lot more powerful than you are; a massive nuclear explosion!"

With that explosive thought in her mind, Elaine went back to taking a few more deep breaths and edged herself closer to the trilo-nuclear mine. When she was just one metre away she stopped and activated the icon that opens the trilo-nuclear mines control panel. The panel opened and then linked automatically with her trilo visor and a trilo-key pad appeared in front of her eyes. All she had to do was mentally input the correct code. Before she tried any numbers, she telepathically asked Notus for help, Notus immediately said;

"Elaine, I have been working with Notus One super computer but regrettably, I do not have the correct codes for you. Just remember that you are unique in this universe, so close your eyes and try to visualise each trilo-number."

What Notus said really did not help, Elaine realised she was on her own and out of desperation she closed her eyes and tried to visualise the trilo-numbers but, as hard as she tried, nothing happened! All that kept distracting her in the quite of space was the heavy thumping of her heart. That's when a thought hit her; she knew it was stupid and illogical but, she had no other option!

She began to count how many heart beats she had in a minute. In the first minute she had sixty eight beats. Elaine then spent the next seven minutes monitoring her heart rate that slowed down each minute. Now with eight different numbers, Elaine used her trilo-visor and called up the triloraptors numerical equivalents. Each number was then converted into a trilo symbol and with that, Elaine had an eight numbered code. Wasting no time, Elaine immediately cross referenced her codes with the fourteen thousand that the trilo-super computers had come up. This exercise came up blank except for one code that had five symbols in the same order! The other three of the trilo-symbols were completely different!

Elaine felt she was on the right road but, she had to make a decision! Use her own unique codes or the triloraptors? Logically choosing the triloraptors ones would make sense. After all, this was their trilo-nuclear mine. But, Elaine still had her niggling doubts! She knew in that instant that she would go for her own 'hearty' combination! And as quickly as she could she mentally entered her own eight digit code and pressed enter. That's when a bright white flash surrounded Elaine, and Captain Elaine Laurence's body was vaporised and she instantly died!

As the powerful nuclear blast spread outwards, the trilo-shuttle craft was thrown several thousand metres backward! But, the blast also detonated every other nuclear trilo-mine around the solar system! This chain reaction totally destroyed the trilo-shuttle craft!

From further out in space, the Universal Interplanetary Congresses news ship along with its neutron engines suddenly re-appeared and everything came back online! Within seconds of coming out of the darkness, Captain Diplad and Dalscar were inundated with all types of questions and problems! But the one item that really caught their immediate attention was the massive explosions in space! Fortunately for Dalscar, the news ships high tech external camera's caught the first and then subsequent nuclear explosions!

Like any professional news team, Dalscar's team were on the ball and within seconds, they were doing live reports to every Universal Interplanetary Congresses planet! The first opening news flash stated; 'Abductees Rescue Mission Marred by Spacial Booby Traps Exploding'. Within seconds, all of this changed when the severity and realisation of the situation began to unfold. The next news flash read; 'Captain Elaine Laurence and her triloraptor team die in daring rescue mission!' Every few earth minutes the new, news flashes and news reports had to be revised! For a short while, every reporter was in news heaven, but, what began to happen next put every news reporter in absolute total shock!

The whole solar system began to collapse in on its self! The first indication was; the ice and rock planets positioned on the threshold of the solar system broke away from their planetary orbits and with the gravitational pull, they began moving towards the gas giants! Before the ice and rock planets had time to collide with the gas giants, they too were pulled out of their planetary orbits and started colliding with each other and their own moons! It wasn't long before the planet Hope and other planets closer to the systems sun joined in with this celestial mayhem!

The gravitational pull was so great that, even the all-powerful space ship, Notus One was being dragged towards the systems sun! Seeing this, Captain Diplad immediately ordered his chief engineer to put their own graviton engine on full power and get them the hell out of there! As they pulled away, they could see Notus One was fighting a losing battle to break free of the strong gravitational pull! Using his uni-net link, Captain Diplad tried in vain to contact Notus One but frustratingly, it was to no avail! Although he wasn't sure, Captain Diplad speculated that the space ships communications and on board systems may have been damaged from the multiple nuclear explosions!

As the news ship cameras kept rolling, billions and billions of beings in every corner of this universe watched with horror as Notus One disintegrated as it was slowly pulled into the systems sun! And the viewing horror wasn't over yet! Over the next few earth weeks, many hundreds of thousands went into shock, as they also witnessed the total collapse of planet Hopes solar system and the birth of a vast, monstrous, all consuming, black hole!

At the request of the chair elect, four earth weeks later. The Universal Interplanetary Congress held its first 'official' emergency meeting over the spacial disaster. All three thousand five hundred elected delegates were present as the chair elect recapped on the events that had happened! The first item that was endorsed by all present was; the U.I.C declared that the area now known as 'the Hope Black hole' a U.I.C spacial disaster area! And because of its hazardous 'black hole,' this area was now a no go zone for all U.I.C space ships! To help enforce this, warning beacons would be placed around the outer perimeter of its system.

At the same meeting, every delegate wanted to know what went wrong with Captain Elaine Laurence's rescue mission? The triloraptor delegate revealed that there trilo-support team had done their best to provide the necessary codes for the disarmament of the trilo-nuclear mine. He continued by saying that;

> "Even with ours and Notus One's super computers working flat out, we could not provide the full coded sequence! This left Captain Elaine Laurence to guess the last few trilo-numbers. This she did, and as you are all aware. She sadly died!

All the U.I.C delegates agreed that this was a tragic accident. It was then that the chair elect said she would like to say a few words. The virtual congress hall went into silence as the chair spoke;

"Members of this esteemed congress. I would like to take this opportunity to pay our respects to the greatest hero this universe has ever had, Doctor Elaine Laurence!

For those who do not know about the history of Doctor Elaine Laurence. This brave female earthling was abducted from an earth orbiting recreational space station by the triloraptors. She was then taken unconscious to a planet on the edge of this universe that we know as Notus and then left their alone! However remarkably, she survived and went on to battle with the triloraptors when they tried to invade the planet Notus!

Members of this congress, it is now an historical fact that Captain Elaine Laurence and her unique space ship, Notus One, defeated the triloraptors. But her victories did not end there; she helped drive the evil overlord from our own universe! So for that one act alone, we at the U.I.C should all be eternally grateful.

But Elaine's sense of righteousness did not end there, she put her differences aside with the triloraptors and they travelled to the overlord's micro universe and freed all of the people there by eliminating the tyrannical overlord and his lord's!

Most beings would have been contented with those achievements but, Captain Elaine Laurence still had one more goal. She wanted to rescue her fellow human beings that were also abducted and placed on several different planets in this universe. Sadly, this was her last mission, and the one she courageously died on!

I therefore have a few proposals that I would like to put to this congress. First, In recognition of Captain Elaine Laurence's unselfish and brave actions that has saved billions and billions of lives. I would like every planet in the Universal Interplanetary Congress to place a statue of Captain Elaine Laurence in a place of prominence.

Second, as a sign of respect to Captain Elaine Laurence, I would like an annual official universal day of respect and mourning where a wreath is placed at Captain Elaine Laurence's statues.

Thirdly, Captain Elaine Laurence and the other four brave triloraptors on the rescue mission should be awarded the Universal Interplanetary Congress's medal of honour for valour.

Fourthly, the humans of the planet Earth do not know of Captain Elaine Laurence's acts of extreme bravery. They also do not know that it was through her actions, the earth was saved from the overlord, and indeed our own invading forces! And finally, they will be stunned to find out that this courageous woman, also liberated this and the overlord's universe from that diabolical tyrant, the overlord! I therefore propose that we send a peace delegation to the planet Earth. With the explicit objective of explaining all what has happened and offering friendship, support and aid from the Universal Interplanetary Congress."

Pausing briefly and feeling quite emotional, the chair elect continued;

"I am sure every human will be extremely proud of Captain Elaine Laurence. And once they know of what she has done and what she has sacrificed. They too will want to pay their respects to the bravest and most honourable person in this universe!

Before I finish, I have one more proposal to put to this congress. It was Captain Elaine Laurence wishes that her fellow abductees be rescued or contacted and helped. I would therefore like to propose that when we contact the humans, we also offer to take a human delegation from earth to the planets where these people are. The humans can then help the abductees and if the abductees wish, they can bring them home."

Within seconds of the chair elect finishing her all inspiring speech, every delegates orb flashed on and off in approval of all five proposals! The chair elect was also pleased to hear that numerous Universal Interplanetary Congress delegates were also planning special events on their home worlds to honour Captain Elaine Laurence.

The whole delegation had one more big surprise. The triloraptor delegate asked if he could address the congress. This was half-heartedly agreed and instantly he changed his avatar from his black orb into his normal triloraptor appearance. And he was now wearing his full trilo-combat uniform, with his trilo-tron by his side! Looking around at all the other orbed delegates, he said with a strong powerful voice;

"Madam Chair elect you are wrong when you stated Captain Elaine Laurence was the greatest hero this universe has ever had! She was the greatest warrior this universe has ever had!

We the Triloraptor's, would like to honour this great warrior by building a new trilo-mother ship that will be shaped as a Marquise-Cut boat shaped diamond. Its exterior colour will be crystal blue. To further honour Captain Elaine Laurence, every facet panel will be an etched with an action picture of the warrior Captain Elaine Laurence!

Every Universal Interplanetary Congress delegate was both stunned and touched by this unexpected gesture from the triloraptors. As the virtual congress chamber was filled with silence, the triloraptor delegate continued;

"The proposal for a statue of the warrior Elaine Laurence had already been approved by all of the U.I.C delegates. We the triloraptors would like to see Captain Elaine Laurence formally dressed in her formal trilo-combat uniform with her trilo-tron by her side!"

The triloraptor delegate then began to stamp his feet; thump, thump, thump, thump, thump. Each of the three thousand, four hundred and ninety nine other U.I.C delegates saw this as a great sign of respect. One by one, they turned off their coloured orbs, and appeared as they normally look. And to show their respects, they also began to clap, stamp and cheer along with the rhythm of the triloraptors foot thumping.

After all the U.I.C delegates finished paying their respects to Captain Elaine Laurence. The chair elect brought up the subject of time travel! She told the congress that the physics, quantum physics and temporal physics experts in the U.I.C had been analyzing all the data recorded and to date, they had not been able to come up with any logical explanations for what had happened?

She also stated that, she had liaised with the triloraptors and between them both and her own experts; no one could explain the disappearance of the U.I.C space ships and the trilo-craft? What was more puzzling to all was how the U.I.C news ship and its graviton engine re-appeared?

By the loud chatter around the virtual congress hall, it was apparent that this open ended explanation was not satisfactory to most U.I.C delegates. To be heard, shouting at full volume over the delegates that were talking nineteen to the dozen, one of the ant specie delegates asked;

"Madam Chair, we cannot go back to our own queen or government without any form of explanation. Surely someone must have come up with some ideas or theories of what happened?"

The virtual congress hall instantly became quite, as the Chair Elect replied;

"Many including the triloraptors have come up with complex theories on what has happened but sadly, that is all they are, a theory. The most popular to date is; when the gravitational field encircled planet Hopes solar system, it caused temporal fractures. As these fractures were caused by gravity they seemed to attract any other form of gravity! It is speculated that that is why all the 'graviton engines' were pulled out of our time zone and into the temporal fractures.

The theory of the U.I.C and triloraptor ships disappearing does require a little bit more of an imagination but, I will tell you and as delegates, you will have to draw your own conclusions.

Each space ship that disappeared had a graviton engine and the theory is; when each graviton engine was pulled into the temporal fracture it left residual graviton particles. Those particles acted like a gravity beacon and they were also pulled into the temporal fracture along with each space ship!

The re-appearance of the Universal Interplanetary Congress news ship and its graviton engines defies any explanation!"

After hearing these 'theories' or the lack of them, a lengthy debate took place with the outcome that was agreed by all. The Universal Interplanetary Congress's knowledge on temporal physics and time travel amounted to almost zero! The delegates also agreed that a new Universal Interplanetary Congress law needed to be past, prohibiting any form of time travel!

For the Chair Elect, the emergency meeting of the U.I.C had been extremely traumatic! Not only had she had to cope with the spacial disaster, she had also lost a person she classed as a good friend, Captain Elaine Laurence!

As the last delegate left the virtual congressional hall, the Chair Elect turned off her uni-net link and instantly she was back in her own watery environment. As she swam around in the clear blue watery liquid, her thoughts drifted to her friend Captain Elaine Laurence and the triloraptors. As the warm liquid flowed over her scaled body, she began to wonder what would have happened if Captain Elaine Laurence had been successful and actually travelled back in time? The thoughts she was having must have crossed many others minds in the Universal Interplanetary Congress;

> "Would the triloraptors have been content with just assisting Elaine? Or would they follow their natural instinctive way, seize the opportunity, and once again try to kill Captain Elaine Laurence?"

As she pondered on that, a more disturbing and realistic thought formed;

> "With Elaine out of the way and the secrets of time travel revealed to them. Would the triloraptors use time travel to satisfy their natural way, and kill and re-kill, time after time?"

The thought of this made her aquatic body shudder. Diving into the depths, the Chair Elect tried to dismiss these thoughts after finally thinking;

> "It's lucky that I and my late friend Captain Elaine Laurence and the whole universe will never know the answer to this! But I for one will always have my doubts on the triloraptors true motives!"

CHAPTER TWENTY THREE

Finale

With the correct time line restored and the Universal Interplanetary Congress passing a law prohibiting time travel, KRONOS's work was done. As he left for the planet Notus, he had to acknowledge that this was the worst time-tastrophe he had ever encountered!

Within a few nano seconds KRONOS emerged on a sandy beach on the surface of the planet Notus. As he had kept his human image, he could feel the hot sun on his muscular body and the light breeze blowing through his hair. As he looked around, everything was exactly as Elaine had described it. The sand beneath his feet was almost white because it had been bleached by the hot sun. He smiled as he looked off in the distance and could see the large sand dunes. His attention was then drawn to the sound of the waves as they gently lapped over the shore line. Looking out to sea, he could see that the ocean waters were clear and crystal blue. As he looked up to the sky above, it was cloudless and a stunning blue colour. This was definitely the beach where Elaine found herself when she first came to the planet Notus. Telepathically he called out to the being Notus;

> "Notus, guardian of this planet, it is I the one you call KRONOS. I am standing on the beach where Doctor Elaine Laurence first spoke with you. It is now time to finish off our business."

Notus had already sensed KRONOS's presence and had been waiting patiently for this moment for over four earth weeks. Replying Notus said politely;

"KRONOS, welcome to my planet. I have followed your orders explicitly; all is ready as you requested."

KRONOS did not say any more, as fast as he came, he left! His plan was not to disrupt the time line on the planet Notus and from his observations, his plan had worked well. As a pure energy being, KRONOS has no restrictions that fasten him in with any laws of physics and quantum physics when it came to travelling through time and space. And at speeds that are beyond the understanding of any life form, he then headed for an artificial planet made by the Salminons in a far distant universe. Once there, he immediately opened up a small time vortex and pulled a powerful but small gravitational sphere created by Notus through it. He then closed the time vortex and gently shut down the gravitational sphere.

As the gravitational sphere closed down, Elaine's pure energy atoms drifted softly into KRONOS's large hands. KRONOS then used his immense powers to systematize each atom so that they once again had a collective meaning and slowly, a pure energy being began to form! Within a few earth seconds, the energy form expanded and this prompted KRONOS to sit down and cradled Elaine's pure energy form in his big muscular arms. It was now time to restore two more vital elements, Elaine's memories and her mental images. This again only took a few earth seconds. With both these tasks done, KRONOS softly whispered;

"Elaine it's time to wake up."

Slowly Elaine opened her eyes and the first thing she saw was KRONOS's handsome face smiling at her. The first thing she did was kiss him. As the sleep cleared from Elaine's mind, she realised she was on a beach? She could smell the sea air and feel the warmth of the sun on her body. Elaine sat up and looked around and to her surprise, everything looked familiar. Smiling at KRONOS, she inquired;

"Are we on the planet Notus?"

KRONOS helped Elaine to her feet. He then kissed her gently on her lips and replied;

"No, this beach has been created just for you. We are now in another universe and I have a lot to explain to you."

Elaine smiled and took KRONOS by the hand and said;

> "If this beach has been made for me, I'm guessing we have plenty of time to go swimming. After that, you can explain all that has happened."

KRONOS scooped Elaine up in his powerful arms and carried her to the water's edge; he then gently placed her feet in the clear blue water and with a big smile on his face he replied;

> "Elaine, one thing we do have on our side is, 'time'."

Back on the planet Notus, Notus was trying to cope with some mixed emotions! Metaphorically speaking, on one hand, Notus was extremely pleased that KRONOS's plan had worked and Elaine was alive and safe. When she was blown up trying to de-activate the triloraptors spacial nuclear trilo-mine, it would have been touch and go as to whether Notus alone could have saved her pure energy atoms. But thankfully with KRONOS's help, Elaine's pure energy atoms were saved and instantly transported to the planet Notus through a small temporal vortex. All Notus had to do was, catch them and shield them in a strong gravitational field until KRONOS arrived.

Notus was also incredibly happy that Elaine had found someone who would love and cherish her until the end of time. With all that she had been through and endured, this plucky earthling, who had evolved into one of Notus's offsprings, had earned that!

On the other metaphorical hand, the sadness came with the fact that Elaine would never be able to return to this universe! If she did, time would once again be thrown into total disarray! Her temporal exile from this universe meant that she and Notus could never see or communicate with each other again!

There was however a glimmer of hope for Notus. In a few billion years, Notus would have to leave the planet Notus and maybe, just maybe, they could once again meet in another universe. But sombrely Notus thought;

> "Only time will tell!"

The End.

ABOUT THE AUTHOR

James was born in 1951 and started school at the age of five in Saint Patricks in Birmingham, England. At the age of eleven, he then went to Cardinal Newman's in Birmingham and left there when he was fifteen to start work. James has had various jobs from a car mechanic, to a baker rounds man and then onto a skilled tool setter.

In 1981, James decided to turn his lifelong passion for martial arts into a career and since that date, he has worked professionally as a professional martial arts instructor. Now, James has achieved a tenth Dan in Jujutsu and also holds numerous other high Dan grades (black belts) in various other martial arts. For almost twenty years, James has owned his own martial arts club in Dudley, West Midlands, England.

James did not turn his hand to writing until the year 2004. Since that date James has written three martial arts books that have then been self published. His books are available from most book internet web sites and book shops to order and are also available as E-Books.

In all three martial arts books, James personally took all of the hundreds of photographs published and also produced seventeen instructional DVD's that cover many aspects of his martial arts expertise.

Ever since he was a young boy, James has always had a passion for science and in particular science fiction. Over the years, he has read many great science fiction novels and has been a fan of star trek, Babylon 5, Battle Star Galactica, Dr who and other great science fiction series on the television. In can also be reasonable to say that James has seen his fare science fiction films. A few of his recent favourites are Star Wars (all), The Time Machine, Terminator (all), I, Robot and Iron Man (all), Thor (all), Avatar, Star Trek and Captain America.

James also enjoys playing science fiction video games like halo, mass effect, gears of war and sky rim. He has completed all of these plus, many more science fiction action and adventure games.

This lifelong interest inspired James to write his first science fiction book called S.P.A.C.E (spacetial populations and cosmic enigmas). After two years of hard work, this was published in May 2013. In this book, James showed his readership that he has a fantastic science fiction imagination, as he undertook to create a science fiction action adventure book based around a complex universal interplanetary congress that is built up of hundreds of alien life forms.

Where the book S.P.A.C.E ends, James's has pushed the science fiction boundaries and his new book T.I.M.E begins! This bold adventurous book covers the intricacies of time travel and also the temporal consequences of meddling with time itself!

SPECIAL THANKS

Special thanks must go to my friend and student Joanne, who has diligently help me correct the numerous spelling and syntax errors I made in writing this book.